This book was written
over the course of a mammoth house renovation.

Huge thanks to Rosemary and Peter
for the part they played in that.

A MIDSUMMER KNIGHT'S KISS

Elisabeth Hobbes

MILLS & BOON

First Published in Great Britain 2019
by Mills & Boon, an imprint of HarperCollins*Publishers*
1 London Bridge Street, London, SE1 9GF

© 2019 Claire Lackford

ISBN: 978-0-263-26936-9

MIX
Paper from
responsible sources
FSC˘ C007454

This book is produced from independently certified FSC™ paper
to ensure responsible forest management.
For more information visit www.harpercollins.co.uk/green.

Printed and bound in Spain
by CPI, Barcelona

Chapter One

The first indication that Rowenna Danby was in
trouble was the honking of the geese. She froze,
standing on the sturdiest branch of the pear tree,
with her hand outstretched towards one particularly ripe specimen. Out of the corner of her eye
she could see the determined mass of white heading at speed towards her. Some devil had let the
geese loose and they were making for their favourite forbidden place: the orchard where Rowenna
was currently standing. She reached the tip of her
fingers out and managed to pull the pear free, only
for it to slip from her grasp and fall to the ground.

'Bull's pizzle!'

No one was around to hear her use her father's
favourite exclamation of annoyance, otherwise
she wouldn't have dared say anything so unladylike. She sat down and lowered herself until she
could drop to the ground. The sound of ripping
cloth accompanied her gasp as she landed in a

heap, scuffing her knees and palms. She swore again, partly from the pain but mostly because of the large tear she now had in her already grubby skirt. She spat on her palm, rubbed it down her bodice and picked up the pear. The windfalls she had gathered before being tempted by the perfect fruit above her were heaped against the trunk of the tree.

The excited honking was growing louder and closer. Rowenna hesitated, caught between the urge to escape and the knowledge that if she returned without the pears it would earn her a whipping from Lady Danby. She scooped the pears up into her grass-stained skirt, then turned towards the path back to Wharram Manor.

Too late. A dozen geese blocked her route to safety. Avarice and determination gleamed in their beady eyes. Their honking became a crooning of anticipation.

'Shoo!' Rowenna stamped her foot. That did nothing to deter them. She clutched her skirts tighter and backed against the tree. 'Hissssss! Get away! They're mine.'

The ugly creatures only saw this as a challenge and edged closer, spreading out to surround her. Rowenna pressed against the tree. She found the smallest pear and threw it overarm, hoping to create a diversion. It disappeared beneath a flurry of feathers but all she had done was confirm that she had what they wanted. Now the geese knew she was the source of food they advanced on her with an alarming turn of speed. She hissed again, hoping to drive off the mob, but knowing she would never be able to get past without a severe pecking.

She bit down a sob of fright, but at that moment a dark-haired figure caught her attention. Rowenna's spirits lifted.

'Robbie! Help me!'

Her cousin Robbie was ambling towards the beck at the bottom of the village. He looked around to see who had called him and grinned at her predicament. Merriment filled his usually serious eyes.

'Are you having trouble, D-Dumpling?'

'You can s-s-s-see I am having t-t-t-trouble, you lumbering oaf!' she retorted, mimicking his hesitant speech. The description wasn't strictly accurate, but his nickname always made her blood boil. He didn't lumber and he wasn't an oaf, but Robbie was going through the awkward stage that afflicted most thirteen-year-olds where his limbs were too long. He moved gracefully, but with maddening slowness. Now he began ambling away from her.

'Where are you going?' she asked in alarm.

He scowled, looking hurt.

'If you're going to insult me, I'll leave you to fend for yourself.'

Guilt prickled Rowenna's neck. Robbie hated the fact that he struggled over some sounds. He would often go for hours without speaking if he was in company with people he didn't know. Robbie had reason enough to be worried today, without Rowenna taunting him.

'I'm sorry, Robbie. Truly, I am. You know I don't think you're an oaf. Please, don't stand there laughing.'

Robbie strolled over, taking his time in retaliation for her meanness. He gave her another slow grin. Uncle Roger often said Rowenna was the only one who made Robbie smile, but now she would happily slap the smile from his face.

'You do look stuck, Dumpling. Lady Stick isn't going to be pleased when she sees what you've done to your skirts.'

Tears filled Rowenna's eyes. The private nickname she and Robbie had for his grandmother reminded her of what was certain to happen when Lady Danby discovered what she had done to her dress and to the fruit.

'Stop jesting! A fine knight you'll make, leaving a woman in distress.'

Robbie frowned and Rowenna knew her arrow had hit the target. He was determined to be a knight like his father and grandfather before him.

'I'm sorry.'

'Well then, Lady Rowenna, if I'm going to be a knight, you must give me a favour.'

'You can have a pear. Not one of the windfalls. I picked a good one from the high branch.'

Rowenna gave him a smile she hoped looked suitably ladylike. One of the few areas her mother and Lady Danby agreed on was that Rowenna should grow up with the accomplishments expected of a guildsman's daughter. She knew by now how to dip a curtsy and show a man how wonderful she thought he was.

Robbie folded his arms and rolled his eyes in an exaggerated manner. She wondered if she had gone too far in her flattery. He was more used to Rowenna beating him at scoring points with the lance and rings or kicking his ankles as they sped round the field after a ball. While the village boys drew back instinctively when tackling her, Rowenna showed no such hesitation and most of them surrendered the ball voluntarily rather than risk being on the end of her solid boots. She vowed to try being a little more gentle in future games, at least towards Robbie.

'Please,' she begged. 'I don't want to get into trouble. It's a very nice pear.'

She cocked her head to her skirts, indicating the fruit. Robbie rolled his eyes again, but he grinned.

'You're behaving more like Eve, tempting me

into sin with forbidden fruit, than a lady at court, only I bet Eve d-didn't have such a foolish smile. I s-suppose I can't leave you there, though.' He flourished an imaginary sword. 'Fear not, fair Lady Rowenna, Sir Robert Danby will save you from these knavish creatures!'

He ran towards Rowenna, circling his arms and yelling at the top of his voice. The geese scattered, their wings brushing Rowenna's skirts as some hurtled past her. Robbie danced out of their way to avoid a couple of sharp beaks that stabbed towards him. He cried out as one scored a hit on his thigh. Emboldened, Rowenna added her voice to the commotion and ran to the safety of Robbie's side. He seized her around the waist and almost caused her to drop her skirt full of pears. Laughing riotously, they ran to safety on the common green and hurled themselves down in a heap on the spongy grass and heather.

When she got her breath back, Rowenna leaned forward and punched Robbie hard on the upper arm.

'Ow! What was that for? I helped you!'

'Eventually!'

'You looked s-so funny, though, huddled in a corner, all wide-eyed and trying not to appear afraid.'

'*And* I've told you not to call me Dumpling.'

She drew her knees up and muttered under her breath, 'You know I don't like it.'

Her father called her solid and her mother said Rowenna would grow more slender as she got older, but that seemed a long way off to the eleven-year-old Rowenna.

'Lady Dumpling!' Robbie crowed. He pointed a finger at her. 'You've got mud on your face.'

'And you've got goose muck on your britches,' she retorted.

'Well, your hair is like s-straw.'

'And your face is one huge spot.'

'But we're both still better-looking than the twins or Henry and John.'

'And more clever.'

They sat back, honour and humour restored by the insults to Rowenna's two brothers and Robbie's twin sisters. Henry was seventeen, John was four and the twins were almost seven. Rowenna and Robbie had grown together as the nearest in age with a strong bond.

'Well, fair Lady Rowenna,' Robbie said when he could catch his breath from laughing, 'You promised me a reward for my s-service.'

Rowenna unfolded her skirt to reveal the bounty that lay within in her lap. She found the finest pear and held it out. Robbie leaned forward and took a bite from it while it was still in her hand. She watched the loss of her prize with a little regret. Robbie, who always seemed able to see her secret thoughts, pushed it towards her.

'We'll share.'

She took a bite; licking her lips to catch the last of the sweet nectar. Robbie's eyes followed her movement hungrily and the strangest fluttering sensation filled Rowenna's belly. He might be suffering the pains of early manhood, but beneath the spots and unsuccessful attempt at growing a beard, Robbie had a nice smile and a good nature. He had been Rowenna's favourite playmate for as long as she could recall.

She reached across and rubbed Robbie's arm where she had punched him and was surprised to feel muscle. She withdrew her hand slowly, letting her fingers trace the unanticipated contours. She wondered what it would be like to kiss him and wished she had suggested that instead of the pear. The thought took her by surprise and she wasn't sure what was more alarming—that she had thought it at all or that she did not feel the slightest shame at the idea.

Mother had warned her that marriage wouldn't be too far away in her future and she would have to become considerably more ladylike. She kept threatening to send Rowenna to live in the town house in York, where she could mix with the daughters and wives of city guild officials rather than the children of villeins and husbandmen in a small moorland village.

Robbie made her laugh more than any of the other boys she knew. He would be a good choice and their parents would be overjoyed. They could live together in Wharram and she wouldn't be too far from home. She absent-mindedly handed Robbie the half-eaten pear, her mind full of visions of a future she hadn't properly considered until now.

Her daydream was interrupted by the arrival of Rowenna's mother striding from Robbie's house. Robbie ran towards her.

'Aunt Joanna, is M-M...?'

He trailed off, unable to finish the question. Anxiety surged inside Rowenna.

'Your mother is well.' Joanna hugged Robbie to her own swollen belly. 'That's why I'm here. She's had her baby. Another daughter.'

Robbie's eyes shone. After three pregnancies that had ended before their expected time, Lucy Danby's baby had survived the birth.

'I'll stay with your mother until your father returns,' Joanna said. 'Go share the good news with your grandfather. I'll follow on with Ro.'

Robbie ran off, long limbs spinning. Rowenna retrieved the pears and walked beside Joanna, no longer caring about the spoiled fruit, the scuffed hands or torn tunic. There would be work to do and a new baby to take care of. Plenty to keep her busy enough to forget about the odd sensation of need that Robbie's expression had caused to spring to life inside her.

Robbie's grandparents were sitting in the Great Hall, Lady Danby at her embroidery frame and Lord Danby listening to a storyteller. Both started in alarm at Robbie's hasty entrance.

Robbie slowed to a walk and halted in the centre of the room. A fire was burning fiercely. It seemed excessive on what was a mild autumn day, but perhaps old people felt the cold more keenly. Even if it had been frosty, Robbie would have chosen a chill over getting too close to the flames. His aversion to fire and his refusal to even step into Uncle Hal's forge was something his cousins endlessly teased him about.

'You look a state, boy!' Lady Danby's voice was sharp. 'Why are you disturbing us? My husband said your duties were done for today and I thought you were gone to your own home.'

Lucy had insisted that Robbie start his knight's training as a page in his grandfather's house rather than with a stranger she did not know. In truth, Robbie would have preferred to be in the smaller, newer manor house his parents had built at the opposite end of Wharram Danby, but once his mother started screaming with birthing pains, he'd been sent back. He kept the thought to himself, though his eyes fell on the slender cane his grandmother used for walking—and for meting out punishments to her grandchildren and any of the village children who displeased her.

He delivered his news, breathing slowly in the hope of lessening his stutter. Sometimes his lips felt like a door that would not open, however much he pushed. It was always worse when he was nervous, which he usually was in the presence of his grandmother.

'Another daughter? Lucy must be overjoyed.' Lord Danby stood and made his way to Robbie, his milk-white eyes crinkling as he tapped his cane across the stone floor.

'A son would have been preferable,' Lady Danby remarked with a thin-lipped smile. 'What a pity Roger will return home to another girl.'

Robbie bit down his retort. There were seven years between him and his twin sisters, and another six between them and the new baby. His mother felt her failure to produce a son, however much his father assured her he was more than content.

'Still, boy, that does not explain your appearance,' Lady Danby continued.

Robbie glanced over his clothes. He did indeed have goose crap on his lower legs, as well as grass stains on his knees and fingers that were sticky from pear juice.

'S-s-someone let the geese into the pear orchard and they w-w-were attacking Rowenna.'

Lady Danby looked down her nose at him. Whatever the reason for his appearance, he suspected she would disapprove. The sight of the twins peeking around the corner of the dais at the end of the hall made him suspect who the culprits were.

'That explains, at least, why my cook has been waiting half the afternoon for the pears. Where is that idle girl now?'

Robbie was saved from answering by Rowenna and Joanna's arrival. As soon as Joanna returned to sit with Lucy, leaving instructions for Robbie to remain, Rowenna was summoned to stand before Lady Danby. She recounted her tale in a trembling voice and displayed her fruit, which was found wanting and sent to the kitchen to be boiled down into sweetmeats.

'You're a disgrace, Rowenna Danby.' Lady Stick reached for her cane. 'I had hoped you would begin to display some decorum, but I see you have not.'

'Decorum wouldn't have picked the pears,' Rowenna retorted, 'or seen off the geese!'

Robbie winced. Rowenna never knew when to hold her tongue. It was infuriating.

'Rude chit! Hold out your hand. You'll get two strokes now.'

Lady Danby's voice was iced outrage. Rowenna whimpered softly. She held her hand out. It was already scraped and red. Small drops of blood welled in places. The whipping would hurt much more than usual.

'It wasn't her fault! My s-s-sisters let the geese out.' Robbie rushed across the room and stood between Rowenna and his grandmother. 'If you're going to punish Ro, you should punish them, too.'

Lady Danby's eyes flickered to the twins playing happily in front of the fire and beckoned them over.

'Does your brother speak the truth?'

Anne nodded shyly. Lisbet, looking amused, scuffed the floor with her foot. They were identical, save for Anne's slightly straighter hair and a small mark on Lisbet's left knuckle, and looked more like their father than their mother. Lady Danby's face softened at the sight.

'That was naughty of you, girls. If you do that again, I will have to punish you. Now, go back to your game and be quiet.'

The girls scampered away, giggling with relief.

'Hold out your hand, Rowenna,' Lady Danby repeated.

Robbie watched with mounting, impotent fury as Rowenna thrust her hand forward and closed her eyes. The stick swished through the air and snapped down. Rowenna gave a wordless wail and bunched her fist tightly. Tears began to stream down her round red cheeks. She opened her hand again and the second stroke caused her to yelp as blood welled in her palm.

'I hope this will teach you to behave more like the lady your parents are trying to make you into,' Lady Danby said. 'It will be hard enough with the stain on your family to find you a place in society without you doing everything you can to thwart it.'

Rowenna flushed even redder, but to Robbie's relief she had the sense not to rise to this taunt.

'Now, Robbie. Your hand, for being so insolent.'

Boldly, Robbie met Lady Danby's eyes. He clenched his jaw and held his breath and was proud that when the stick met his palm he allowed no sound to escape him. He kept his hand outstretched until Lady Danby had lowered her cane before slowly closing his fist. He bowed deeply and asked to be dismissed, and it was only when he had left the room that he allowed hot tears to fall as he clutched his palm beneath his armpit to stop the pain.

Despite the unpleasant interlude, the evening meal was a merry affair. Robbie's father, Sir Roger, returned at sunset. He called on Lucy, then visited Wharram Manor, greeting his daughters by swinging them high into the air until they squealed. He enveloped Robbie in a strong embrace.

'Lucy is going to be vexed with me, I fear,' he told Robbie with a broad grin. 'My business was successful.'

Excitement coursed through Robbie. He had told no one of the business Sir Roger had left on, though he had found it hard to keep the secret from Rowenna.

His father named a place and person, but looked solemn. 'We'll talk more this evening when we're in our own home.'

As soon as he was able, Robbie sought Rowenna out and pulled her into Lady Danby's garden, determined that she should be the first to hear his news. He had been allowed more ale than usual and felt as though his head was padded inside with raw wool.

They sat side by side on the stone bench and listened to the bleating of the sheep on the moors. Rowenna ran her fingers over Robbie's palm. 'I'm sorry you got a whipping,' she said, fingertips tracing the lines on his palm. 'It was my fault.'

It was intended to be soothing, but made Robbie's chest tighten. He was becoming uncomfortably aware how even the glimpse of one of the village girls' legs could make his body do all manner of alarming things. Before today Rowenna had never had such an effect on him and he was unsure he was comfortable with it.

He concentrated on examining her hand, unwrapping the wide blue ribbon she was using as a makeshift bandage. The skin on her palm had broken in three places and was dotted with raised weals across the mounds below her fingers where she had previously scuffed them. They would scab over in time, but were now weeping a little. The fury that had boiled inside him began to rise once more.

'I'm not sorry,' he said. 'But why did you have to be rude to her and earn yourself a second strike?'

'Why should I keep quiet when she is being unjust?' She gazed at him, eyes full of rebellion and outrage.

'Is s-speaking out worth the pain of a whipping?' he asked gently.

'Sometimes it is. Lady Stick didn't have to punish either of us. She just doesn't like us.'

Rowenna wrapped the ribbon round her hand once more and bunched her fist. Her expression grew fierce. 'She never tells Anne and Lisbet off the way she does us or John. She dotes on them! Mother says its because my father isn't her true son so I'm not really her kin. I don't know why she dislikes you, though. She loves your father and one day you'll be Lord Danby.'

Robbie's heart filled with pity. Uncle Hal was a bastard: the illegitimate son of Robbie's grandfather. He would never hold rank or title and nor would any of his children.

'She thinks I'm stupid because I s-speak poorly,' he muttered.

'But you aren't at all!' Rowenna exclaimed. She twisted round to face him. 'You're clever and kind *and* brave. That's twice today you have defended me. Thank you, Sir Robert.'

Robbie couldn't contain his excitement any longer.

'I will be Sir Robert,' he said, facing Rowenna. 'Father has secured me a place as a squire. I shall have to serve two years as a page so I'll be fifteen rather than fourteen before I become squire.'

'Are you going to go?' Rowenna asked quietly.

'Of course,' Robbie exclaimed. 'Why wouldn't I?'

Rowenna pouted. 'You'll become Lord Danby anyway one day. You could just stay here.'

'I can't just wait here until I inherit my title. I need to earn it. I want to serve in another household.'

'Then I'm very pleased for you. It's what you've wanted for as long as I can remember!' Rowenna was beaming, but her smile didn't reach her eyes. 'Where will you be going?'

'Wentbrig. To Sir John Wallingdon, who owes fealty to De Lacy of Pontefract.'

'That's so far,' Rowenna breathed with excitement. 'The same distance again as from here to York.'

Robbie looked towards the beck, even though it was too dark to see the moor or stream. His whole life had been spent in Wharram Danby or Ravenscrag. The furthest he had been was to York, when Uncle Hal stayed in his town house and invited Roger's family to visit. When he had to leave, a part of his heart would be torn from his chest, remaining in the home he loved.

Rowenna's eyes shone with dreams. 'I wish I could go with you. You'll get to see the whole country while I have to stay here.'

He took her hand and was surprised by the strength in hers when she gave his a squeeze in response. He cared a lot for her, for all the trouble she caused.

'I'll miss you most of all,' Robbie said. 'I'll write to Father and get him to tell you everything I say.'

'Perhaps I'll work harder at learning my letters so I can read them myself,' she replied. 'Father wants me to read and write as much as Mother nags me to learn to sew and sing. I'll have to if I'm to ever become a lady and satisfy Lady Stick. "A bastard's daughter who can't behave might as well be a dairymaid",' she said, mimicking Lady Danby's cold tones. 'I'll have to catch a husband somehow.'

Robbie couldn't imagine his best friend as a grown woman. She would for ever remain a wild, unruly girl who joined in with the village children kicking a blown-up bladder through the beck, or dirtying her skirts playing Blind Beggar Catch. For that matter he could barely see himself as the knight he hoped to become. He pulled Rowenna to her feet to stand opposite him. She smiled and her hand tightened on his, causing the hairs on his arms to rise. She was quite pretty, really.

'I would marry you,' he declared nobly.

She burst into peals of laughter. 'Yes, we should get married! Can you imagine what fun we'd have?'

Robbie blinked. He didn't think marriage was supposed to be fun. It should be passionate to the point of mortifying onlookers like his parents', or serious and prickly like his grandparents'. He couldn't marry Rowenna. Once more it struck him how unfair it was that she was a bastard's child. She couldn't help who her father was.

'Perhaps I'll meet a lord who will marry you and you will be Lady Rowenna after all. Lady Dumpling.'

Robbie ducked his head to avoid the playful

swipe of her hand and they stared at the sky in silence. The stars pricked the blackness like gems on a velvet cloak. He plucked a rosebud and held it out to her.

'We'll always be friends, even if I become a noble knight and you're still hurling yourself out of trees,' he said.

She unwound the ribbon from her hand and held it out to him. 'Here. You asked for a favour earlier. Take this. I hope it brings you more luck than the pear did.'

Robbie coiled it around two fingers, then slipped it inside the pouch at his belt.

'I'll be returning to Ravenscrag tomorrow morning with Mother,' Rowenna said. 'Will you come visit us before you leave?'

'Of course.'

Father had said he could leave as soon as he liked, but he might delay for a few weeks. He lifted Rowenna's hand to his lips and kissed her knuckles lightly in the manner he had been taught, bowing low with a flourish. Her face grew uncharacteristically serious.

'Promise you won't forget me.'

Robbie put his sore hand to hers, palm to palm. They linked fingers and another rush of fondness for Rowenna filled him.

'I promise. We'll always be friends.'

She smiled widely, then unexpectedly leaned

close and kissed his cheek. The sensation lingered long after she had darted back inside the house.

Roger was sitting in the kitchen when Robbie returned home. He looked up when Robbie entered.

'We need to talk.'

He gestured to a chair. Robbie sat, unnerved by the serious tone. Roger had poured two cups of wine and was turning one between his fingers. His hands were mismatched: one pink, smooth and hairless. Robbie had never asked why.

'Is something wrong with Mother?'

'Lucy is well. She's sleeping. This concerns you. What I am about to say must never be spoken of to another,' Roger continued. He stood and paced around the room. Robbie's heart began to pound a slow drumbeat.

'I have considered how to tell you and there is no easy way of doing it.'

'Tell me what?' Robbie urged.

Roger poured himself another cup of wine and drained it in one gulp.

'Robbie, I am not your father.'

The world folded in. Robbie lifted his cup to his lips, but it was as if someone else was drinking the wine because he tasted nothing. He thought about protesting that his father was jesting, or there was a mistake, but the look in Roger's eyes told him it was futile.

'We always wondered if you would remember the time before I met your mother, but you never did.' Roger twisted his cup between his hands and bowed his head.

'And now you have told me, you are s-s-sending me away?'

'You are not an exile,' Roger said. 'You want to go.'

Robbie stared around. He could remember nothing before this stone house full of laughter and affection, but now the walls trapped him.

Robbie's throat seized with an unspeakable pain. It was not in his nature to shout or rant, and experience told him that he stuttered worse when he did.

'Why are you telling m-me now?' he asked in a low voice.

'You have a right to know.'

'It's something I should have always known!'

Roger reached out a hand, which Robbie ignored, his heart tearing. The father who had soothed Robbie when he fell, played with him and taught him did nothing to ease the grief and confusion beyond offer a hand.

'You were too young to understand before and we couldn't risk you revealing it. There were reputations to consider. But you are almost a man and should know the truth about yourself.'

Robbie balled his hands. Roger's reputation was the least of his considerations when his world had been shattered. He flung himself from the stool, sending it crashing to the floor. He winced at the noise. The wine made his head spin, adding to the fug of emotions that surged inside him.

'Sit down and be sensible,' Roger said.

Robbie glared, bristling at the command in Roger's voice, and stood his ground.

'Is Sir John my father?'

Roger shook his head.

'Who is?'

'That doesn't matter.'

'It matters to me!'

'It is not my place to tell you.' Roger looked away. 'This changes nothing. I have no son of my own.'

Robbie glanced at the closed door to his mother's room. Acid filled his throat. If the new baby had been a son, Robbie would have been an outcast by now.

'You're my only heir. Titles can pass to adopted sons if there is no legitimate heir.'

Roger smiled, as if this negated years of deceit. Robbie had often marvelled at the way his father—no, his stepfather—swept through life with a carefree manner as if nothing had consequence. Did Roger not understand how completely he had destroyed everything Robbie had believed to be true?

'But you haven't adopted me. You've kept it secret.' Robbie began to shake.

'William of Pickering believes only true bloodlines matter. His son, Horace, might see differently when he becomes the Earl, but it is too much of a risk to reveal the truth. Secrecy is better. For now, at least,' Roger said.

'Lies are better, you mean?' Robbie exclaimed. 'What if I reject your plan and refuse to be your heir?'

'Then Wharram could pass to a stranger when I die. Everything my family has created will be lost.' Roger eyed him sharply. 'Would you do that?'

The portion of land owned by the Danbys, including Rowenna's village of Ravenscrag, was held in fief from the tenant-in-chief, William of Pickering. Whether or not Robbie cared if the manor passed to another of William's vassals—and at this point he was not sure he did—there were tenants who relied on the Danbys. Another nobleman who was unfamiliar with the area might be less generous and fair with the serfs and peasants. Robbie couldn't be responsible for jeopardising so many lives. He shook his head.

'Does anyone else know?' he asked.

'Hal and Joanna, and my parents.'

Which was why Lady Stick had no liking for Robbie. He was not her blood any more than Rowenna was.

'Your reputation is safe,' he said stiffly. 'I shall tell no one and I shall be your heir. I'll leave for Wentbrig at first light.'

'There's no need for that.'

Roger looked distraught. He raked his fingers through his hair, a gesture that Robbie had unconsciously adopted. Robbie stared at the man, who he resembled so closely in manner and looks. No wonder the deception had been so easy.

'There's every need. You've done your duty and found me a position. I shall take it.'

He had promised to see Rowenna. Though he would break his word, how could he face her knowing what he did now, but unable to share his burden? He did not know what the future held, but it was not in Wharram.

He bowed curtly. 'Please tell my mother I am sorry not to see her. Farewell, Sir Roger.'

He left the room before he cried.

Chapter Two

June 1381

Her name was Mary Scarbrick and he loved her more than life itself. Robbie Danby knew with absolute certainty she was the woman he wanted to marry. She had hair so blond it was almost white and eyes the colour of his mother's sapphire rings. True, he had only known her a month, but it had been a month filled with the greatest passions and despair he had ever experienced.

Riding towards York in the retinue of his master, Sir John Wallingdon, Robbie passed the time in two ways: he searched as he always did for a hint of the father whose unknown identity plagued him whenever he was in the presence of noblemen and knights, and he dreamed of Mary. There was plenty of time to do both as the procession of entourages all converging on the road to the city stretched seemingly for miles and was making slow progress.

Mary was among them somewhere, though Robbie had lost track of which covered litter she was travelling in. The ladies seemed to move from one to another as they kept each other company. As lady-in-waiting to Lady Isobel, Sir John Wallingdon's wife, Mary would follow her mistress wherever that woman desired her to go.

Robbie sighed, thinking of the curve of Mary's lips, the tilt of her nose, the smooth whiteness of her cheeks. No woman in the country could come close to her perfection. He would do great deeds in her honour. He would write poetry that would cause the hardest heart to weep. He would dedicate his life to her happiness if she would let him.

All he had to do was be able to speak to her without his throat seizing and his tongue becoming lead.

As a squire in the service of an elderly knight of middling wealth he had little to recommend him, but one day Robbie would be a knight, Sir Robert. With the expectation of one day inheriting the title of Lord Danby, Baron of Danby and Westerdale, he would be a much more attractive prospect to a young woman.

His stomach squirmed as it always did whenever the matter of inheritance occurred to him. He had kept The Great Secret buried within him, but never a day went by that he was not conscious of the deception he was party to, simply by living under the name he bore. His conscience would not permit him to deceive a wife over his origins.

With the prospect of Mary in his future, he was more determined to win his knighthood on his own merit. Robbie pictured himself taking Mary back to Wharram Danby, his childhood home. His mother would naturally love her as much as Robbie did himself. Even old Lady Stick would have to unbend when introduced to someone of such elegance, despite her dislike of Robbie. His twin sisters would fall over themselves to gain her notice while his cousins would look on in envy at the woman Robbie had won.

Most of his cousins, at least. Robbie slowed his horse a little, dropping back to the middle of the cavalcade as he pondered what his cousin Rowenna would make of his intended bride. He couldn't imagine the meeting between the elegant Mary and spirited Rowenna, though they were similar in age. He would have to make time to travel to Ravenscrag and visit his cousin now he was home in Yorkshire. It had been abundantly clear in each of the notes she sent along with letters from Robbie's family that she was desperate to visit the city more frequently than her father allowed.

'What's wrong, Danby? Forgetting how to

ride? Are you going to travel to York at walking pace?'

A mocking voice pulled Robbie back from his reverie. He ground his teeth and looked into the eyes of the squire who had come alongside him. Cecil Hugone had been Robbie's rival and friend—he was never sure which—since they had joined the same household within six months of each other as untrained pages and become squires together. Hours of work under the hard eye of their master had gradually changed both boys from scrawny youths into well-built young men, but while Robbie was tall and leaner than he would have liked to be, Cecil was thickset and squat.

Robbie took a deep breath to steady his voice. 'Just thought I'd l-let you have a chance to ride in front without having to half kill L-Lightning to keep up with me.'

Cecil pursed his lips and Robbie knew his well-aimed arrow had found the intended target. Cecil never liked reminding he was not the best at everything.

'We both know my Lightning could beat your Beyard without you needing to draw back. You were thinking of a woman, weren't you, and I'll wager I know which one.'

Robbie couldn't prevent the blush rising to his cheeks. He wished he had grown a fuller beard to conceal it rather than the close-trimmed dust-ing he wore.

'You aim high for a poor Yorkshire squire,' Cecil said with a lift of his eyebrows.

Of course Cecil knew which woman Robbie had given his heart to. High indeed. Sir John was childless and his niece was rumoured to be the beneficiary of his fortune. Whoever caught the heart of Mary Scarbrick would find himself set for life and every man in Sir John's household, old or young, had been admiring the nobleman's niece when she had left her convent a month ago to serve as attendant to Lady Isobel. Cecil was in-cluded in that number and Robbie was certain he was equally determined to win Mary's hand. The thought that Cecil might win the woman Robbie loved drove him to despair at night.

With a full beard and corn-blond hair, Cecil drew admiring glances from every quarter. He was the third son of a family who had first come to England from France with Edward Long-shanks's second wife. He was charming, hand-some, good-humoured—and Robbie didn't trust him not to put his own interests first any more than he would trust a fox in a henhouse.

Roger, now Lord Danby, could trace his line back for three generations of nobility, but as for Robbie himself...

He furrowed his brow. The deception he was

party to was a weight on his mind, as was the fact he had no idea who his true father was. Despite the letters Robbie had written requesting, demanding and cajoling, his parents had refused to name the man beyond saying he was of noble birth. By hoping to win Mary as a wife, Robbie aimed considerably higher than even Cecil suspected.

Cecil laughed, mistaking Robbie's discomfiture to do with their conversation. He threw his head back in a careless manner that Robbie knew for certain he practised when he thought no one as watching.

'That's it! You can't sit straight in the saddle because you're worried you'll snap your swollen prick in half!'

Robbie winced inwardly at Cecil's crudity. His intentions towards Mary were pure and Robbie himself was chaste. He yearned to marry her, not dally with her, then move on to another conquest as Cecil frequently did, if what he boasted about was true. Having said that, the affliction Cecil described did cause him trouble at times. That was only natural. There were nights when it felt like a knife was plunging into his groin and he was sorely tempted to seek out one of the maidservants of the household who had hinted that his particular attention would be received gladly. Sir John was elderly and presumably unaware of the behaviour of some of his household. For all Robbie knew, he was the only person not slipping from one bed to another after dark.

He loosened his cloak a little at the neck to allow the breeze to play about his throat. The weather in early June was warm and he could attribute some of the heat that flushed his body to that.

Robbie had learned over the years to speak through gestures to save his voice catching—a nod or wink, a shrug or a smile could make his meaning understood without having to endure the expression on the face of a listener who was no doubt branding him as feeble-minded. He had also discovered that enduring Cecil's taunting with good humour was the quickest way of putting an end to it and that replying in kind was even better.

'It's true,' he said with mock regret. 'I am considering having a s-special s-saddle made that is much longer at the front in order to accommodate my inhumanly large member. How fortunate you are, that you have never had to fret over such matters!'

Cecil laughed coldly and punched Robbie on the arm. 'A sting and a good one! So, tell me— what were you thinking about the fair Mary?' He leaned closer in his saddle and lowered his voice conspiratorially. 'How she'd be to kiss? What it would be like to bury your head between those tender breasts—or those supple thighs?'

'None of those!' Robbie said.

Cecil smirked. 'Something more dissolute than that, even! Between her rounded—'

'Guard your tongue if you w-wish to keep my friendship!' Robbie growled. He sat upright in the saddle and let his hand drop to the sword at his belt.

Cecil eyed the sword and the hand tightening on the grip.

'My apologies.'

Robbie took hold of the reins again, his temper, which was always slow to flare, subsiding.

'If you really m-must know, I was w-wondering how M-Mary would greet my cousin Rowenna.'

'A cousin! Is she fair?'

Robbie had last met Rowenna on a brief visit to York two years after he had left Wharram Danby to join Sir John's household. His memory was of a thirteen-year-old, still far too ungainly and unladylike in her mannerisms and interests, but who was showing signs of becoming a comely woman. Dark, unruly curls came to mind, along with a plump form and a determined expression.

He enjoyed a private moment of humour as he considered the likely outcome if he introduced Cecil to Rowenna, remembering the many times she had trounced him at games and scorched him with her tongue, but this ended abruptly as he thought of the games Cecil might introduce *her* to. He felt a curious prickle at the base of his neck, as though someone had blown on his neck with ice-cold breath. The idea of Cecil showing interest in Rowenna was not something he wanted to encourage. He shrugged in an offhand manner.

'She may be fair. I have not seen her for five years. She writes to me from time to time and tells me of home.'

Cecil wrinkled his nose. 'A writer. I suppose she reads also and is grey-complexioned and furrowed of brow from the effect of concentrating.'

'Possibly. I don't think she is too serious. She used to get us both into trouble. There was one time she made me drive the sow into the beck and…'

He tailed off. Cecil was losing interest already, Robbie noted with some relief. Women were made for dancing and wit and seduction in Cecil's world. A woman of a scholarly nature would bore him, though Rowenna's descriptions of life in Yorkshire had always been a source of pleasure to Robbie and a link with home.

Now he thought of it, a studious woman of letters did not seem like the Rowenna he recalled from their youth, and little like the author of the letters, which were witty and exciting, painting a vivid picture of home and of a vibrant girl who seemed to delight in living, for all she grumbled about how quiet the village was. She had always seemed more alive than anyone Robbie knew and he loved her for it. Loved her for the way she could draw him out of his inclination to solitude—though more often than not into mischief and trouble—in a way no one else managed.

He'd sought her out eagerly on that last meeting, hoping to share his tales with his closest friend, but she'd been too busy drubbing some sense into her youngest brother to properly listen to Robbie's tales of life in the nobleman's house and his duties as a squire. Once he had done with his business in York he would make a point of visiting Ravenscrag and seeing Rowenna in person.

'Come on, Rob, let's not idle here in the middle of the party,' Cecil urged. 'It's hard enough we are journeying north when there is fighting to be done in the south without having to travel at the pace of a grandmother walking to market. Let's work up some sweat on these beasts.'

Robbie glanced back over his shoulder, as if he would see evidence of the unrest that had recently arisen in response to the newly introduced Poll Tax. Thanks to Sir John's age and preference for dwelling at home, they had missed most of the riots that had supposedly taken place in the south of England.

'The last to the bridge pays for the wine to-night!' Cecil said.

He cracked the reins with a cry and cantered away. Robbie could afford to give Cecil a head start. He was the better rider and had more affinity with horses than Cecil did. He always had loved them since the time when his stepfather had put him astride his great destrier despite his mother's protests. Robbie took his time to scratch Beyard in the soft spot behind the bridle before he gathered the reins. The bay rouncy tossed his head and snorted, eager to let loose and put the ground beneath his hooves.

Robbie's spirits rose once again as he recalled that a tournament was planned for the assembled nobility once they arrived in York. He would take part in the *bohort*—the games for squires. He knew, without feeling the sin of pride, that he was a far better archer and swordsman than Cecil and that performing well was sure to win Mary's notice.

He clicked his tongue, urged Beyard into a canter and chased after Cecil. He reached the bridge first, overtaking Cecil and Lightning with ease.

Cecil bought the wine as promised and not too grudgingly. They sat in the noisy inn that evening, sharing it companionably and joining in the arguments regarding the rebellions, some knights sympathetic to their cause and others outraged that common men might rise up against the King. Robbie drank slowly and listened with interest as both sides made strong cases, but before long he found the heat and noise too great and his thoughts drifted once again to the matter he had been thinking of before Cecil's interruption on the journey.

Mary and Rowenna. That was it. They would love each other, of course. How could they not, when he loved them both so deeply?

York was much as Robbie remembered it from his last visit. After the small market town near Sir John's manor house, the narrow streets felt oppressive and the buildings imposing. As they rode through the streets, Cecil once more came alongside. He gestured to the building site where a new Guild Hall was being constructed. It would eventually replace the current Common Hall, but would not be ready in time for the feasts and banquets that were to take place over the next month.

'I've never been to York before. Are the women worth spending money on? You'll have to try find me an alehouse where we won't catch more fleas or the pox.'

Robbie grimaced at Cecil's condescending attitude. He knew the streets well enough and his mother had been professionally scathing enough about other brewers she had encountered for him to deduce where he would find decent ale.

'I can take you to the best alehouses, but I don't know many women of the sort you'd be interested in,' he said. 'I was a boy when I was last here! The only woman I know is my Aunt Joanna and she'd have your eye out with her adze if you tried your sweet tongue on her!'

Cecil laughed and slung an arm about Robbie's shoulder. 'Then we'll have to discover the delights together, won't we! Not tonight, however. I'm too weary after the early start and for once have a craving for my bed with no company in it.'

They travelled at a walking pace through the city to the bank of the smaller of York's two rivers. The inn was nestled into the walls, close enough to allow easy access to the tournament grounds and festivities that would accompany the summer pageant, yet far enough away from the stench of the city and the early-morning cries of street hawkers selling their wares.

Robbie settled into his quarters in the inn that had been commandeered by Sir John's steward for the household. He was sharing a room with Cecil, two pages and four of the menservants. He would have preferred more space and privacy than the cramped attic room of eight men would allow.

'I still would have preferred the camp with the other knights,' Cecil grumbled. 'Don't you wish sometimes that Sir John was young enough to compete and had the inclination?'

Robbie made vague noises of agreement. He was fond of his elderly master, who had long since retired from active service to the King. The squires and servants had been dismayed to discover they would be quartered in an inn rather than the tents beside the ground itself. As Robbie inspected the straw mattress that was to be his bed for the month for obvious fleas, he had to admire the steward's choice. The room was clean, the straw likewise. Robbie unlocked the small chest where he kept his personal effects and checked his savings. Rowenna's ribbon, faded with age, was nestled in a corner. Robbie ran his fingers over it, remembering the night she had given it to him.

The night he had learned of his true birth. Even now the bitterness of Roger's betrayal and his blundering attempt to act as if the secret was of little consequence made Robbie's stomach lurch and fill with acid. Since they had parted that night with Robbie furious and Roger refusing to comprehend why, Robbie had seen Roger only once. That had been Roger's brief visit to Wallingdon four years previously, where they had spoken stiffly and publicly, aware of Sir John's presence and neither mentioning their argument. He would have to visit Wharram and see Roger at some point, but the idea filled him with anxiety and could wait.

He made his way downstairs and busied himself unpacking and polishing the armour Sir John no longer wore, until he was summoned to the main room of the inn, where the household would eat. He took his place at the table. His mind was only half on the prayers that Sir John intoned before they ate and half on when he might catch a glimpse of Mary. Unfortunately the litter bearing Sir John's wife and her attendants had travelled at a slower pace and would not arrive until the following day. Even when it did, the women would be eating with Sir John in the small chamber that had been set aside for their private use.

Robbie ate with enthusiasm, scooping up barley-thickened pork stew, and listened to the other men trading insults and jokes. Their language was coarse and their wit quick. Even without the affliction that caused his words to become trapped behind his tongue he did not have much to add. The meal was drawing to an end and the household beginning to drift away on private pursuits. The segregation between the male and female members of the household relaxed, someone struck up a tune on a pipe and Robbie sat back, contented to watch others conversing. He began composing a verse to Mary in his head, wondering if he had the courage to commit it to ink and try passing it to her. Perhaps before he fell asleep he would write it down. It was only doggerel, but he knew Mary had simple tastes and was a poor reader. He hoped the effort—and brevity—would gain him some standing.

Before long, however, he tired of the heat and bustle and allowed Cecil to persuade him to join a game of jacks in their attic room. As they were halfway to the staircase, a rapid and insistent knocking on the door to the street sounded throughout the room. The innkeeper hurried to open it.

'We're full. No rooms to spare.'

'I don't need a room,' came the reply. 'Is there a Master Danby here?'

Robbie stopped, surprised to hear his name spoken and in a female voice. He could make out the form of a cloaked figure in the doorway, partially masked by the innkeeper. Cecil, who was three steps ahead of him, grinned and whistled.

'You've lost no time in finding yourself a diversion for the night! I thought you didn't know where to find women and you've called for one already.' He thrust his crotch out and made an obscene gesture with his fist.

'I didn't call for a w-woman. There m-must be a m-mistake.' Robbie glared at Cecil in outrage as humiliation caused his cheeks to burn.

He gestured fiercely to Cecil to go on up the stairs, then walked back down, his curiosity piqued. He crossed to the doorway where the woman stood. She was clad in a deep blue cloak of light wool with the voluminous hood pulled over her face, obscuring her identity. Her head was downcast and her hands folded neatly in front of her.

'Who w-wants me at this hour?' he asked. 'I'm M-Master Danby.'

The woman drew her hood down to reveal neat black curls caught beneath a simple white cap. She raised her head and her dark-lashed eyes travelled upward and met Robbie's. They widened briefly and her face broke into a beaming smile, small dimples appearing in each cheek.

'Of course you are Master Danby,' she said. 'Don't you recognise me? I'm Rowenna.'

'D-Dumpling?'

Robbie couldn't help himself. The old name he used to call her slipped out amid the words that caught in his throat. With her arched brows, straight nose and high cheekbones she looked so unlike the round-faced Rowenna he had nestled in his memory and even further from the greypallored mouse Cecil had described. He was not even sure she was who she claimed to be.

This woman was stunningly beautiful.

She also looked furious at being reminded of the childhood name. Her eyes glinted. Her smile froze. Vanished completely. The smooth forehead ruffled into a familiar scowl.

Robbie knew then, in no uncertain terms, this was his childhood friend. He prepared himself for a smack on the arm and began to blurt out apologies, but Rowenna gave an imperious wave of her hand to silence him and her smile returned much quicker than Robbie was expecting. She lifted her chin and set her shoulders back, all sign of displeasure gone from her expression, which was tinged now with aloofness. The mannerism reminded Robbie of his grandmother.

'I had hoped your years away would have taught you how to speak to a lady,' she said.

Her voice sounded oddly dignified, coming from the girl who used to bellow in his face when they argued.

'I'm sorry! I w-was just s-s-s—'

'Surprised to see me?' Rowenna finished for him. Robbie stiffened instinctively, his eyes narrowing, and her expression became one of anguish. She put one hand to cover her lips, which Robbie noticed had become fuller and redder over

the years, and placed the other on his arm in entreaty.

'Oh, Robbie, I'm sorry!' she gasped. 'I know
you hate people finishing your speech. Forgive
me!'

Her fingers slid slowly down his sleeve, coming to rest on his bare wrist. Her fingers were
warm against his flesh. He was acutely aware of
how the hairs on his arm stood on end at this unexpected contact. He shook his head, smiling to
show she had not offended him, though inside he
writhed with shame that he could not even greet
his old friend with ease.

'I think we have both offended each other adequately so the s-score is s-settled.' He managed to
spit out his words without too much faltering and
was touched to see Rowenna waited patiently for
him to finish, watching him with bright eyes that
called to mind an inquisitive blackbird watching a worm. She inclined her head gracefully to
one side, displaying an elegantly curved neck that
made Robbie think of fresh cream.

'I agree. Greet me properly, then, Cousin Robbie,' she said.

And waited.

Fingers of fire raced over Robbie's body.
Clearly she expected him to take the lead and
set the tone of their reunion, but he had no idea
where to start, being so unprepared for this mo-

ment. He leaned forward instinctively to embrace her and show how glad he was to see her again, but drew back as his heart gave a violent throb. Taking her in his arms after so long apart felt too intimate. A kiss on her cheek would be acceptable, though this led to the thought of kissing her lips, sending shivers racing over his skin in the most alarming fashion.

He settled for taking her hand and lifting it to his lips, combined with a quick bow. She curtsied gracefully.

Robbie became conscious that they were standing in full view of those members of Sir John's household who had not departed. Cecil's assumption that the unexpected visitor was a whore came to mind.

'Why are you here?' he asked.

'I want you to come for supper tonight. Father was going to ask you tomorrow, but I begged him to ask for you tonight. You will come, won't you?'

'Tonight?' She had clearly lost none of her impulsiveness in the years they had been apart. He had other plans, but they had gone clean out of his head in the presence of Rowenna. He pursed his lips doubtfully.

'I shall have to ask permission from Sir John. The hour is late.'

'But will you come if he allows it?'

She didn't wait for his answer before continu-

ing, 'Let me ask him, I'm sure he would not refuse the petition of a lady. Where is he to be
found?'

Robbie glanced to the large recess where Sir
John's private table was veiled by a thick curtain. Following his eyes, Rowenna walked purposefully through the room towards the alcove,
her heavy cloak swaying from side to side. Robbie half expected her to pull the curtain back and
demand entry in the direct manner she had dem-
onstrated as a child. Robbie strode to Rowenna
in consternation and caught her by the arm. She
stopped, cocked her head at him and raised her
eyebrows in surprise.

Robbie's lord and master was a kind man.
Robbie had no complaints about the treatment
he had received in the many years he had been
in Sir John's service. He could be stern, however,
and had very definite and fixed views on how a
woman should conduct herself.

'I'll speak with him,' Robbie said firmly. 'You
w-wait here.'

He slipped between the curtains, clenching his
jaw in exasperation at Rowenna's assumption he
had no plans of his own. He made his apologies
for the intrusion and explained to Sir John that
his cousin wished to address him. The old man
listened, then gave a brief smile.

'Your cousin? Bring her in, then, Master

Danby. I should be happy to speak a few words to her as she has come so far at such a time.'

He settled himself upright in the high-backed chair while Robbie slipped out to beckon Rowenna.

'He will see you. Be polite,' he cautioned.

Rowenna gave him a withering look in response to his warning and declined to answer. She adjusted the ribbons on her cloak, which had come slightly askew, folded her hands neatly and followed behind Robbie, head bowed submissively.

'M-may I have the honour to present my cousin Rowenna Danby, my lord?'

Sir John's expression when displeased had been known to reduce a clumsy kitchen skivvy to tears from across the Great Hall. He fixed Rowenna with such a gaze, his gimlet eyes examining her from head to foot.

'I believe you wish to speak to me regarding my squire.'

Like Robbie, Rowenna had grown up under the eye of Lady Danby and such attempts to intimidate her were sure to fail. He only hoped she would not speak as forthrightly as she used to when addressing Lady Danby—something that had landed her in trouble on many occasions.

To his relief—and slight surprise—Rowenna averted her gaze modestly and smoothly dropped into a deep curtsy with surprising elegance. She remained silent. Robbie glanced sideways and saw Sir John's expression soften, filling with approval. He motioned Rowenna to rise with a quick shake of his hand.

'I crave your pardon for the lateness of my visit, but my family are all eager to have my cousin with us again. It has been many years since we last saw him.' She looked at Robbie and her smile deepened, causing the dimples to return. 'Far too many years.'

Robbie smiled in return, his eyes meeting her dark-lashed pair. Surely they had not been that long when he had last seen her? He took her hand, fondness rushing through him.

'Are you here to ask my permission to marry?' Sir John asked.

'To marry!' Robbie exclaimed. A peal of laughter burst from Rowenna as if such a preposterous idea was the most amusing thing she had ever heard. She clasped her hand across her lips.

'I… No… I merely wish to claim him for a night… *We*… For an evening!'

Rowenna stumbled over her words as though her tongue was as awkward and disobedient as Robbie's and she had begun to blush as red as Sir John's wine. Her eyes flickered to Robbie's and widened. The two of them could once again have been children awaiting judgement from their parents. Robbie bit back a smile.

'I have no intention of marrying yet,' Rowenna added.

'Good. A squire is in no position to wed.' Sir John nodded at Robbie. 'I would advise a man to have made a name for himself before he takes a wife.'

Robbie's scalp prickled as he wondered if Sir John suspected his hopes towards Mary. Sir John addressed Rowenna once more.

'Young woman, where is your attendant? You have brought a chaperone, I assume?'

Rowenna gazed on him with clear eyes. 'Father planned to send the servant to ask, but I decided I would come instead.'

Sir John was stone-faced for what felt like a year. Then he chuckled. 'Neatly ensuring I am in no position to make you return home unescorted. Very well. Robbie, you have my leave for a short while. Go visit your kin, but be warned, I expect you attending to your duties as usual tomorrow morning. If you hope for any success tomorrow, you will not be late to bed.'

Robbie wondered whether his lord meant success in the *bohort*—the games for squires to take part in—or with Mary. He was still pondering that when he bowed and took Rowenna's arm to escort her from the alcove. He left her waiting in the outer room while he rushed two steps at a time to the bedroom and gathered his cloak and money scrip. Cecil and his companions were engrossed in their game of jacks and showed only mild interest in what he was doing. His inability to answer concisely worked in his favour as they returned to their game before he could explain.

He paused at the turn of the stairs and walked the bottom half slowly to give himself time to look at Rowenna. As a child she would have been scuffing her feet or twisting her ribbons into knots, but now she stood perfectly still, hands folded placidly and face serene as a marble statue in a cathedral. Only her eyes gave life to her, darting around the room and taking in everything that was happening.

She slipped her hand on to the arm he held out and they left the inn. A boy was sitting against the wall to the side of the door, his knees drawn up and his feet drumming a repetitive beat on the stones. He had a small brown puppy on a leash that began barking as soon as it spotted Rowenna, racing round in circles in a tangle of long hair.

'Get up out of the mud, lazy-legs,' Rowenna said cheerfully.

'You brought him!' the boy exclaimed, looking at Robbie in delight.

Before Robbie knew what was happening, the boy had hurled himself upright and barrelled into

Robbie, flinging his arms about Robbie's waist. Rowenna was smiling. Robbie raised his eyebrow.

'You haven't met my brother,' she told him.

Robbie disentangled himself from the boy and held him back to examine him. The child bore the Danby black curls and had inherited his sister's determined expression. This must be Ralf, the child Joanna had been carrying when Robbie had left Wharram.

'I thought you said you had no escort,' he said, narrowing his eyes at Rowenna.

'A child is hardly a chaperone. Besides, if I had admitted he was here, your master might have sent me away empty-handed.'

She gave him a smile that radiated the innocence she had displayed to Sir John, but her eyes gleamed with a wickedness that made Robbie's toes curl in a thrill of surprised delight. Before he could answer she drew up her hood and turned away.

'Come on. Father will be worrying why we aren't back. The city isn't as safe as it used to be.'

She began walking swiftly ahead. Robbie threw his cloak over his shoulder, checked his sword was buckled securely at his side, Rowenna's mention of safety setting his senses on edge. With Ralf clinging on to his arm and asking a dozen questions, he followed her into the city. It was only when he crossed in front of the passage that led to the stables that he remembered he had intended to write his poem to Mary. Just as in his childhood he had been swept up in Rowenna's plans and had been as incapable of disobeying her as he would be the pull of the tide.

Chapter Three

Rowenna glanced back over her shoulder. Robbie and Ralf were walking side by side a few paces behind. Ralf was looking up at Robbie with eyes already filled with hero worship even though Robbie was swathed in a plain green cloak that covered the blue-and-orange livery of Sir John's household. When Robbie was knighted and dressed in finery or full ceremonial livery he would look even more attractive.

She stopped walking abruptly so that Robbie and Ralf nearly collided with her. Where had that description sprung into her mind from? She hadn't meant to consider his looks, only his bearing and the fact that Ralf was obsessed with knights. Ralf was bombarding Robbie with questions about life in Sir John's household, but giving him no time to answer any of them. His dark eyes were serious and he nodded politely. It occurred to her that he might have had other plans and that her arrival had not been welcome, but she had been so eager to see him again. The years apart had increased her fondness for him rather than diminished it.

She fell in beside them, with Ralf between her and Robbie, and gave him a furtive look from beneath her hood. A delicious fluttering filled her belly as she looked at him. The letters he had written to her had been packed full with details of his life, the places he had been and whom he had encountered. She had relished every one he sent, but nowhere had he mentioned how tall he had grown or how he had changed. In her mind he had been the same as when she had last seen him, only beginning to take a man's form with legs and arms too graceless and long. He had grown into a man and a remarkably handsome one at that.

Very handsome!

Rowenna bit her lip to stop a smile spreading to her lips at what she saw and looked again. His hair was cut short in the fashionable style, barely grazing his angular jaw, which bore only the slightest hint of beard. Unlike the rest of their family he was not cursed with unruly curls, and his dark brown locks were smooth and thick, parting to one side.

Her eyes travelled further downward. He had grown taller still since she had last laid eyes on him, but from what she could tell, the rest of his body had filled out a little to compensate. If his arms were any indication, he would be toned and muscular all over.

Watching her brother impulsively throw his arms around Robbie's lean frame, Rowenna had been filled with the almost uncontrollable urge to do the same. She recalled the awkward dance they had performed when they had greeted each other. Once she would have thought nothing of behaving in such a familiar manner as Ralf and hugging him. This Robbie was no longer the boy she had played rough and tumble with, but a grown man, and she was a woman now. The years apart had created a formality between them and to behave in such a forward manner would be unacceptable and unladylike.

Besides, when Rowenna thought of the word *hug*, a wayward part of her mind replaced it immediately with *embrace* and sent her thoughts running head over heels down unexpected paths. She burned inside with curiosity to see if the rest of Robbie's body really was as firm and taut as the arm she had taken hold of. It was an outrageous thing to think of her old friend, but she could not suppress the way her blood grew hot as it raced through her veins.

Despite her wish to get safely home, she slowed her pace. Ralf was still talking, describing a joust he had seen and tugging on the leash in his hand in a way that caused the puppy to be tugged back.

'Careful, you'll hurt Simon's neck. He's only small still,' she cautioned.

Hearing the name, Robbie grinned over Ralf's head and his eyes crinkled at the corners with amusement.

'Another Simon?'

Rowenna grinned back. Her mother had owned four dogs in succession and all had been called Simon. It seemed to be a private joke between her parents.

'Mother says if something works she doesn't see a reason to change it.'

She stopped short of grumbling that Mother would be content to stay in Ravenscrag for her whole life, despite having been born and brought up in York. She led Robbie into a narrow street between two closely packed rows of houses. During the day the shutters were thrown back so shopkeepers could display their wares. The street would be alive with noise and bustle. Now it was quiet and, though the evening was light, the houses loomed above, blocking out the rising moon. Rowenna edged a little closer to her companions and saw Robbie's hand slip to the pommel of the sword at his side. He saw her glance and grinned, drawing his cloak back to reveal more of his weapon. The gesture was heartening. Robbie would have spent much of his time in Sir John's service learning to fight. If they did encounter any danger, he would protect her, as he had always done.

They walked in silence. Rowenna's mind had been overflowing with things she wanted to say ever since she had learned Robbie was returning, but now they all seemed dull or too personal.

'You don't mind me claiming you tonight?' she asked eventually.

'Why would I mind?'

'I thought perhaps you might have other engagements, having just arrived in the city.'

He was silent for a moment, his brows knotting as if some matter had only just occurred to him, but then he shrugged.

'I did, but nothing that could not wait until m-morning. When I have not seen you for so long I would be glad for you to claim me at any time you choose.'

'Sir John said you hope to be successful tomorrow. What are you doing?'

'Tomorrow is the first day of the tournament.'

Ralf had been listening quietly, but could not help interrupting with excitement, tugging on Robbie's sleeve. 'You are competing in the tournament? But you aren't knighted yet!'

Rowenna hid her annoyance that her brother

was intruding. If only Father had allowed her to collect Robbie alone as she had begged.

'There will be a *bohort* for anyone who is not yet knighted, as well as the formal tournament,' Robbie explained, smiling at them both. 'I sh-shan't be competing against knights, only squires.'

'Will you joust?' Ralf interrupted.

Robbie shook his head. 'I may take part in the ring tilting, but I'm better with the sword and better s-still with a bow.'

'Not the joust?' Rowenna asked. 'You used to enjoy that. Your father will be disappointed.'

The joust was the most prestigious event and the one with the chance of winning the greatest prize. Uncle Roger, Robbie's father, had apparently been a keen jouster when he was younger. An injury at some point had weakened his shoulder and now he rarely held a lance.

'I used to, but then I stopped. I will shine on my own, not walk in his shadow.' A determined light filled Robbie's eyes and his chin came up, giving his face a startling vitality. 'I prefer to choose my own path to success.'

Rowenna bit her lip to hide her astonishment, hearing the fire in his voice. For his son to reject the discipline he had loved would strike Roger hard. Perhaps Robbie would say differently when he arrived at the house to discover his parents present. The street was busier as they rounded the corner into Aldwark. The small herb garden in front of the Smiths' Meeting Hall was one of Rowenna's favourite places to slip away to and watch the busy streets. Her home was only two streets beyond that, and when they arrived Rowenna would have to surrender Robbie to her family and his. She had so much she wanted to ask him about life in a nobleman's household, the places he had seen and people he had met while she had stayed at home on the moors.

'Ralf, run ahead and tell Mother that Robbie and I will be along shortly.'

Her brother raced off with Simon the puppy at his heels. Rowenna stopped beside the old fountain with the weathered stone lion's face that stood at the edge of the garden. The fountain had long since lost the cup on a chain so Rowenna dipped her fingers in the basin of the fountain and rinsed them as an excuse for lingering.

'Rowenna? I did not know you were in town!'

Surprised at hearing her name, Rowenna turned to face the sombrely dressed young man who was striding towards her. She recognised Geoffrey Vernon, her mother's cousin and a member of the same guild as Rowenna's father. Now she would be trapped in conversation until Judgement Day.

Her heart sank at the interruption, doubly so

as she recalled the discussions between Geoffrey and her father regarding marriage with Rowenna.

Don't reject Geoff. You might find it harder than you think to find a husband in York.

The regret in her father's voice as he warned her cut deeper than any of Lady Danby's jibes. It would not do to snub Geoff, who, for all his lacklustre conversation, did not openly shun the daughter of a bastard. She discreetly wiped her hands dry on her skirts and dropped into a curtsy, while Geoffrey bowed in turn.

'I arrived yesterday and am here for the next fortnight,' Rowenna replied.

Delight filled Geoffrey's ruddy face and he filled the next few minutes with a succession of pleasantries and broad hints that he hoped to see Rowenna again before long. He allowed her no time to respond even in the short time he drew breath, but she listened with all outward appearance of interest, while inwardly cursing him for interrupting her time with Robbie.

'But you are out without the protection of your father! This will not do in these troubling times!' Geoffrey exclaimed. 'Please permit me the honour of escorting you home.'

Before he could take hold of her arm and forcibly enclose it under his, Rowenna slipped to one side. 'Thank you, but I am not alone. My cousin is with me.'

She glanced around and discovered Robbie had stolen round to the other side of the fountain while Geoffrey commanded her attention. He stood with arms folded, watching the exchange take place. In his dark cloak he blended into the shadow, but as Rowenna caught his eye he stepped forward and bowed with a flourish. He came to stand close at Rowenna's side. Geoffrey's face fell at the sight of the handsome young squire. He quickly made his excuses and left with a hasty bow to Robbie and a longer one to Rowenna, who acknowledged it with another graceful curtsy and a smile.

When Geoffrey had disappeared round the corner Rowenna turned back to Robbie, intending to apologise for the unwanted intrusion. She found he was looking at her with interest and amusement in his deep brown eyes. A grin was spreading across his lips. She folded her arms and held his gaze.

'Is something wrong, Robbie?' she asked sharply.

'Nothing is wrong at all. I am merely remembering how the Rowenna I left s-seven years ago would have responded to your acquaintance's none-too-subtle hints.' His eyes flickered downward, then settled on her face. 'Have you become a lady, Ro?'

Approval and wonder were clear in his voice, laced with something else.

A touch of jealousy as he spoke of Geoffrey?

Admiration?

Attraction?

The idea thrilled her. Years of mastering her impulses and behaving with decorum and grace had paid their dues. The urge rose up to throw her arms round Robbie's lean frame and pull him into a wild dance. She fought it down, knowing that would prove the lie to what he had said. Instead she inclined her head in acknowledgement, regarding him with a half-smile, though inside she sang triumphantly at his words.

'I'm trying to be. As you say, Robbie, that was seven years ago. Did you really expect me to be running around barefoot chasing after a pig's bladder?'

He looked a little guilty and she realised with a jolt of dismay that must be exactly what he was thinking.

'I finally tired of your grandmother's cane,' she said. She drew her hand out from beneath the cloak and held it out, palm upturned. 'Do you remember the whipping we got after the geese in the orchard? I still have a scar.'

She rubbed her thumb over the soft, plump mound between her first two fingers. Robbie took hold of her hand and lifted it to the light, cupping it in his palm. His hand was warmer than hers and the small hairs on the back of her hand and arm stood on end. Robbie was looking at her hand and to avoid looking at his face in case hers revealed something she did not want him to see, she kept her eyes on the scars. They were small, white marks about the size of grains of wheat along the ridge between her palm and fingers.

'You grazed your hand falling from the tree. I remember.'

'Jumping! Not falling!' Her pride momentarily overcame any intention to act as a lady. 'You're right, though. It bled and hurt so much when she whipped me, too. After you left I vowed that would be the last time she would use her cane on me.'

'I'm pleased she didn't hurt you again.' He looked at her earnestly. She saw the boy's eyes peering out from the man's face, bearing the familiar expression of protectiveness and outrage he had worn whenever Lady Danby disciplined Rowenna too harshly.

'Oh, Robbie, I have missed you. You always think the best of me. Of course, it wasn't the last time, but I made an effort for it not to happen without very good reason.'

She didn't tell him about the deeper wounds that had left scars on her heart, not her flesh— that a bastard's daughter would never have a place in society. Widowhood had released Lady Danby from the trial of tempering her nature in front of her late husband and as she had aged her tongue had become freer and crueller. But she was still Robbie's grandmother and he would not learn of her unkindness from Rowenna. If she had not loved Robbie so dearly she would have been racked with envy that his birth and position ensured him a path through life with an ease she would never have.

Feeling more confident in their intimacy, she put her arm under Robbie's, drawing him close to her side. He looked at her and his eyes flashed with a new light of interest that made sparks burst in Rowenna's chest like a hammer striking hot iron.

She stumbled, turning her foot on a pile of rough stones and slipping from the kerb, bumping into him in the process. His hand shot out, catching her in the small of her back to steady her. He slid it further around her waist until it came to rest on her hip and drew her close to his side. Rowenna bowed her head to hide the flush of embarrassment that raced across her cheeks. She, who was as sure-footed as a goat and could walk these streets with her eyes closed, had no reason to be stumbling and tripping in such an ungainly manner.

'Here we are,' she told him. They stopped opposite a large two-storey house set back from the road with Hal's workroom on the ground floor and their living quarters above. Robbie let out a low whistle of surprise and appreciation. Rowenna grinned, realising he had not seen the new house.

'Father bought it last year when he received a commission for ten swords for the Sheriff of York. He's determined to have a house that reflects his wealth and status.' A great throb of love filled her heart for her father. 'He's worked so hard to ensure his children would not be blighted by his birth.'

'Is his birth such a blight?' Robbie asked quietly.

A rich man who was still shunned by some members of York's society? Whose wife and daughter were not acknowledged as they passed through the marketplace? Robbie would never understand that all the wealth in the world could never compensate for the taint of illegitimacy.

'What else could it be?' she asked, bitterness creeping into her voice.

She gripped Robbie's hand tightly a moment longer, then tucked it under her arm and led him to the door. She had kept him to herself for long enough. Now she had to let his family claim him.

As Rowenna had suspected, as soon as they entered the house she no longer had sole claim on

Robbie. Rowenna's parents greeted him with delight and Robbie's three sisters hurled themselves at him with shrieks of joy, even though small Joan didn't know him, but the warmest reunion was between Robbie and his mother. Aunt Lucy burst into tears and clutched Robbie to her tightly as if she never intended to release him. Finally she surrendered Robbie to his father, who had waited silently at her side. Robbie had grown taller and leaner than his father, and there were grey hairs in Roger's darker curls.

The two men faced each other and said nothing for what felt like a decade. Silence descended. Rowenna looked from adult to adult, all of whom stood watching closely. The feeling grew on her that she was missing something that everyone else understood.

Finally, Robbie took the hand that Roger held out.

'Good evening to you, Father.'

The tension lifted. Robbie dropped Roger's hand and turned back to Rowenna. She could not read his expression.

'You devious wench! You gave me no idea my family was here also.'

'I wanted to surprise you,' she said. It had seemed such a good idea, but now she was not sure.

Robbie crossed the room and took her face between his hands, turning it up to him, his marble expression softening. Her skin began to prickle with the anticipation that he was about to kiss her, but he only laughed.

'That you did.'

For the first time they were looking properly into each other's eyes in the light. She examined Robbie's with interest. They were greenish brown with flecks of a darker shade that reminded Rowenna of the burnt-sugar syrup her mother made to drizzle over Lent cakes. She licked her lips at the thought of them. Robbie smiled, creating tiny half circles at each side of his mouth. Rowenna wanted to dip her fingernails into them and trace the shapes.

She became aware that they were being watched. All four parents were standing by, observing Robbie holding her in such a familiar manner while she gazed at him like a newborn calf at its mother. An unfamiliar feeling of self-consciousness overcame her and she stepped back hastily before she inadvertently let anyone guess that her thoughts were careering off in wild directions.

If anyone noticed her reaction, it was her mother alone. Joanna Danby called Rowenna through to the storeroom to help serve the wine.

'Robbie is looking well, isn't he?' Joanna remarked as she placed cups on Rowenna's tray. 'He looks so much like Lucy it's quite startling.'

If this was a hint that Rowenna should spill out her thoughts of how well Robbie had grown, she was determined to ignore it. The strength of the feelings that had assaulted her on seeing him again was something she wanted to consider in private.

'He's grown too tall to be Lucy's son,' she said gaily. 'He even towers over Uncle Roger. They look nothing alike.'

Joanna looked at her daughter thoughtfully and it seemed as if she was about to speak, but Rowenna was well practised at holding her mother's gaze with an innocent expression and Joanna said nothing more to her. Rowenna bustled back through with cups of wine to discover that already the men were already arguing.

'By unorthodox means, but de Quixlay is better for the city than Gisbourne was!' Her father clapped his hands together loudly in emphasis. 'He's less corrupt and the fines he imposes are fairer.'

Uncle Roger strode towards Rowenna and scooped up a cup with a nod of thanks, then turned back to his brother. 'That wasn't the tune you were dancing to when the Common Hall was stormed last year!'

Hal glowered. 'Of course not! Only a fool

would welcome violence in the streets, but Gisbourne had been minting his own coin and ruling by means that…'

Rowenna never discovered what means he had been ruling by, because her mother marched to the centre of the room in a flurry of skirts and held her hands up.

'I will not have this argument again!'

Joanna folded her arms over her chest and Rowenna knew the matter was finished. Her mother was a short woman, wide-hipped and buxom, who had raised four children and could command attention from everyone in the building with a single frown. She gave such a look to her husband and brother-in-law, who both became intensely interested in the contents of their wine cups. Joanna smiled.

'Not when we have guests and this should be a night of celebration. Rowenna, bring your cousin a cup of wine and we'll toast his safe return.'

Rowenna did as bid and squeezed beside Robbie on the settle beside the hearth. It was her father's house, but Hal held his hand out, palm upward, and invited Roger to speak. Roger formally welcomed Robbie back and wished him well in the tournament. Everyone cheered. Aunt Lucy sniffed. Roger slung his arm around her and kissed her full on the lips, which caused his daughters to protest loudly with embarrassed groans and Lucy to swat him away with a hand. Despite her outward disapproval, she leaned against him and rested her hand on his waist, Rowenna noticed. The argument was forgotten and the mood was merry.

'Do our fathers quarrel often?' Robbie asked quietly.

'Oh, all the time. They never fight in a serious manner, but more so since the unrest in the city last year,' Rowenna replied, taking a sip of wine. She wrinkled her nose, never much liking the sickly burning sensation in this particular wine. 'Both of them are as determined to be right as they always were.'

Robbie looked across at his father and his expression darkened a little. Did that explain the unexpected coolness between them?

'I remember. It seems there is unrest everywhere,' he said with a frown.

'Oh, don't say that or they'll start off again. You have no idea how persuasive I had to be to get Father to let me come to York this week! He thought I should stay safely in Ravenscrag in case there was any more trouble. I have to behave or he'll never let me attend the feast at Midsummer and I can't bear to miss that.'

Robbie gave a deep-throated laugh and tilted his cup towards her in salute. 'I can imagine you could persuade anyone if you got it in your mind to do so.'

Rowenna leaned back contentedly, wriggling the brightly coloured, padded mats into place behind her. The settle was small and her leg and arm were squashed slightly against Robbie's, which Rowenna was more than happy with. The room was slightly stuffy and she felt a little sleepy. It would be so nice to rest her head on Robbie's shoulder and drowse beside him. Joan went to bed, complaining she could not stay up. Anne and Lisbet sat with Ralf and teased Simon the puppy and two of the young cats that had slunk in. Her father and uncle had taken seats beside their wives on the settle opposite Rowenna and Robbie.

The evening passed far too quickly. Robbie obligingly answered question after question about his life in Sir John's household, though Rowenna could tell he found speaking so much a trial.

'I m-must leave now,' he said eventually.

It was a signal for everyone to go to bed. Rowenna began to gather the cups and took them into the storeroom. Robbie followed, bringing the jug. She stowed it back on the shelf and turned to go back into the room, but Robbie caught her hand to hold her back. She was startled when she saw how serious his expression was.

'Is something wrong?' she asked.

'Dare I tell you?' he asked, more to himself than her, glancing back to the noisy room they had just left.

'Tell me what? You know you can always tell me anything.'

'When Sir John talked of us m-marrying earlier, what did you think he meant?'

Rowenna tilted her head thoughtfully. 'I suppose he thought that as cousins we might be expected to wed. I haven't really given it much thought.'

'What if I told you I do plan to m-marry? That is, I hope to…' he said, his voice low.

He looked hesitant, his warm eyes filling with a light that could only be described as adoring. Rowenna blinked. The conversation had taken an unexpected, but not unwelcome, turn. Her heart began to race, drumming a beat beneath her ribs that felt violent enough to break them.

'Tell me,' she breathed.

She would accept him, of course. For years she had idly daydreamed that Robbie would return and marry her since his jest the night before he had left. She had never met another man she preferred and she would be able to enjoy her stay in York without the task of trying to find a husband who would marry a bastard's daughter.

'Her name is M-Mary.' Robbie's eyes burned with passion.

A deep blush rose to Rowenna's throat. She hoped it would not creep higher than the top of her bodice. He loved someone else, not her. Embarrassment filled her belly, made her writhe inwardly, and for once she was thankful for the lessons that had been drummed into her by Lady Danby. How fortunate she had not blurted out the answer to a question that had not been asked, nor ever would be.

'Is something wrong?' Robbie was waiting patiently for her reaction with a solemn expression that made him look vulnerable despite his strength and height. Rowenna shook herself from her reverie and waved a hand as if blowing away cobwebs.

'I just thought… After you mentioned Sir John's mistake, I thought you were going to ask me. Can you imagine? How foolish you must think me!'

She giggled to show how amusing the idea was. Robbie looked confused, then gave a quiet laugh.

'Who is your Mary?'

'She is Sir John's niece.'

A knife buried itself in Rowenna's breast. Of course Robbie would have been introduced to many young women. That was one of the in-

tended consequences of living in another nobleman's household. The letters she and Robbie had
exchanged had always been warm and affection-
ate, but ink and parchment could not compete
with a flesh-and-blood woman. Rowenna had
been cloistered away in the middle of the moors
as surely as if she had taken holy orders.

The disappointment that was beginning to fill
her belly felt too acute for the dashing of a hope
she had not even been completely aware of and
she couldn't honestly say at that moment whether
she was more envious of Mary for capturing Robbie's heart, or of Robbie's opportunities to meet
lovers.

Robbie's eyes took on a faraway look. Rowenna wanted to clap her hands in his face to
wake him from his daydream.

'She has golden hair and the bluest eyes you
could imagine. She is tall and slender and graceful.'

Everything Rowenna was not.

'You wrote nothing of this to me!' She slipped
her arms around his neck and scolded him in as
light-hearted a manner as she was able to muster.
Robbie slid his arms around her waist. How cruel
that he could touch her in such a tantalising, tormenting way and suspect none of the emotions
that swelled inside her.

'And does your Mary return your affection?' she asked.

'I do not know. I have never spoken to her. She arrived only last month from a convent and already has m-many suitors.' Robbie looked wistful. 'You know I struggle to speak, but if I prove myself worthy in the tournament perhaps I can find the courage.'

Rowenna raised her eyebrows in astonishment. 'You don't know if she cares for you, but you intend to ask for her hand?'

Robbie looked doubtful. He was still embracing Rowenna as he talked about Mary, which no devoted suitor should contemplate. She unwound her arms from about Robbie's neck and took his from her waist, holding them before her.

'I did not believe you to be so bold. I wish you luck, if that is what you desire.'

'And what of you?' Robbie asked. 'Does anyone own your heart?'

Rowenna walked to the window, tossing her hair back over her shoulder breezily so he didn't read the answer in her eyes. 'Who is there in Ravenscrag who could? That is why I begged Mother and Father to let me come to York during the tournament. To find a husband.'

Did his smile falter? Was the slight twitch of his eyelid any indication that this news was unwelcome to him? Rowenna gave a careless laugh that belied the longing that was now churning within her breast.

She peered out of the window across the city. Who else was arriving for the tournament, preparing to be knighted, seeking someone to fall in love with? Robbie was not the only man in York. There was no need for him to ever know that he had been one of the potential suitors she had hoped to attract. If he thought her affections lay elsewhere, that might spark his interest.

'I intend to marry well, Robbie. I won't settle for anyone less than a knight or nobleman. Or a merchant who is hugely wealthy, at least. Then I'll take him to Wharram Danby and parade him before Lady Stick and she'll have to admit she was wrong.'

Robbie looked surprised at her ferocity. 'Do you w-want a loving husband or a prize stallion to show off?'

She burst into peals of laughter and was pleased to see Robbie start to grin.

'You once promised you would find me a husband, do you remember? On our last night together.'

'Yes. I do.' Robbie gave her studious look and she wondered if he was recalling what he had said just before he had promised that.

'I'm not sure I know anyone worthy enough

to do you credit.' His face broke into a grin. 'Or brave enough.'

She laughed and swiped a hand out to bat him on the arm as she had used to. Not ladylike, but intimate in a way she would not dare to be with anyone else. He reached out and caught her wrist, trapping her hand in his. They stood together in the shadowy storeroom, hands clasped. Rowenna squeezed his fingers.

'I've missed you.'

'And I you,' Robbie said. 'May we both find what we're looking for and achieve the happiness we deserve.'

He kissed her cheek, then ducked through the low doorway. Rowenna rinsed the cups and left them to dry. When she returned, Robbie was at the door, bending to kiss his mother's cheek. He gave Rowenna a wink and left.

As she prepared for bed, Rowenna's thoughts kept returning to the way her heart had leapt as Robbie mentioned marriage. She could be happy with him.

Most of the times when she had imagined the grand knight whom she would marry to prove she was a lady, he had borne Robbie's face. Now they were reunited she could not shake the image from her mind. The disappointment had been over Robbie, not envy for his opportunities.

She sighed deeply as she unlaced the ribbon of her bodice, causing Lisbet to give her a strange look. She slipped into bed, wriggling down between the twins, and closed her eyes.

The way Robbie had spoken about Mary sounded more like infatuation than true love. He barely knew Mary and would be slow to muster the courage to speak to her. Meanwhile Rowenna would contrive to spend as much time with him as she could. Robbie's affection might kindle into a hotter flame than the one that burned for Mary. And if it didn't, then as she had told him, there would be men aplenty to win her heart.

Chapter Four

Robbie brought his buckler up in front of his face and twisted at the waist. He succeeded in deflecting his opponent's sword before it struck him full on the helmet and the sword glanced off the edge of the small round shield instead.

Spectators roared. Beneath the cries of excitement, the whining scrape of metal on metal set Robbie's teeth on edge. He stepped back, feet apart, together, apart once more, light on his feet and bracing himself for another onslaught. He shifted his hand on the grip of his short sword and prepared to duck again. Deflection was the key here. That and not receiving too many blows that would leave his body pummelled to wine pulp.

Was Mary watching? Robbie gritted his teeth, knowing that to risk even the quickest glance towards the fences that held back the crowds would leave him open to attack. He had beaten his first opponent, a red-haired squire from Derbyshire, but lost to his second, so this bout would decide his fate. He swore inwardly that he had been drawn against Cecil. There were friendly grudges that both would like to settle, and an opponent with no reason to fight him beyond the competition would have been preferable.

Cecil raised his sword once more. He grunted, giving Robbie enough forewarning to be able to skirt to one side and receive only a light strike to the hip with the flat of the blade.

Now he was behind Cecil, who had foolishly manoeuvred himself into one corner of the square. It was Robbie's turn to strike a blow. Cecil was short, which gave Robbie an advantage, but thickset and powerful, which did not. Cecil lunged forward as Robbie brought his blade around. He drove his buckler flat into Robbie's belly and managed to knock Robbie off balance, but carried on lunging. Recovering quickly, Robbie brought the sword around in an arc and caught the flailing man across the shoulder blades. A second blow delivered rapidly to the lower back sent him sprawling forward. His buckler fell from his hand and another roar went up. Cecil raised his hand in submission and Robbie had won.

He lowered his sword and held out a hand to help the fallen man to his feet. They clasped hands, bowed and faced the arbitrator.

'Robert Danby, squire to Sir John Wallingdon of Wentbrig, is victor in this round.'

A pennant bearing Sir John's orange-and-blue standard was added to the growing line on a board showing which squire had won honour. Robbie felt a warm rush of pride at the sight, mingling with impatience. Today he had fought under his lord's colours. How long before he would be a knight and fight for his own honour and name? The two men retrieved their weapons and left to loud applause. They slumped beside each other on a bench and wearily removed helmets and breastplates. Half the day had passed before Robbie had taken his turn in the square. The sun was high overhead and the slight breeze did not even begin to penetrate the thickly padded layers each man wore beneath their mail shirts.

'Well fought.' He held his hand out to Cecil, who shook it before running his hands through his corn-blond hair. 'I thought you had me once or twice.'

'Perhaps next time I will. Are you competing again today?'

Robbie shook his head. 'Tomorrow I'll try my hand at the archery butts, and of course, I'll join the melee on the third day.'

Unlike Cecil and a number of the other squires who entered their name into every event, Robbie was content to watch the knights demonstrating their skill. The longing to prove his worth was almost a physical pain, but he reminded himself there would be enough time to once he was knighted. The chance to observe and learn was rare.

A pageboy brought ale. Robbie downed his in three gulps before untying his hood and letting it fall to the ground. His damp hair was plastered to his head and when he finally removed the padded gambeson, his hose and the usually loose-fitting linen shift beneath it were sodden with perspiration and clinging uncomfortably to his body. He thought longingly of the fast-flowing beck at Wharram, where the water rushed ice-cold even in summer, and felt a sudden pang of homesickness.

He peeled off his shift and plunged his head and shoulders deep into the trough. The water was not as cold as he would have preferred, but was still invigorating. He held his breath and scrubbed at his scalp, face and body, then righted himself, tossing his head back. The water streamed from his hair, down over his chest and back in cooling rivulets that ran down until the tape at the waist of his hose was damp. He could already feel the muscles in his thighs, torso and arms beginning to stiffen from so much exertion.

He drenched and wrung out his shift, and began to vigorously wipe away the sweat from his body until his skin was damp and tingling. He dropped the now-sodden and grimy cloth over the edge of the trough.

'Can you find my clean shift?' he called to Cecil.

The requested garment was flung at his head from behind, flopping over his face, but an accompanying giggle in high female tones told him it had not been Cecil who had carried out his request in such a silly manner. Robbie pulled the shift off his head. He looked around to discover Rowenna standing behind him. Lisbet and Anne stood to one side of her, arm in arm. The twins had grown into bonny girls, but were so similar that Robbie couldn't immediately tell which was which.

'You were talking to yourself,' Rowenna said, her voice bubbling with amusement. Robbie glanced around. Sure enough she was right. Doubtless Cecil had returned to Sir John's company, leaving Robbie to follow at his own pace.

'How did you get in here?' Robbie asked. This area was reserved for the competitors and their aides.

Rowenna's eyes gleamed. 'One of the guards comes to Father's workshop from time to time. I smiled sweetly and said I had a message for my cousin. Who is Cecil?'

'Cecil is my friend. Does your mother know

you are here?' Robbie asked, unable to imagine strict Aunt Joanna sanctioning her daughter sneaking into a camp filled with young men, even if her target was a cousin. Guilt flitted across Rowenna's face.

'She told me to be quick and not tell my father. Is Cecil a squire like you?'

'Yes. He's Sir John's Squire of the Table. I'm his Squire of the Body. I care for his armour and horses. That's my favourite duty.'

She giggled. 'Cecil's role seems a better thing to be. Less chance of being bitten by a horse and more opportunity to eat the best sweetmeats.'

'I like the horses. They're peaceful to be around. Placid and uncomplicated.' And they didn't care if he stuttered his way through life, Robbie mused.

'Is that what sort of company you like? I think I'd prefer the sweetmeats.'

Rowenna laughed and licked her lips, the pink tip of her tongue skimming slowly around them as she presumably imagined the sweet delights Robbie had access to. He looked at her thoughtfully, remembering he had offended her by using her childhood nickname the night before. The description of dumpling was no longer appropriate.

A slight annoyance at being abandoned by Cecil fought with relief that his companion had done so before Rowenna arrived. Cecil had dropped heavy hints after Robbie's return the previous night about the identity of Robbie's mystery visitor, which Robbie had shrugged away with tales of his family. Unable to forget that Cecil had dismissed Rowenna as a grey-faced scholar, he was in no rush for them to meet and disprove the assumption. It would not do for the fickle Cecil to develop an interest in Rowenna.

Rowenna's eyes were dancing and her rosy lips creased into a wide smile as she stared at Robbie. Today the front of her hair was pulled back from her brow, parted in the centre and pulled into submission in tight, beribboned braids that looped down at either side of her ears. The braiding had pulled her skin taut, drawing her eyes wide so they reminded Robbie of a cat. She licked her lips once more with the tip of her tongue and fixed him with a firm look, which only served to increase the comparison and make him feel like the mouse she was about to pounce on.

'I didn't expect to see you today. Did you watch my bout?' he asked.

'Oh, no, we were watching the jousting.'

Disappointment pricked his chest that his family, not to say his dearest friend, had not found him enough of a draw, but before Robbie could express his regret Rowenna broke into another laugh.

'Oh, I'm only teasing. Of course we watched

you! How could we not? We all did.' She tossed
her head towards the lists, causing the loops of
hair to sway back and forth against her cheeks.
Robbie wondered if the tight braids gave her a
headache and found his fingers longing to undo
them and free her dark locks from their captiv-
ity. He still had the blue ribbon she had given
him, kept safely in his travelling chest, and the
notion of claiming another to keep it company
appealed to him.

Lisbet and Anne rushed forward, hugging him.
Lisbet, Robbie deduced, spoke for both of them to
praise his efforts while quiet Anne held his hand.
At Rowenna's suggestion they released him and
skipped off arm in arm to look for the woman
selling candied plums. Robbie and Rowenna were
left standing alone among the bustle that carried
on around them. She had not offered her own
congratulations yet.

'Did I impress you? It's been a long time since
you last saw me fight,' Robbie asked with what
he hoped was a light-hearted tone.

'I've never seen you properly fight, only play-
act,' Rowenna said. Her merry expression grew
serious, the elegance reasserting itself in her face
as it had the previous night when she had spoken
to Sir John and then the fawning cousin who had
interrupted their walk home and briefly claimed
her attention.

'You were magnificent, though I barely could stand it at times. I was so worried you would lose. It looked so dangerous!'

She stepped closer to him, reached out and put a hand on Robbie's aching ribs, right over the tender red place where he had received the worst blows at his left side.

'Are you badly hurt?' she asked anxiously.

Her palm covered what he already knew would become a livid bruise and her slender fingers spread wide beneath his arm while her thumb rested unsettlingly close to his nipple. Her hand was soft and warm against his moist, naked skin. No woman had touched him so intimately before and the nerves in his flesh, which had already been stinging from the vigorous scrubbing down, began to burn hotter from the contrast with her cool palm. He instinctively flinched at the gentle touch. Rowenna flinched, too, and jerked her hand away hastily.

'I'm sorry, that was forward of me.'

'No,' Robbie rushed to reassure her with a smile. 'I'm feeling a little tender, that's all. You made me jump.'

In truth, her touch had been confusingly soothing and stirring at the same time and now she had removed her hand he wished he had let her keep it there. She could stroke those gentle fingers across the bruises that were starting to appear and ease the ache in the muscles that protested in his back and abdomen, arms and legs.

He blinked, wondering how Rowenna's innocent attempt to soothe him had led him to imagine her touching him so intimately and in other places. He dragged his eyes away from her and fixed his eyes instead on the shift in his hands. He must appear so dishevelled, standing there wet and half-clothed. He thanked Providence he had kept his hose on rather than stripping down to the loincloth he wore beneath. That was not remotely appropriate a sight for a maiden to witness!

Living in a busy household and travelling about England, Robbie had shared rooms and beds with Sir John's other squires. And since the abominable embarrassments of early youth had passed, he had ceased to care about nakedness. Appearing half-clothed in front of his fellow men was one thing, but in front Rowenna, Robbie felt a curious coyness.

It wasn't helped by the way Rowenna continued to stare at him openly as if she was looking at an elephant or manticore, or some other such oddity rather than a man. Her father and brother worked in unbearable heat in the forge and often worked bare to the waist, so she must have seen male bodies before. Why she was regarding him with such wide eyes was something Robbie could not explain.

'Thank you for the shift. I should dress. I need to go speak to Sir John.'

He thrust his arms into the voluminous linen and pulled it over his head. When his head emerged he was surprised to see an expression of disappointment on Rowenna's face.

'I hoped you would join us.'

Robbie's stomach clenched at the sight of her disappointment. If it had been Rowenna alone he might have considered it, but he had been unnerved by the sudden reunion with Roger and did not want to repeat that in public. There would have to be a meeting at some point, but he would delay that as long as he could.

'I can't come with you. I know today is a holiday for you, but I must attend my master and his retinue.'

'Must you really? Father has secured seats in one of the front stands thanks to his influence with the Mayor. We have the best view of the lists you could imagine. Your father was speechless when he saw where we were going to be sitting.' Her eyes gleamed once more, her momentary disappointment vanishing.

Roger loved to watch the jousting. Robbie shared Rowenna's smile at the thought of his stepfather's enthusiastic response.

'It's so exciting! I've never seen so many things

all happening at once. You'd hate to miss out,' Rowenna wheedled.

He folded his arms across his chest and looked sternly at her. She gazed back boldly and Robbie sighed. He took her face between his hands, his thumbs resting in the hollows beneath cheekbones that had not been there when she was younger. He was taken aback by how much he longed to study and trace his fingers over these fascinating new contours. He tilted her face up so he could smile down at her and she would understand his regret was genuine.

'You know how to tempt me, Ro, but I'm not free to do what I wish as you are. I have obligations.'

'Ah, that is a shame. We had hoped to see more of you before you leave.'

'You'll see me often enough, don't fear.'

'Until you leave and I get sent back to Ravenscrag.'

She pouted, then gazed up at him with eyes that were ringed with thick, dark lashes. Her lips parted a little. Robbie felt his own do the same. He gave a wistful sigh and saw a flicker of something in Rowenna's eye that he didn't fully understand. He withdrew his hands slowly, reluctant to break the contact with her soft skin.

Robbie walked to the bench and began shrugging on a tunic and fresh hose. He craned his head over his shoulder to look at Rowenna, who was folding his discarded tunic. She looked downcast, her full red bud of a mouth in a pout. As soon as she glanced up and saw he was looking at her, the pout vanished. He felt a little stab of remorse.

Robbie pulled on his orange-and-blue tabard, buckled on his sword and added his light wool cloak of deep green. There was no need to feel remorse, really. He had to attend to his master's wishes and could not dance to Rowenna's tune simply because she wished him to. Besides, as much as he wanted to spend time with Rowenna, his heart tugged him to Sir John's stand. Mary was there. He might catch her attention. He'd already delayed following Cecil because of Rowenna's arrival.

'I'll walk with you as far as the stands,' he said, offering her an arm. 'But then I will have to leave you.'

She placed her hand lightly on his arm and he felt that same tingling as they made their way slowly through the crowds. It was odd. That arm—that whole side of the body—felt more sensitive than the other, more aware of her touch and presence than the casual jostling of other people against his body in the crowd. They were buffeted as they passed through the narrow gate to the main pavilion and Robbie instinctively drew

Rowenna closer, slipping his arm from beneath hers and putting it around her shoulder. When she offered no objection he slid it to her waist and drew her close to him in order to shield her from the worst of the crush. Once through the worst of it she stepped free of his embrace and frustratingly did not take his offered arm, but instead walked beside him, striding along with her head high.

'You don't want my arm?' he asked.

She gave him a wicked smile and raised a single eyebrow—a trick Robbie had never managed to perfect. 'I am trying to catch a husband, remember. I can't be seen to be claimed already by you, otherwise no one will want me and I'll have to settle for Geoff.'

Claiming Rowenna…

The idea sent a shiver down Robbie's spine; a frisson of excitement he was unprepared for. He shuddered and glanced at her to see if the words had any effect on her, but she was seemingly unaffected, with not even a hint of a blush on her cheeks. Clearly she did not mean the words to take on the significance they had. It was Robbie alone whose mind had fixed on such improper thoughts. Spending time in her company made him feel as if he had drunk a bottle of strong wine.

Rowenna wove her way between the tents and

stalls, greeting people with a deferential nod here, a graceful curtsy there. She seemed pleased by the admiring looks she provoked, of which there were many. Robbie noted every one. He tried to swallow down the possessiveness that made his throat seize. After all, she had every right to try catching the eye of any man she chose.

'Would you marry your cousin?' he asked.

'My cousin?' Rowenna's eyes flickered over his face and she looked astonished at his question.

'Your cousin Geoffrey.'

'Oh.' She covered her mouth briefly, turned away and carried on walking. 'Father would like me to. It would strengthen his business connections if the two branches of the family allied. If I can't find a better husband soon, I expect I'll have to agree.'

She dropped her shoulders and sighed. 'I wouldn't be *un*happy, I expect. Geoffrey travels from time to time, so I could see the country. I know him well enough to be sure he wouldn't beat me and he already knows I like to speak my mind so he couldn't be too disapproving when I did.'

'Those are your criteria for a husband?' Robbie asked.

'Those are what I would settle for if I could not have a man who loved me.'

She'd laughed the night before when Robbie

had teased her about wanting a stallion to parade, but now he saw she was speaking seriously. He could not imagine her with the overly earnest young man he had met the night before.

'I thought you had higher ambitions of knights or noblemen,' he reminded her.

Rowenna stopped abruptly and looked at him with a more serious expression than he could ever remember seeing on her face. 'I'm the daughter of a bastard, Robbie. Don't you realise what that means? If I had time, I could take you past five or six families who would pretend to have something caught in their eye rather than acknowledge me and I don't even blame them.'

She didn't even sound angry, as if she had passed through bitterness and arrived at resignation. Robbie's stomach knotted. Her words applied to him equally and more than ever he craved the time and space to tell her his secret. But doing so would open him up to the censure she spoke of and dash any chance of marrying Mary. He pressed her hand and the hardness in her eyes softened.

'Anyone w-with s-sense would see past a misfortune of birth and count himself honoured to be noticed by you,' he said.

She blushed and her cheeks dimpled.

'I should go. Mother says it isn't seemly for a

young woman to be alone somewhere like this,' she said. 'Farewell, Robbie.'

She stood on her tiptoes and brushed her lips lightly over Robbie's cheek before dropping down too quickly for Robbie to respond. She walked away towards the bustle of food stalls, but turned back to him in a flurry of skirts.

'If I don't see you again today, search for me at the feast on Midsummer's Night,' she called. 'And promise me a dance.'

'Even if it means your potential husbands m-might think you already claimed?' he answered. His hand twitched with the urge to cover the spot on his cheek where she had kissed him. He kept it firmly by his side.

'That won't matter. Everyone dances with everyone, I believe. I intend to.'

She laughed and walked off, her hips swaying in a manner Robbie found distracting. He promised himself he would indeed find time to dance with her at least once.

He waited until she had vanished, then straightened his cloak and belt, ran his fingers through his hair and made his way hastily to Sir John's stand at one end of the lists, picking out the orange-and-blue flags which decorated the rail. Cecil Hugone was already sitting on a stool on the level beneath Sir John. A little way further along the party, Mary Scarbrick and two other attendants sat below Lady Isobel, their mistress.

Robbie bowed deeply to Lady Isobel, then knelt before his master. He made sure his eyes did not stray to the object of his desire, though he dearly wished to know if Mary had noticed his arrival.

'Master Hugone tells me you won your bout and my colours are flying in yet another area,' Sir John said. He broke off to applaud loudly, as behind Robbie a knight was unseated from his horse and crashed to the sandy floor of the tilt yard.

'I am pleased to bring honour to your name.' Robbie spoke slowly, choosing his words carefully so that he would not stumble over them. 'I hope I will do the same tomorrow.'

'You have my congratulations. Rise, Master Danby, and join us.'

He rose to his feet and at last permitted himself to look at Mary. Her pale hair was caught beneath a wide silk band that matched her gown and her blue eyes were focused on the embroidery she held. If she had noticed his arrival, she gave no sign. Robbie made his way along the row and gave Cecil a pointed stare. Cecil grinned lazily and moved over one stool to let Robbie take his place beside Mary. She gave him a brief flicker of a smile.

'Good m-m-m—' Robbie stopped and bit his

tongue. His hands curled into fists. How could he hope to charm Mary when he could not even greet her? Good day? No, he might stumble over that, too.

'Are you well?' he said finally.

She looked at him, then at the lists where the knights were waiting to charge for the third time. She sighed and folded her hands over her embroidery.

'I am, though I will be glad when today is over. I have been sitting here all morning with only jousting to amuse me.'

Her expression made it clear it had not worked.

'Perhaps I could amuse you?' Robbie said, sliding his stool a little closer to her.

She did not appear to object, nor did she seem particularly enthusiastic. Undaunted he continued.

'Have you seen no other events?' His hopes that she might have watched him fight faded.

'No, only this.' She sounded exceedingly bored with the jousting that was taking place. 'You did not take part?'

'I fought with s-s—' He took a deep breath, conscious of perspiration beginning to bloom on his brow. He gestured to the sword at his side.

Mary gave another faint smile, still looking bored.

'Not everyone has the skill, I suppose.'

'I enjoyed jousting as a child, but I lost my interest when I left home,' Robbie said. No need to explain how the rift with Roger had destroyed his love for his stepfather's favourite pastime and replaced it with an association too painful to think of.

Mary looked thoughtful. 'I expect it costs a lot to take part in such an event as this, whereas a sword is cheaper to come by.'

It sounded like a slight, but Mary spoke so sweetly Robbie could not believe she intended it to be.

'Everything costs a lot of money nowadays. Fortunately my family lives comfortably in Wharram Danby,' he said.

Mary's eyes brightened. She sat straighter, turning her knees towards Robbie and asked him where this was. Robbie began hesitantly to describe the rolling moors that surrounded the village, the busy inn his mother brewed ale for and supervised with frightening efficiency, the flocks of sheep Roger had inherited on his father's death. The effort was exhausting.

'Ale and sheep. How…unusual,' Mary said drily. 'Tell me more about where you live.'

Robbie began hesitantly to describe the village with the manor houses at each end. He exaggerated slightly, embellishing the grandeur of the buildings, the size of the flocks and succeeded in capturing Mary's attention until a fanfare sounded and Mary turned her attention to the two knights on horseback who entered the lists.

Robbie sat back on his stool, thinking of his stepfather. Roger carried out his required number of days of service to Horace, the new tenant-in-chief of Pickering, but was otherwise content to live quietly with his wife and daughters. He had never sought to take prizes in the tournaments as far as Robbie knew.

Hal had been the ambitious brother, determined to amass greater riches and more influence in the guild until he had risen as high as he could. Consequently Rowenna's dowry would be double what Anne, Lisbet and Joan's might be. To Robbie's mind it was another example of how feckless Roger had been over the years regarding matters that would affect his family.

He sat forward again and began to search the crowds for a sign of Rowenna, but couldn't spot her. Perhaps she was with their family, or perhaps she was lingering by the arena gate, hoping to catch the eye of one of the young knights waiting to take his turn. He was overcome by a sense of restlessness, a need to be walking and easing the ache in his ribs that felt suddenly tight and constricting his lungs and heart. He did not wish to spend the rest of the day sitting here, even if that meant leaving Mary. He could not simply rise and leave, however. As he had tried to explain to Rowenna, his time was not his own to command. He pulled surreptitiously at the neck of his tunic. It was a fiercely hot day now and a solution came to him in a flash. He turned to Sir John.

'My lord, the day is hot. Will you permit me to bring d-drinks to cool everyone's thirst?'

'A sound idea. As a reward for the victories you and Master Hugone have achieved, I shall bear the cost myself.'

Sir John passed Robbie a small pouch of coins. Mary gave him her warmest smile so far and he replied with a bow, holding her gaze in what he intended to be a devoted manner.

'What should I bring you?' he asked. 'Or perhaps you would care to walk with me?'

'Through the crowds?' Mary wrinkled her nose doubtfully. 'I'm not sure a lady should. I think I would fear too much what might befall me.'

Robbie hid a smile, preparing to offer himself as her protector, but was interrupted by the sound of his name.

'There you are, my boy!'

The sound of Lord Danby's voice booming across the crows caused Robbie's stomach to plummet. Was it not enough for Roger to have destroyed Robbie's belief in his past without now sabotaging his chance of future happiness? Now was the most intrusive time for his family to appear, but sure enough, strolling towards the stand were his parents, aunt and uncle.

'This is your family?' Mary asked.

Robbie admitted they were, but was surprised to see Mary looked on them with interest, not disdain. It was clear to see why.

Walking four abreast, the elder Danbys were an imposing sight. Each wife was on the arm of her husband and they were laughing heartily at some matter. The younger children followed behind and only Rowenna was missing. She, unlike Mary, had no qualms about walking alone in the castle grounds.

The adults were dressed in their finest clothes. The two men were still vital and handsome, even though grey flecked their hair and beards, and their bellies hinted they were used to eating well. Roger wore his rich wool cloak thrown informally back over one shoulder, revealing a tunic edged with embroidery a finger's length thick and an intricately decorated scabbard hanging from a glossy leather belt. Uncle Hal's velvet doublet, robes and chain were a sign of his status in the guild for all to see.

The crespine that concealed Aunt Joanna's hair was red silk that seemed to give out its own light as it flowed down her back. Robbie's mother wore a shorter veil of light blue—similar in colour to that worn by Mary—clearly chosen to best display the three sapphires set into an intricately worked gold necklace that she wore around her neck. The sapphire ring that matched her husband's caught the sunlight, glinting on her hand where she rested it on Roger's arm.

The effect was only slightly spoiled by the long-haired puppy that twisted and pulled at Aunt Joanna's side on the end of a leash, but Robbie heard Mary give a soft moan of delight as the animal gambolled about. He vowed to present the fifth Simon with a pig's knuckle as soon as he was able.

The two couples drew to a stop in front of Sir John's stand. This was a planned visit rather than a stroll about the tournament grounds. Robbie wondered what part Rowenna had played in it. She was still nowhere to be seen.

Roger bowed with a flourish.

'Sir John, permit our intrusion on your party. I wanted to pay my respects and thank you for the care and attention with which you have raised Robbie. He is grown into a fine young man.'

'Your son has proved himself a worthy and able squire. I have no doubt he will continue to do so after he is knighted.'

Sir John gave Robbie a penetrating stare that made Robbie shiver and wonder if the elderly knight suspected he harboured an imposter beneath his roof.

Roger made the introductions for the rest of his party. Sir John's smile grew warmer as Roger named Hal's position in the guild. He smiled at Robbie.

'I was unaware until today you had such influential connections, Master Danby. I was admiring the new sword of the Sheriff of the city this morning. I hope I might be fortunate enough to commission your uncle to furnish me with a new pair of daggers.'

Lucy stepped forward and curtsied to Sir John and Lady Isobel. She, too, thanked them, expressing her hopes that Robbie had not been a troublesome pupil in a forthright manner.

'I read poorly so he writes seldom to me,' she grumbled good-naturedly. 'I have to learn everything from my husband or niece, but I believe he has a good hand.'

Everyone laughed except Robbie. It had been a source of frustration that he could not write to Lucy and beg her to reveal his father's identity without Roger being a party to it. Writing such a letter via Rowenna was inconceivable. Robbie took a quick look at Mary, whose eyes were fixed on Lucy. Her eyes were shining. Sir John invited the Danbys to join them and explained Robbie's intention of bringing refreshments. Aunt

Joanna sat beside Mary, who began fussing over the puppy. Roger escorted his wife to the seat beside Lady Isobel and returned to Robbie.

'I'll go with you.'

Without appearing rude, Robbie could hardly refuse. 'If you wish.'

He walked silently from the stand towards the stalls selling wine. If Roger wished to speak, let him begin.

'You fought well this morning,' Roger said. 'A little too far back on your heels when you attack, but that will come.'

'Rot!' Robbie exclaimed. He folded his arms and faced his stepfather. 'My balance was faultless!'

Roger laughed. 'You do have some fire! I know you find speech hard at times, but I was beginning to worry you had grown so courteous or quiet you didn't know how to hold your own.'

Robbie picked up the wine. 'I just d-don't feel the need to bluster and strut around like a cock in a henhouse. When I have nothing to say, I say nothing.'

'You learned that lesson quicker than I did,' Roger said, scratching his chin. 'You didn't enter the tilting, I noticed'.

It might have been an offhand comment, but Robbie bristled again. 'I did not.'

'I hoped you would at least try. You could have been good and it is the sport of noblemen.'

Noblemen. Robbie grunted, wondering if his father could see the irony in his words. Roger seemed determined to treat Robbie as if he had not torn his world apart with a single word before he left Wharram Danby. He strolled through life as if nothing had repercussions. Robbie almost envied him, but for the harm such a carefree attitude left behind.

'I lost the taste for it,' he said coldly. 'I'm sure you will understand why.'

Roger lowered his gaze and they walked side by side in uncomfortable silence to the stalls. Roger reached into his scrip for coins to pay the vendor, but Robbie stayed his hand.

'I have money.'

Roger raised an eyebrow, but put his scrip away.

'I meant what I told Sir John,' Roger said as he stacked beakers to take back. He lowered his voice and drew closer to Robbie. 'We have not spoken for far too long and now you are a man. I would like more than anything to claim the credit for that, but it is Sir John's doing. And yours. You've done well, Robbie.'

Whatever Robbie had expected to hear, it had not been such honest praise spoken with sincerity from the man who usually joked about everything. He felt an unaccustomed flicker of affection for the man who had given him a name and home. It was something he thought had long died. Memories of a childhood filled with laughter and warmth passed before his eyes. Not everything had been a lie. Roger had been a good father to him.

'You and Grandfather gave me a good grounding before I went to Wentbrig,' he admitted grudgingly. He was startled to see Roger's eyes soften with emotion and felt his throat tighten. The secret had caused him to exile himself, not just from Roger, but also from the rest of his family. How different would the past seven years have been if he had not left with such anger between them? 'Lord Danby always treated me fairly. It was a shame I could not return to see him before he died.'

'You would have been welcome at any time,' Roger said huskily. 'You still are.'

Embarrassed by Roger's earnest tone, Robbie slowed his pace, eyes roving the crowd as they walked.

'Who are you looking for?' Roger asked.

Robbie hadn't realised he had been so obvious. He set his jaw.

'I just wonder if I'll ever see a face that looks like mine.'

Roger frowned. 'What purpose would it serve if you did?'

'It would stop me wondering. Everywhere I go, I wonder if he's there.' Robbie faced his stepfather and folded his arms. His brief rush of fellowship subsided, replaced with the habitual resentment at only knowing half the truth. 'I hate not knowing who he was. Why won't you tell me who he is?'

'Is this a conversation for now?' Roger sucked his teeth.

'It's one I mean to have before I am knighted. Don't I deserve to know what name I could have owned now I'm a man?'

'Perhaps you do. But as to whether you could have owned the name is for your mother to say.' Roger pursed his lips. 'You should talk to her.'

Robbie frowned, wondering what darker secret his mother would reveal. He shifted the bottle from one hand to the other, but almost dropped it when a tall man dressed in a riding cloak barged between him and Roger and continued on into the crowd.

What he was shouting pushed all concerns from Robbie's mind.

'Take me to the Lord Mayor. I bring news from London. Wat Tyler is dead!'

Chapter Five

Rowenna left her family when they decided to go pay their respects to Sir John. As much as she wished to spend more time with Robbie, she was reluctant to stand before Robbie's master and repeat her strange encounter from the previous night. She bit her lip thoughtfully. What had the old knight seen in their faces or postures to suggest she and Robbie would be thinking of marriage to each other? She could think of nothing.

She made her way out of the tournament ground and headed to the temporary market outside the tournament. Weaving her way through the tightly packed stalls, past trinket sellers, food vendors and entertainers, she could still hear the noise coming from the events. She bought a warm rosemary-and-curd pastry to nibble as she walked, greeted acquaintances, then stopped as the bundles of ribbon on one stall caught her eye.

She smoothed down the skirt of her sensible

brown cote-hardie, longing to wear something brighter. She had still not decided what to wear for the Midsummer's Night Feast and new ribbons might help her make up her mind. Pale blue to go with her favourite dark blue gown, or gold to match the fine caul of wire that went with the new wine-coloured silk? The two surcoats were similar in style; both had a row of buttons from neck to waist to fasten them over the kirtle beneath, but the deep red gown could be laced tighter at the sides to give what Rowenna knew was a much more slender silhouette that emphasised the fullness of her breasts.

Rowenna's hand wavered over the gold ribbons. Her mother would not approve. She should wear the blue gown. It was pretty and the colour suited her complexion, but she had worn it so many times. The decision was an important one. The feast would be Rowenna's best opportunity to find a husband.

There was a swell of noise from behind her. Something interesting had clearly happened and she had missed it. Perhaps a bout had ended badly or unfairly. She turned to face the wall of the castle, head on one side to listen. The shouts were louder in the main arena, where the jousting and tilting were taking place. Rowenna had given up watching the contests, finding nothing excited her as much as Robbie's fight had. Now she wondered what she was missing. There was another roar, different in tone to the first. She could not readily identify the source of the noise or the emotion they represented.

'Do you know what is happening?'

The stallholder, who was still holding up the ribbons, shrugged. 'Not out here.'

Rowenna looked again at the ribbons. Mary would be at the Midsummer's Night Feast.

Her stomach clenched. She half wished she'd gone with her parents to pay respect to Sir John and could have satisfied her curiosity. She wanted to see what sort of woman had won Robbie's heart. She would watch them together and see whether she had been right to suspect infatuation. If it was that, she would have some hope of turning Robbie's affections to her. If not, then she hoped Mary would be as kind and beautiful as Robbie deserved. A woman who would be as fond of him as Rowenna was.

Robbie had promised her a dance and would surely keep his word, even if Mary was there. She hoped Robbie would be a good dancer. If he were as swift and graceful with a woman in his arms as he was when he had a sword in his hand, he would be a delight to dance with.

The stall-keeper gave a meaningful cough. Rowenna's mind stopped wavering. The atmosphere in the market had changed. More people were stopping to turn to the grounds. The cries that filled the air were transforming from excitement at the combat taking place to something else.

Fear?

Anger?

Rowenna frowned. There was something significant happening and she was missing it.

'I'll take both colours, please.'

She stuffed the ribbons into her bag, bunched the hems of her kirtle and cote-hardie in one hand and began to push through the crush of people to get back to the gate. The guards on the bridge that served as passage to the entrance looked troubled, gripping their pikes firmly. Rowenna feared they would not let her in. They smirked as she pushed towards them.

'Better head the other way, lass. There's trouble inside.'

Rowenna's scalp prickled with annoyance at his condescending manner. She held her back straight and head high, and gave the most dignified look that she could muster. One Lady Danby would be proud of.

'Thank you for your caution, good sir, but please let me pass. I need to speak urgently with my father. He's Master Danby of the Smiths' Guild.'

The description impressed these men, even if

people of a higher class scorned the family. The guards looked at her with slightly more respect and waved a hand in the direction of the bridge. Rowenna crossed it slowly, caught between the throng of people leaving and those pushing along in the same direction as her. Once inside Rowenna was caught in a fresh swell and bundled along towards the row of stands where the crowd seemed to be converging.

Someone shouted, 'Is it true? The uprising is over?'

'Tyler is dead. The revolt is ended,' a voice roared.

'What did he say?'

'Who?'

The crowd began to take up the name.

The man who had told them the news shouted over the muttering, 'Wat Tyler has been killed. A messenger arrived from London bringing the news for the Lord Mayor.'

Rowenna recognised the name, but it meant little to her. It was just one of many that was thrown up in arguments at home or in the inn, where men gathered to discuss the evils of the hated Poll Tax imposed by the King. To many in the crowd it must have a greater significance, because a murmur began in the crowd: a ripple that began quietly but that raced around the field, gaining in volume until the air was filled with angry mutterings and shouts. Rowenna couldn't tell whether the anger was at Walter Tyler for daring to behave so insolently, or against King Richard for allowing the killing of a man with legitimate grievances. Either way it served to hasten the speed at which the crowd pushed forward.

'De Quixlay will speak,' one man roared.

'He'd better,' another growled. 'We'll not stand to be squeezed and ignored any longer by those rich leeches! The time for the Poll Tax is over.'

It was a living nightmare. Rowenna's feet were trodden on, her hair snagged on buckles and cloak pins, her body jostled from side to side, back and forth. She was certain the hand that at one point caressed her buttock and thigh was intentional. She did not want to think about what else was pressing up against her hip. Her stomach rolled and she began to elbow herself forward. She wished, not for the first time, that she was taller and could see more than the backs of the men surrounding her. She tried to turn back and make her way to the gate, but it was as useless as swimming up the Ouse at a spring tide.

A pile of barrels and crates was stacked by the side of a tent selling wine. Rowenna clambered on to the smallest one and looked over the mass of heads. Her luck changed and she cried aloud, 'Robbie!'

She glimpsed his dark hair over the top of a

group of women. Uncle Roger was by his side. Just the sight of them gave Rowenna the courage she had been lacking. Robbie would protect her as he always did. Rowenna waved a hand to catch their attention and called their names, but they didn't notice her. They both wore expressions of concern, heads bowed together as they spoke. She jumped down from the crate and tried to make her way to them. The crowd surged towards the stands once more, taking Rowenna with it. Even if she had not wanted to go in that direction, she would have had no choice.

She caught another glimpse of Uncle Roger and Robbie, and began to slip through the gaps towards them. She was closer now, almost with them. She stood on her tiptoes again and screamed their names in quick succession, hoping to be heard over the other cries that filled the air. Robbie's head turned. Rowenna jumped into the air, waving her hand desperately, and shouted again and again. Robbie raised his eyebrows in surprise, then frowned and spoke to his father. He began to move towards her, parting the people separating them with forceful swipes of his arms.

Someone barged into Rowenna from behind, a sharp blow in the centre of her back that sent her flailing forward to her hands and knees with a cry of alarm and pain. Before she could push herself to her feet she was caught in the rush and knocked down again. A wicker basket that must surely contain cannonballs from the weight of it caught her across the side of her head, catching at her hair and ripping it painfully from the tight braid. She yanked on the strands to pull free. She crouched down, trying to make herself small so she would avoid injury, and kept still, clutching her bag to her. The air had a warm and oily texture, thick with the smell of bodies and mud, and it felt as if her lungs would not fill properly. Her heart was thumping in her throat with fury that her predicament was going unnoticed and fear that she would remain on the ground for the rest of the day. She was unimportant compared to the news that was driving the crowd beyond her, but surely someone would help her to her feet?

Someone did. She ceased to be battered and sensed a body standing over her. In a matter of breaths, the unseen person was gently pulling her upright. She found herself face-to-face with Robbie. She drew fresh breath into her lungs and let it out in a loud exhalation of relief. He had come for her, as she knew he would.

He gripped her lightly on the shoulders, turning her this way and that as he inspected her. 'Are you hurt?'

Rowenna shook her head. She tried to smile at him and blink away the tears that had only sprung to her eyes once she was safe again. Robbie clearly did not like what he saw because his forehead wrinkled. Without a word he drew Rowenna to him, holding her against his body. His arms enfolded her protectively, locking firmly around her so that she could not even wriggle.

She heard a sigh escape her lips that was more pleasure at the comforting intimacy than relief at being rescued. Let the city rant and riot over the killing of a man none of them had ever laid eyes on. With Robbie standing as tall and firm as an oak, Rowenna felt safer than she had since her foolish decision to come back inside the grounds.

'What's happening?' she asked, her voice muffled against his neck. 'I heard the name they were shouting.'

'Wat Tyler insulted the King at Smithfield and got a sword to the neck for his troubles.' It was Roger who spoke as he strode towards them. Clearly he had not moved with the same speed as his son.

Robbie unwound one arm from around Rowenna and reached for the sword at his side. Rowenna noticed his father doing the same. They weren't alone in drawing their weapons, though the sight of rough labourers feeling for knives did not reassure her as much.

'Can you stand unaided, lass?' Roger asked.

She nodded but was in no hurry to let go of Robbie.

'Best find your family and go home. I suspect we're not too long away from a riot ourselves here. Robbie, take her to safety and see what your master bids you to do. I'm going to stay here and make sure the way into the city is free.'

Roger issued his orders briskly. Rowenna felt Robbie's arms tighten around her. She recognised the irritation she felt when her mother treated her like a child, too. It must be worse for Robbie, who had grown into a man out of sight of his father, to now have Roger taking charge.

'I can go myself,' she said, trying to placate him. 'Tell me where to look.'

'Not in this crowd,' Robbie said firmly. 'I'm taking you with me. Come on.'

When she did not move he took hold of her upper arm. His face showed no fear or anxiety now, but the way his fingers dug into her flesh made it clear he was deeply worried by the commotion going on around them. Knowing this made Rowenna's stomach clench.

'You're hurting me!' she gasped.

Robbie murmured an apology and loosened his grip a little. He moved so he was standing much closer, half behind Rowenna with his right hand on the centre of her back, and took hold of her left arm with his left hand. It felt like he was beginning the measure of a dance and she had the urge to skip her feet to an imaginary beat. She giggled loudly and he flashed her a look that quelled the urge to laugh. There was nothing funny after all.

Robbie walked swiftly, the firm weight of his hand on the curve of her spine compelling Rowenna forward as they moved through the crowd. He set the pace and the direction. She could possibly have resisted if she tried hard enough, but in truth she did not really want to try. Ordinarily, being ushered along like a sheep to market would have set her temper flaring, but she was certain that she would wake in the night for days to come with the memory of the crowd pushing down on her and the sense of helplessness.

'This isn't the way to the gate,' she said. 'Where are we going?'

'To Sir John. Your parents are there along with mine.'

'Oh.' The urge to stay by Robbie's side was stronger than she expected. 'You can't take me home yourself?'

'No. I have to return to Sir John. I have already been gone too long. I'll take you straight to your father. He'll be worried about you. Thank goodness he did not see you as I did or he would have turned grey on the spot!'

He flicked his own hair back from his eyes, as if checking it was still dark brown.

'What were you doing by yourself in the crowd?'

His mouth was close to her ear and he almost shouted the words. He sounded furious and there was no hesitation or stumbling over them. He had always been so slow to anger as a boy that it was a shock to hear him so agitated. Rowenna turned her head. It brought her lips disconcertingly close to his. Robbie stopped walking abruptly.

'I heard cries so I wanted to see what was causing them,' she murmured.

Robbie raised his eyebrows, looked at the ground, the sky, back at Rowenna. He gave a humourless laugh and his brow knotted.

'You thought there was t-trouble, so instead of seeking safety you rushed straight to it. You haven't the sense of a chicken!'

Rowenna's eyes began to sting. It sounded reckless now that he said it, but Robbie's disapproval after what had been a frightening ordeal was the last thing she could stand. She wrenched her shoulder free from his hand and began to walk off.

'Ro, wait!'

He skirted around her and spread his hands wide to prevent her walking past him. She folded her arms and glared, willing herself not to burst into tears. His face was grave and filled with such concern her anger died away. She allowed him to tug her arms gently from the tight knot she held in front of her chest. He held her hands, his thumbs a soft pressure on her palms that made her quiver, and fingers laced between hers.

'I'm not angry,' he said more gently, 'but you need to take more care. If you hadn't seen me, or if I hadn't got to you when I did...'

He left the thought unfinished, but for a gasp, snapping his lips shut and pulling her close. Rowenna suppressed the shiver of anticipation that raced across her skin and stepped eagerly into his embrace for the second time. Now her heart was no longer racing with fear, Rowenna had time to explore the sensation of being held in a man's arms.

Despite the firmness of his grip, Robbie held her tenderly against the chest that had transfixed her when she had seen him earlier.

That chest.

Pictures danced in Rowenna's mind of Robbie naked to the waist, standing before the water trough, using his shift to wipe away sweat and grime when he had not known she was watching him. In her memory, the muscles undulated in his back and arms, toned from years of exercise and work, shapely and firm and sharply defined.

No wonder she had not been able to tear her eyes away. No wonder she had been unable to resist reaching out to feel for herself the perfect, beautiful smoothness of his chest where it had been marred by bruising. She had done so without permission, a liberty that unnerved and confused her. Now he had invited her touch and she felt no qualms about taking full advantage.

She slipped her hands around Robbie's waist and let them settle in the small of his back. She rested her head on his chest in the place where her hand had caressed his bruised flesh, closed her eyes and let her entire body melt against him.

She took another deep breath and her breasts pushed against Robbie's chest in a manner that caused them to throb. Fingers of heat raced down every limb, turning them to liquid. Her chest tightened once more and she took another lungful of air, then another, savouring the deliciously wicked sensations that the closeness of their bodies awoke in her.

She could have stayed in that position for the rest of the day, but she felt Robbie shift a little. To claim him as her protector was selfish when he undoubtedly needed to be elsewhere. Reluctantly she opened her eyes again and her vision was filled with Robbie's face. His hair fell forward as he looked down at her and his soft brown eyes brimmed with concern. He held her gaze, unblinking. His pupils grew wide until they almost obliterated the brown of his irises, leaving only blackness that drew her in.

Rowenna's skin prickled and grew hot, yet a cold shiver ran down her spine. Perhaps she was starting to fall prey to a fever. She surreptitiously wiggled a hand between them and loosened the neck of her gown. She hoped she would not be indisposed before the feast. She wanted to dance so much. She wanted Robbie to be there to dance with her and to hold her like this again.

'You're safe now, I promise.'

Robbie loosened his embrace a little, but made no move to remove his arms from around Rowenna. She cherished the small moment of peace in the middle of the field that was now rapidly emptying as guards marched through the stalls and stands, ushering the spectators out none too gently.

'I'm glad you did come to me,' she whispered. She lifted her head up to kiss him, but it felt too intimate. Instead she brushed her fingertips over the line of his jaw.

'Thank you.'

His face twisted into something that was not quite a smile and he unwound his arms from around her. 'Come on.'

He took her by the hand, his fingers enclosing hers, and led her through the crowd.

Sir John's stand was close to the Lord Mayor's. Rowenna's father was striding back and forth in the company of the burgomaster's deputy and one of the councillors Rowenna was familiar with. Their faces were grave.

Robbie apologised for his slow return and explained in a few concise words how he had encountered Rowenna. He spoke slowly, carefully choosing words that he would not stumble over as much as possible, but Rowenna noticed the tension in his throat and the slight deepening of colour in his neck and cheeks.

'A man of sixty-two would be of no use in a skirmish,' Sir John announced. 'I shall return to the inn.'

Rowenna hoped Sir John would send Robbie to escort her home after all, but her father stepped in.

'I need to gather some documents from the house before I meet with the other guild members. I'll take my women home.'

The Danby women began to make their farewells and edge towards the end of the stand. Hal threw an arm around Rowenna's shoulder.

'My thanks for keeping Rowenna safe, lad,' he said, swinging her round to face Robbie. 'Come by the house when you are able to and I'll make sure I have a flagon of fresh ale waiting.'

Robbie bowed and turned to go, but Rowenna caught him by the hand. He looked at her expectantly, his eyes searching her face.

'My thanks, too,' she said in a low whisper.

She lifted on to her toes and wrapped her arms round his neck. He stiffened and his eyes slid to the stand. Rowenna's heart clenched. Of course his Mary would be there and Robbie would not want another woman behaving so intimately in front of her. She wondered if Robbie would have been so eager to relinquish Mary to a father's care. A sob rose in her throat and she swallowed it down painfully. She unwound herself from around him with reluctance and followed his gaze. A cluster of young women was helping to gather Lady Isobel's possessions. Rowenna could not tell which attendant Robbie had been looking at and she had no more time to find out because Joanna tugged at her arm.

'We need to leave.' She cocked her head at Robbie's mother. Lucy looked stricken. Rowenna's stomach twisted in sympathy. A son and husband both about to be caught in the middle of inevitable violence must be unendurable. She was glad for once that her own father took no part in such dangerous acts. She took Lucy's arm and patted it, and was gratified by the warmth that filled Robbie's eyes.

'Ro will stay with you and the twins.' He kissed his mother's cheek, then smiled at Rowenna.

'Look after her for me.'

He straightened his cloak and left without another word or checking if she agreed. He knew her well enough to know it was not even in doubt.

Rowenna watched Robbie walk away to join his master. The walk transformed into a stride in one fluid movement with no sign of the loping gait of a youth whose limbs were too long, which she had held in her memory. He had grown into his body and wore it well.

'He'll be safe. He fought so well this morning,' Rowenna said reassuringly to Lucy. Her throat tightened at the thought that Robbie might come to harm. Losing him was more than she could bear to imagine.

'Ro's right,' Joanna added, drawing Lucy's other arm under hers. 'He's been well trained by Sir John, I'm sure.'

Rowenna was ushered away by her father, but as she looked back she caught a final glimpse of Robbie flanking Sir John along with another squire. He held his head high and his eyes roved keenly for any trouble. He reminded Rowenna of a cat, poised to leap on prey. No, not a cat, she considered as she made her way through the crowd to the safety of the town house. He was more like one of the hunting dogs Roger favoured, shaggy haired, with meltingly soft eyes and a mild nature, but with powerful muscles concealed beneath their skin. A whistle or word would have them springing to alertness, ready to defend their pack. Robbie was the same, his body hardening to iron and hinting at the strength he bore. She hoped that would be enough to keep him safe because the thought of losing him so soon after having him return was almost unbearable.

Chapter Six

The simmering anger that had begun to brew during the tournament was only the start of what proved to be a long night. The unrest caused by the announcement of Wat Tyler's death boiled over into a riot that spread throughout the city. Every available man who could fight was called upon to patrol and stop the violence when it occurred, walking in groups of three or four: a constant presence on the streets and squares.

Robbie found himself with a pair of knights in their fourth and fifth decades and a squire of seventeen. He was the only man in his group who knew the city well so he found himself taking charge, despite his youth and status. A squire commanding knights! After his triumph in the arena earlier in the day, the blood sang in his veins at this opportunity to prove his worth as a leader. Keeping a watch out meant there was no need to speak and reveal how hard he found it.

The largest part of the unrest seemed to centre around the religious houses and the Mayor's dwelling. As Robbie guided the men down snickets and through squares, he could not tell how much of the raucous language and fighting as men spilled out of the inns and taverns was related to the news from the south and how much was simply the usual drunken behaviour of York's population. He suspected many were taking the opportunity to settle personal vendettas as much as express their anger at the death of the rebel leader from the other end of England.

The sun was setting, but the temperature was still stuffy and overbearing. Robbie led his companions past the Smiths' hall and through a narrow passageway that opened beside the herb garden where he had paused with Rowenna the night before. He gratefully took a drink from the fountain, hoping Uncle Hal had managed to take the women safely home. He had been instructed to finish his patrol at the Dominicans' House on King's Toft and assist with ensuring the curfew was obeyed, but decided to walk past Hal's home and try to catch a glimpse through the window to reassure himself his cousin was safe after her ordeal.

As Robbie and his companions rounded the corner, they came face-to-face with Roger striding in the opposite direction. Roger sheathed his sword. His eyes looked weary from patrolling, but his broad frame exuded vitality. Robbie wondered whether his father missed the excitement of a battle. He had volunteered to join the watchmen eagerly.

'Heading to Hal's? You had the same idea as me, lad,' Roger said.

It was hardly an original idea and didn't merit such commendation, Robbie thought.

'Has Rowenna recovered?' he asked.

'She has.' Roger smirked knowingly. 'Your mother and sisters are well, too, in case you were wondering.'

Robbie's neck flushed hot at Roger's implication that he cared only for Rowenna. 'They had never been otherwise,' he retorted. 'Rowenna suffered a fright so naturally she is my first concern. It was difficult to relinquish her knowing she was upset.'

'I'm merely jesting. Lucy and the girls are safe at Hal's house. Rowenna made sure Lucy had a bottle of Mistress Jackland's ale to criticise so she hasn't time to fret over what we are doing.'

Robbie grinned. His mother was never happier than when she was passing judgement on the quality of a brew other than hers. He had been right to leave her in his cousin's care. Rowenna might seem flighty, but she was warm-hearted and had always possessed a quick mind and determined nature. He knew no woman more capable.

'When I bade them goodbye Rowenna was making light of the riots and explaining to Joanna why it would be safe for her to attend the Midsummer's Night Feast. She's her mother's child through and through.' Roger laughed, then grew serious and clasped Robbie's hand. 'You did well to reach her so rapidly when you did. She could have been badly hurt.'

Robbie shuddered. Seeing Rowenna quaking with fear as she was swallowed and felled by the crowd had shocked him to his core and he would have cut down a hundred men to reach her if necessary. He would not soon forget the way she had trembled from head to toe as he held her in his arms to comfort her. She could not have been aware of the way her breasts had pushed against him, or that her hands brushed against the sensitive flesh at his waist as they tightened around him, but these unconscious actions only served to strengthen Robbie's urge to protect her and to hold her closer and longer. Releasing her afterwards had been harder than he'd thought.

He ran his fingers across his jaw where she had stroked her fingers and was lost for a moment in a reverie involving the soft curves he had felt beneath Rowenna's clothes. He did not hear his father speaking at first until his name was repeated.

'Where are we going now?' Roger asked, adjusting his hood and nodding at Robbie's companions.

'We?' Robbie frowned.

'I might as well add my strength to yours,' Roger said.

Robbie didn't relish being accompanied by his stepfather, but Roger's face glowed with life. 'With your permission, that is,' Roger added.

The addition of the request was a surprise and it would be churlish to refuse.

Childhood tales of his stepfather's escapades and battles came back to Robbie. Moonlit chases through forests, days spent on horseback travelling the country, facing opponents on the battlefield. Lucy had always disapproved of the stories, hushing Roger whenever she caught him spinning them, but Robbie had gloried in them. Roger must miss that life now he was lord of Wharram. If they focused on the patrol, there would be no opportunity to reopen the awkward conversation that had been interrupted.

Robbie pointed back the way he had come from. 'We're going towards King's Toft.'

'Where's the glory in that? There is better fighting to be had and more opportunity for distinction.'

'This isn't about glory,' Robbie said. 'It's about defending York.'

Roger rolled his eyes. 'We should go towards the river. There is unrest near the castle and we can skirt round the outer wall.'

Robbie's jaw clenched at the way Roger immediately assumed leadership. He glanced at the other two knights, who were looking impatiently between father and son. He would gain no respect by agreeing timidly with his father, but the route to the river would take Robbie close to his lodging. He belatedly wondered if Mary was safe and felt a small stab of guilt that he had not considered her well-being before that of Rowenna and his family. It was fortunate Roger hadn't spotted that or he would have been insufferable.

'If you w-wish to join us you may. But w-we'll cut by the river and go to the D-Dominican friary as I s-said. If you prefer to go another w-way, do it alone.'

Robbie could hear himself beginning to stutter at the effort of speaking so much in front of strangers. He would lose the argument if it came down to words. He shifted the bow on his shoulder and planted his feet further apart. His jaw tightened as he drew himself tall. Much taller than Roger. His unknown father must have been a large man. He held Roger's gaze, waiting for his response. Roger nodded briefly.

'We'll do as you say.'

Cheering inside at this victory, Robbie fell

in beside Roger and they walked side by side towards the friary. The road was littered with rocks and makeshift weapons that had been discarded. Men dressed in everything from tatters to fine homespun lurched about or slumped against walls, passed out from drink.

'This rabble needs whipping until they bleed,' growled the elder of the knights, kicking a prone figure out of the way. The second knight grunted.

'Insolent upstarts should know their place and keep to it.'

Robbie shook his head, eyeing the rich nap on the tabards the knights wore and the gems ornamenting their scabbards. The expense of even a modest pageant such as the one taking place this week must seem sickening to men living on next to nothing.

'When Adam delved—' Robbie said.

The knight interrupted. 'And Eve span, who then was the gentleman? I've heard what John Ball is said to have preached and my answer is this—I was. Me and my father. And yours here. And theirs before them.'

Robbie's chest tightened. He glanced at Roger. He was no more entitled to a name and title than a man who tanned the leather or tended the horses. One such man could have sired him after all.

'Wh-why shouldn't the poor object when the King squeezes them so hard?' he asked.

The knight guffawed. 'You're a soft touch!'

'He has a good heart,' Roger said, shooting the knight a look of animosity. 'I doubt half the men out this evening have heard the names John Ball or Wat Tyler, but the lad is right. The government raised the tax by three times the original amount. Can you imagine what that did to the needy? I had to look my vassals in the eye while I held my hand out to them and took their means to buy bread.'

Robbie heard approval in his father's voice, but he set his jaw, again resenting the older man coming to his defence. Years living away from Wharram meant he had forgotten how stifling his father could be, however good his intentions.

'I do not need you to speak for me and I'm not so naive to think there aren't people here taking the chance to cause trouble simply for the devilry in them.'

He strode faster, not caring if Roger and the others kept pace. The bell of St Peter's Church tolled, signalling curfew, and the sound was taken up by others across the city. As they passed the Council Hall, Roger slowed and his face became thoughtful. Dusk was falling and the flickering of oil lamps lit the small windows as figures passed back and forth in the chamber.

'My poor brother will no doubt be in there trying to make his rational voice heard above the braying of the aldermen and bailiffs,' Roger said.

'He left his house unguarded?' Robbie asked in consternation. Horrors filled his imagination of rough men breaking down the door of Hal's shop, of Rowenna once more falling beneath the swell of their bodies as she had in the crowd. 'You should go back there.'

'Trying to get rid of me? Don't fear. I think anyone attempting to gain entry will wish they had not, if I know your mother and aunt.'

Roger's eyes glinted with wicked amusement. Robbie felt himself grin. People never managed to stay angry with Roger for long when he decided to be charming. It was a knack Robbie envied.

'It's a cruel injustice Hal will never be elected Master of the Guild. He would do so well.' Roger sighed, his eyes still on the window.

Robbie followed his father's glance. Rowenna might find it harder to find a husband than she hoped. Hal's lineage would reflect on her, too, and would limit the number of men who would court her.

'Bastardy is a curse,' he muttered.

'If you consider a man is only what he is at birth. My brother has spent his entire life proving a bastard of good family and good character

can be worth more than a legitimate son who is
a wastrel like myself.'

'I mean no criticism of Uncle Hal,' Robbie
said.

'I know,' Roger said. 'A man with strength
of will can rise above his circumstances, if he
strives hard to make the best of his opportunities. Remember that.'

He gave Robbie an earnest look for a long time.
Robbie shifted uncomfortably and looked away.
His stepfather's meaning was clear.

'A man who knew his background would do
better,' he retorted in a low whisper. 'Knowing
whether he was the son of a swineherd or a passing pedlar.'

Roger's jaw tightened, the tendons in his throat
knotting.

'You insult your mother when you say that,'
Roger muttered, leaning in close. 'Nothing so
base.'

He walked off, the others falling in behind him
in silence. Robbie followed last, keeping watch
for any danger and chewing over Roger's insinu-
ation that he was not of low birth.

The route to the river took longer than anticipated. Carts had been upturned in the streets and
they had to double back on more than one occasion. Once they came across a row of houses on
fire. Women passed buckets of water in a chain to

quench the flames. Robbie recoiled, the heat and smell of burning wood reaching into his stomach and making it heave. Nevertheless, he was already starting to unbuckle his cloak when Roger took his shoulder, holding him back. He pushed the squire towards the line of women instead of Robbie.

'Stay and help. We'll carry on,' he ordered and for once Robbie did not object to Roger taking charge.

No one spoke again until they reached the gates of the friary. This was where the largest gathering was, where all the various groups of rioters and peacekeepers seemed to have converged. The heavy gates were closed, but the way they rattled when a makeshift battering ram beat against them indicated they would not last long. Robbie and Roger exchanged worried glances.

'Have you fought before?' Roger asked.

'Never to kill.'

'Well, you won this morning, so there's hope for you,' Roger said.

Robbie shifted uneasily. His victory in the arena, the odd exchange with Rowenna, the conversation with Mary, all seemed much longer ago than this morning.

A man with strength of will, Roger had said. Robbie could be that. He regarded the mob, which was hurling rocks, sticks, vegetables, anything they had laid their hands on at the door to St George's Chapel. He drew his bow and loosed off three arrows in quick succession. They embedded themselves in the door just above the heads of the rioters. He was gratified to see Roger raise an eyebrow in surprise.

'A lance would be no use now,' he said, smiling. Roger bowed his head in acknowledgement.

'Get to your homes!' Robbie bellowed.

The mob began to fall back. Robbie's party drew their swords and joined the line that was steadily pushing the rioters away from the friary and back towards the river. With the night finally cooling and faced with a line of armed, trained men, the mob quickly dispersed. Robbie walked back to the centre of the city in Roger's company.

'You resented me being here this evening,' Roger said. 'I'm sorry for forcing myself on you.'

The apology took Robbie by surprise. He was on the verge of denying he had cared so much, but Roger would not believe that. Instead he lifted his chin and looked Roger in the eye.

'I need the chance to prove my worth on my own. As you say, a man with strength of will can rise above his circumstances.'

'You'll have the chance, there's no doubt about that,' Roger said grimly. 'I doubt this will be the end of the troubles. You've not had the opportunity to do it during war, but you should count yourself fortunate there. A ragbag of a few hundred dissatisfied city dwellers is not the same as an army determined to slaughter you.'

He rubbed his right shoulder and rolled it back. It was an old injury from before Robbie was even born. Roger never talked about how he had received it, but clearly it still troubled him years later.

'Not returning to France was the best decision I made. I have your mother to thank for that. And you, of course.'

Roger's face lit at the mention of Lucy. Whatever else Robbie doubted, he knew their love was the strongest he had ever seen. Even the passion he felt for Mary could not compare.

'I would never want to part from the woman I love,' he said.

'I was right, your mind is on marriage.'

Robbie looked at him sharply and Roger grinned widely.

'You have your eye on someone. I thought so last night. I confirmed it when I saw you together today. You have the same expressive eyes as your mother and your whole body proclaims your heart as clearly as if you had written the words on your chest.'

Robbie hid a smile. He had thought his brief conversation with Mary had been discreet and short enough not to attract notice, but something in his manner had clearly given his feelings away. He resolved to be more cautious, if merely exchanging a few words about a walk had been enough for Roger to guess the emotions that churned inside him.

'If I w-were to ask the woman in question for her hand, would I have your blessing?' he asked.

'Need you ask? I think I can say with confidence that you would have the blessings of every Danby in Yorkshire.'

Unexpectedly, Roger drew him into a brief embrace, clapping him on the back hard. Robbie's heart swelled at the sanction so much he didn't even object to the embrace.

'Then wish me luck at the feast.'

The unrest had continued into a second day and night. The only thing Rowenna had to be thankful for was that she did not develop the fever that she had feared was upon her when she had become weak, hot and shivery in Robbie's arms. The flames that had shot through her while simultaneously making her tremble like a newborn lamb had obviously been the temporary result of her escapade in the tournament ground.

Uncle Roger called by the house early on the second evening. Rowenna rushed to him eagerly, hoping for news of what was happening, but he refused to speak in front of his daughters, saying it was men's business. He chucked her under the chin, turning her face to the light.

'You look brighter than you did yesterday,' he said.

Rowenna hushed him quickly. 'No one knows about what happened beyond you and Robbie, and I intend that no one will, if I'm ever to be allowed to leave the house again.'

'A Danby woman sneaking around against all good advice. How unusual!' Roger gave her a conspiratorial wink. 'Don't fear. We'll keep your secret.'

'Have you seen Robbie since we parted?' Rowenna asked, trying to keep her voice light. 'I hoped he might be able to call.'

'Last night, yes. Not today, though I'm sure he will be safe. He's a brave lad and knows how to handle his weapon. You saw him in combat yesterday.'

Once again a vision came to Rowenna of Robbie dancing about on light feet to avoid his opponent, thrusting and blocking with the short sword. It was replaced almost instantly with one of him standing at the water trough after his fight, naked to the waist with his skin slick and glowing from his exertion in the bout. Why could she not rid herself of that memory? Why did it cause her skin to burn inside and out whenever she pictured the dark hair travelling from his firm chest down between the supple muscles of his abdomen?

Somewhere, out in the city, Robbie was patrolling and facing the fury of the citizens who had decided they would accept unjust treatment no more. She might even have taken arms herself in protest if she had been a man, if it had not meant standing in opposition to her cousin. Those men would not be battling with blunted swords. She bit her lip and turned pleading eyes on her uncle.

'If you see him, will you watch over him?'

'Do you think he needs guarding?' Roger patted her hand. 'He's not a child. I doubt he would welcome my intervention but I'm sure he will be glad to know he is in your thoughts. If you wish, I will try to find him tonight.'

Roger kissed his wife with a thoroughness that made Rowenna's cheeks flame and departed. Rowenna ran to the window in time to see Roger striding away and meeting a group of cloaked men. They exchanged words. One dropped his hood down and stared up at the window. With her heart racing, Rowenna recognised Robbie. She waved the candle, hoping he had seen her, and received a brief wave in return. She darted from the window and down the stairs into the workroom at the front of the house, ignoring her mother's protests. The door was bolted and her fingers fumbled in her haste to open it.

'Bull's pizz—' She caught herself midoath and bit her tongue. 'Oh, why won't you open?' She succeeded and flung the heavy door open. She ran out into the street in time to see him striding away, bow in hand.

'Robbie, wait!' she called.

He halted, spun on his heel and strode back to her. She met him halfway and flung her arms around him. Her breasts pressed against his chest, her arms around his neck. Her lips grazed against the stubble on his cheek, sending a delightful thrill through her.

'You're safe. I was so worried.'

She drew back and looked at him, smiling widely, but he looked furious. Her heart lurched. He tugged her arms from around his neck and held them firmly by her side.

'Get back inside!'

When she did not move, astonished at his ferocity, he scooped her up with a low growl and carried her bodily back into the house and kicked the door shut behind him with a thump. He deposited her on to the workbench. She sprawled in a graceless heap while Robbie glared down at her, hands on hips. His eyes flashed and, with his dishevelled hair in tangles and leather jerkin, he looked alarmingly dangerous.

And astonishingly handsome. The feverish chills threatened to return.

'Have you lost your senses?' Robbie thundered. 'It isn't safe out there!'

Rowenna hopped from the table and faced him, arms mirroring his. 'I was standing in front of my own house!' she exclaimed.

'Which was no doubt bolted and the windows shuttered for good reason,' Robbie snapped. 'I've spent most of today doing my best to avoid being hit by rocks or worse hurled by an angry m-mob and keep the peace. Believing you were all safe inside was the one worry I didn't have to consider.'

'And I worry when the people I care for are marching around the city at risk of death!' Rowenna's cheeks flamed. 'I didn't think it would be dangerous outside here.'

'Of course you didn't.' He rolled his eyes, but there was humour in them. 'What did you want?'

'Just to see you and check you were safe. Your father said he hadn't seen you today. I asked him to watch over you if he saw you.'

Robbie's brow knotted. 'There was no need to do that. I can look after myself.'

Rowenna bit her lip, realising she'd blundered. Roger had been right to predict Robbie's resentment. 'He said the same, but it eased my mind. You must both indulge me. I know you can look after yourself, but don't turn away anyone who wants to do the same.'

Robbie looked slightly mollified. Rowenna put her hand to his chest to pacify him, feeling the shape of the muscles beneath his leather jerkin.

'Will you please tell me what is happening? Your father said there was nothing to trouble us with, but I don't believe him. He grows too protective over us. I'm not too stupid to understand, or too weak to withstand the knowledge.'

Robbie's eyes lost a little more of their annoyance. A flicker of a smile crossed his lips.

'No one would ever call you weak or stupid.'

He wrapped his arms around her, giving her a brief squeeze. Rowenna smelled smoke and earthiness and had to resist burrowing in closer to drink in his scent. She leaned back to stare at him.

'Tell me, then. I know you don't keep things from me.'

'Very well, if it means you stay indoors. The friary has been breached. The city militia are attempting to suppress the violence and force the mob back, but it is proving difficult. My skill with the bow was brought to the attention of the commander this morning.'

His voice brimmed with pride. Rowenna hugged him tighter. 'Well done. Is it over now?'

'Not yet. I'm being sent to guard the bridge at Lendal and fire warning volleys at anyone who attempts to cross.'

He unwound his arms from around her. Rowenna reluctantly let him go. 'I'm needed. Before I go, can you spare me a cup of wine? I'm a husk.'

Rowenna took the stairs two at a time. When she returned, he was staring through the half-closed door at the road. His shoulders were tense and his manner watchful. Real fear flooded Rowenna and she had to force herself not to beg him to stay with her. He needed to do his duty and she would not stand in his way. She held the cup out to him and he took it, fingers brushing against hers. He drank slowly, looking at her over the rim. His gentle brown eyes were shadowed from not enough sleep. Remorse flashed through her at having created problems by distracting him.

'You look a mess,' she said with a forced smile.

She ran her hands through his hair, rearranging it in a neater fashion across his forehead, tucking stray curls behind his ear as if making him neat would ward off any danger. Her fingers brushed against the lobe and his eyes widened.

'What are you doing?' he asked.

'I cannot arm myself and fight at your side and I have no favour to give you.' She bit her lip. 'I shall make you presentable enough so that if you meet with the Mayor himself he will marvel at your knightly bearing.'

She straightened his collar and unexpectedly her eyes stung. It would most likely be Mary's place to do this before long. She widened her fingers over his neck, leaned in and, with her heart in her throat, kissed his cheek. She felt his jaw tighten, but he rested his face against hers and they stood motionless together.

'I can't stay,' Robbie said.

'I know. Stay safe,' Rowenna answered.

'I should be saying that to you.' Robbie felt for her hand and squeezed it. 'Stay indoors now and bolt the door after I go.'

She nodded obediently, determined not to cause him any more concern.

He strode away, bow across his back and the hood of his deep green cloak pulled down to hide his face. At the corner he turned, saw her standing there and pointed at the door.

'In! Now!'

She darted back inside and bolted the door.

She lay in bed that night, unable to sleep and listening to the cries grow quieter until the only sounds were the usual indications of life in the city. Her father returned late, her uncle later. Robbie was not with them, but knowing Roger and Lucy were drinking with Hal and Joanna put her mind at ease. He was safe, otherwise they would not sit and drink so easily. He must have returned to his lodging at the inn. He was probably sitting with his Mary while she was lying in bed alone.

Robbie's face rose in her mind, his warm eyes looking into hers, full lips drawn slightly to one side as he smiled, and her heart thumped. She rolled on to her back with a sigh of frustration, tangling her legs in her shift. She unwound the shift and smoothed it down again, letting her hands linger as they travelled across the linen, feeling the shape of her body beneath it and remembering the way Robbie's hands had caressed her and tried to remember exactly what it had been like to be in his arms.

Was this infatuation or something deeper? Or simply her body responding to the physical sensations she had never experienced before and seeking further explorations? She couldn't say.

His jaw had been stubbly when she touched it. She wondered what it would have felt like on her lips or brushing against her throat. She stroked her fingertips over her throat and could almost feel the roughness against her skin. She rolled on to her side, clenching her legs together and drawing her belly in, imagining Robbie's lips in place of her hand. A sensation of warmth began to burn in her core and a gentle tremor passed through her body. Finally the sleep that had evaded her came upon her. Rowenna was lulled to sleep by the sound of voices, low and peaceful, coming from the room below.

Chapter Seven

Robbie woke to see Cecil's face looming over him. He had been dreaming of dancing with Mary, whose wide brown eyes had been sparkling with laughter and desire. Cecil interrupting his sleep was a poor substitute.

'Shift yourself, Rob, Sir John wants to speak with you.'

Robbie rolled from the low truckle bed and pulled on his clothes, wincing as he did. It was only as he followed Cecil downstairs that it occurred to Robbie that Mary's eyes were blue, not brown. He hadn't been dancing with her after all, but try as he might, he couldn't place the familiar eyes.

Sir John was breaking his fast alone at the long table. The dividing door was half-shut across the private area and a heavy curtain covered the rest, blocking the women from Robbie's sight, but the sound of Mary's lute and female voices raised in laughter filtered through the cloth. The women of the household were occupied with their own diversions. The three men glanced towards them and shared a smile.

'Master Hugone, shut the doors fully,' Sir John instructed.

Robbie waited anxiously, but when Sir John faced him, the old man's expression was one of approval.

'I was woken early by a communication from the Mayor's office this morning,' Sir John said. 'He wishes to reward those who have played their part in defending the city and to provide a celebration to divert attention from what has taken place. In the next week he intends to hold a public ceremony to knight five of the squires who showed particular devotion to their duties.'

He held out a scroll to Robbie, who looked at it uncomprehendingly.

'My heartiest congratulations,' Sir John said, smiling. 'And my thanks for bringing such honour on my household.'

The meaning became clear. Robbie's hand shook as he took the scroll and read it. His name was undeniably written in black ink above the seal of Simon de Quixlay. Sir John continued speaking, but Robbie could barely take in his words. To be knighted so soon—and in York, where his family might be able to attend and where the nobility of York would watch him—was beyond his expectations.

His heart rose. His stomach plummeted. He stammered his thanks, his words twisting in his throat even more than usual. He listened calmly while Sir John explained the time and place of the dubbing ceremony.

'I have an errand for you now. I have a commission for your uncle. Please visit his workshop and take him this letter. I am sure you are anxious to inform your parents of your good fortune, but please keep the knowledge to yourself for the time being until the formal announcement is made.'

Robbie bowed, thinking that he was in no hurry to tell Roger of his news. Still, he was grateful for the opportunity to clear his head with a walk and to try to master the smile that he knew was emblazoned on his face.

'My congratulations also.' Cecil's eyes were flint as they walked away. 'You were fortunate indeed to be sent out into the city rather than protecting Sir John and his women.'

'I did not choose where I w-was sent,' Robbie said. 'Cecil, your time will come.'

'Of course it will, though not as soon as it would have if my noble father and wealthy uncle of the guild had been available to lobby for me. I much preferred staying at the inn and reassuring the womenfolk of their safety.'

Robbie's jaw tightened, but he said nothing. If Cecil knew the true relationship between him and Roger, he would not be so brazen in his insults. He let the accusation of nepotism slide off him. Any acclaim was due to his actions alone. Robbie was no longer a squire but formally a knight-in-waiting, and could forgive Cecil his jealousy. Within seven nights he would be knighted. He grinned, hoping the response would irritate Cecil more than angry words. Oddly, the implication Cecil had been comforting Mary did not disturb him as much as it should have done.

'It's a pity you couldn't be knighted before the feast,' Cecil continued. 'It would have been much easier to find a woman willing to have a fumble in the corner with a knight than a squire, though I imagine there will be plenty willing to play with one so close to being dubbed. You'll have some fine sport.'

'And corrupt the oath I w-won't have even m-made?' Robbie retorted.

He thought of the vows of chastity and honour he would have to declare before everyone assembled at the ceremony. His stomach twisted into a tighter knot and he felt queasy.

'You had better practise making it quicker than that or I'll be knighted ahead of you even if I start a week later.' Cecil smirked.

Cecil's final arrow found its mark. Robbie

should be elated, but Cecil had made a fair point. He would stumble and halt his way through the ceremony and disgrace himself, his master and his family.

He made his way through the town to Hal's house. The shutters to the ground-floor shop that had been closed and barred during the unrest were thrown back and the door was propped open. He peeked through the window.

Hal was not there, but Rowenna was sitting at the trestle table they had sat on together the night before. She was dressed in the same brown kirtle she had worn at the tournament, now with a sleeveless blue cotte over the top. Her hair was loose and swept back from her brow with a filet of matching blue cloth to keep it out of her eyes as she worked. She seemed happy in her work, her head bent over a pile of papers, and her pen moving swiftly down the page before she wrote carefully at the bottom. Robbie was about to call to her but hesitated, reluctant to break her concentration. She dropped the pen and turned to piles of herbs that she began laying into bunches as she sang softly to herself. She wrapped twine around the stalks to tie the bunches together and laid them out on the table side by side. When she was finished she picked one up and held it to her nose, inhaling deeply. She raised her head, finally saw Robbie at the window and jumped, putting her hand to her breast. She beckoned him in.

'You made me jump. How long were you watching me?' she asked suspiciously.

'Not long,' he lied. He leaned against the table beside her and they smiled at each other. He indicated the herbs with a tilt of his head. 'Can I smell them?'

She held a small bunch out to him at arm's length. He leaned close to her hand and sniffed, catching the scent of lovage and thyme. He breathed deeply, the rich spiciness tickling his nose. He took it from her and tucked it into his sleeve.

'Are you here to see your mother and father before they leave for Wharram?'

Robbie tensed. During the first night of the patrol, he and Roger had come closer to speaking frankly than ever before. Knowing Roger approved of Mary made Robbie feel a little warmer towards his stepfather. He should have the conversation he needed before they returned, but his stomach felt hollow at the thought.

'Not now. I might if I have time, but I have a letter from Sir John for your father. Are you here alone?' he asked.

'Father is working at the foundry on St Andrewgate. I offered to write up the accounts for him. It's more satisfying than sewing or weaving.'

Rowenna stood and began to gather her papers. 'Do you want to go see him? I would welcome the opportunity to escape the house.'

Robbie caught her hand to stop her. 'I'm happy here.'

Her eyes scoured his face and she frowned before understanding filled them.

'You still hate the forge?'

'The fires,' Robbie explained, shuddering at the thought of the vast blackness of the furnace and the flames he was sure would consume him if they were able. 'I don't know why.'

'Well then, will you walk awhile with me?' Rowenna asked. 'I've been inside all morning and the room is stifling. We could go to the herb garden with the fountain and sit there.'

'It could be dangerous,' Robbie said.

'In the garden? Even if it is, I don't care! My parents refused to let me leave the house, saying the same thing, but they'll be happy if you're protecting me.' Rowenna took his hand, dropping her eyes to the sword at his waist before raising them to look at him beseechingly. 'I know you won't let me come to any harm. You fight so well.'

She spoke with such confidence in his abilities that Robbie was swayed. What fool would resist the opportunity to spend time with a woman as appealing as Rowenna?

'Only for a short while,' he agreed, tucking

her arm into his and relishing the way she nestled against him as they strolled out.

They made a circuit of the garden, but despite Rowenna's company, Robbie could not shake the melancholy that possessed him.

'You're troubled,' Rowenna said. She stopped by the fountain and put her hands on his shoulders, peering into his face.

'Yes. No. I...'

He untangled himself and leaned back against the stone lion, dropping his head. The worry Robbie had pushed from his mind since Sir John had announced his impending knighthood rose up. He could no longer ignore it. He found himself keen to share his trouble with Rowenna, who he knew with certainty would not mock him. He sat on the step and studied his hands, bending his head so he didn't have to look at her.

'When I am knighted I will have to s-speak. To m-m-m-make m-my oath at my dubbing.'

Tearing each word from his throat was agony and took more difficulty than anything he could remember for a long time. If he hesitated and mumbled like that, his investiture would make him a laughing stock of the city.

'That will not be for months,' Rowenna said. 'You will have time enough to prepare and you will be word-perfect.'

Robbie bit his lip. He was allowed to tell no

one what Sir John had told him, but his heart yearned to share the news with Rowenna. His oldest friend would share in his delight and understand his fears. It pained him that he could not tell her. One more secret that lay between them.

'However soon it comes, I will not trust myself,' he replied.

'I have faith in you.' Rowenna slipped her hand into Robbie's and rested her head on his shoulder. He leaned his head to the side so it rested on the top of hers and closed his eyes. The scent of the herbs she had been tying was on her skin and mingling with the smell of rosemary in her hair. He inhaled deeply and sighed. He could not remember the last time he had felt so at peace. Warmth spread through him, knots in his shoulders easing as he relaxed beside her. If only he felt so at ease in Mary's presence. He would never struggle to speak to Rowenna about anything. A troublesome fluttering in his chest stirred his conscience, telling him that such a thought was disloyal to Mary, but he ignored it.

'I don't think I can do it without shaming myself and everyone I know. I can't speak without the words choking me.'

'You're doing it now,' she said gently. 'You often do.'

He shrugged. 'With you perhaps I do. I always feel at ease with you.'

She twisted round to face him and put her free hand to his cheek, giving him the sweetest smile and causing his heart to melt.

'Why not imagine you are talking to me alone when you repeat your oath? I'll make sure I'm there. We could practise now.'

Could it work if he imagined Rowenna was the only person in the church? The only person in the world? He considered her words for a long time. The garden was deserted and no one would come across them.

'It might work.'

He moved to kneel on one knee. Rowenna stood before him with an expression of such uncharacteristic gravity on her face Robbie had to fight hard not to burst into laughter. He suppressed it, knowing she was trying to help, looked up into her eyes and began to recite the vows he had learned by heart years ago.

'I will observe fast days and abstinences.'

He was hesitant at first, pausing between words, but the oaths that he had spoken in his mind so many times came more easily to his lips than he anticipated.

'I shall not traffic with traitors.'

Rowenna's face changed slowly from solemn to smiling and she gave him encouraging nods. Robbie smiled up at her from his position at her feet. Her face filled his vision. Sunlight lit her from behind, turning her dark curls to burnished bronze.

'I will not give false counsel to a lady.'

Rowenna bit her lip and her shoulders shook a little. Robbie stopped speaking.

'I'm sorry.' Rowenna giggled. 'Only you made me remember the times you gave me bad counsel when we were children.'

Robbie grinned. 'I can recall enough times when you did equally!'

'A fair point. In that case, I dub thee Sir Robert.' She extended a hand and tapped him lightly on each shoulder. Her hand brushed the bare skin at his neck as she withdrew it and he shivered. He pulled on his collar, remembering the way his skin had fluttered where Rowenna had touched him the night before. He stood and brushed the dust from his knees.

'Thank you. I do believe that was easier than I feared. I shall think of you while I stand my vigil.'

'Aren't you supposed to be contemplating your future as a knight and praying for strength?'

'Maybe I need to pray for strength to contemplate you!' he teased.

She laughed and tossed her head back. Robbie stared at her, enjoying the way her eyes danced and her curls fell softly back around her jaw and neck. Contemplating Rowenna was a much more appealing proposition than anything else he could think of.

'I should keep you with me for counsel and to practise all my speeches on,' he said wistfully. 'If only speaking to M-Mary was as easy as talking to you.'

'Isn't it?' Rowenna looked at him keenly. 'You shouldn't find it hard to talk to someone if you love them.'

Robbie bowed his head. It made no sense. Speaking to Mary should be as effortless as talking with Rowenna.

'I find that almost as daunting as the prospect of knighthood. I plan what to say when I'm alone, but the thought of speaking to her makes my throat seize.'

After the exchange with Roger, he knew he could approach Mary with the blessing of his family. If he could find the words to approach her at all.

'You need to rehearse beforehand as you did with your vows,' Rowenna said.

'You would let me practise on you?' Robbie asked. It was an odd idea, but now Rowenna had put the thought into his mind it took root.

'That's not what I mean at all.' Rowenna backed away, arms folded. 'You don't need a real person. A dummy in the tilt yard would suit perfectly well, I imagine.'

Robbie chuckled at the idea of speaking to the padded figure. 'You were happy to pretend to be knighting me.'

'That was different. I'm not Mary. I'm not the one you want to say words of love to.' She pulled a bough of rosemary from a nearby bush, shredding it on to the ground.

'I know you're not. Not Mary, I mean,' he added quickly, realising how rude his words sounded and fearing he had offended her. He ruffled his hair. 'I never run out of things to say to you. I'm just asking you to listen while I say the words. You don't want me to seem a dullard, do you?'

'Oh, I certainly think you're a dullard!' Rowenna said sharply, turning to face him. 'I'm not going to listen to your words of love for another woman. Would you pretend to be Geoff and let me coo into your ear so happily?'

'Geoff? Do you want to coo into his ear?' Robbie's skin prickled. He really didn't want Rowenna to be entertaining thoughts of that stuffed tunic when she was with him.

She crossed her arms and pouted. 'You know I don't! I just can't think of anyone else to name. I haven't had the chance to meet anyone!'

'You're right, I was stupid.' He sighed.

Rowenna took his hand. 'No, you aren't. If you love her, the words will come, and if she loves you, she won't care how hesitant they sound. I could think of a hundred things to say to the man I love if I had the chance.'

Her cheeks turned so pink Robbie wondered if she had anyone in particular in mind. Not Geoff, but he couldn't think who else she might be fond of.

'I'm s-sure you could, but my tongue is not as quick as yours,' he replied.

'Not for speaking, but I'm sure it works adequately for other purposes.' She gave him a wicked look from beneath her eyelashes, curving her mouth into a pouting bud that begged to be kissed.

'Ro! You scandalise me!'

She giggled, a rippling sound that infected Robbie like a fever.

'I don't mean to. Or possibly I do.' She put her hands on his arm in mock entreaty. 'Forgive your poor cousin her wanton behaviour.'

A laugh erupted from deep inside Robbie. He lifted her chin with a fingertip and gave her a stern look. 'I'll pardon you if you help me. I won't say anything to scandalise *you*.'

'I doubt you could!'

'Is that a challenge, Ro?'

She looked up and caught his eye. He held her gaze, slipping his hands from her wrist along her arms to rest on her shoulders. She sighed and looked away.

'Very well, I'll do it, only to see if you do manage to shock me. Tell me where your Mary will be while you are declaring your love to her.'

Robbie shrugged. He hadn't given that much thought. 'She'll be sewing or playing her lute.'

Rowenna arched an eyebrow. 'The life of a court lady is so diverting. I wonder sometimes how I have lived so long without it.'

Robbie scowled. 'You seem eager enough to marry a knight so you can do it yourself.'

Rowenna jutted her bottom lip out, scowling back. 'I'm not planning to marry so I can sit idle and look like an effigy waiting for a tomb to grace. I want to marry a man who will take me to see the country when he travels. I certainly won't marry a man who leaves me alone and expects me to sit quietly all the hours of the day. Think of my parents or yours. Can you imagine either of our mothers sitting placidly, sewing in solitude?'

Robbie conceded the point. His mother and aunt both played full roles in their husbands' lives and work. He could not imagine Rowenna doing anything different.

'But I'm being unkind,' Rowenna said. 'I shall be your elegant lady.'

She walked between the neat rows of lavender and betony, hips swaying distractingly, and positioned herself on the edge of a stone bench with an elegant movement. She did an exaggerated mime of strumming a lute. Robbie sniggered.

'Good morrow, Master Danby,' she said. She spread her skirts out, cocking her head to one side with an expression of coquettish challenge that he was certain would never appear on Mary's placid face.

Robbie took a deep breath, doing his best not to be distracted by the delicious frisson that shot through him. He dropped to her side, going on to one knee. 'M-Mary, I adore you.'

'That's very forward.' Rowenna laughed. 'Perhaps converse a little first. What do you usually talk to her about?'

'I don't. That is, we've only spoken once or twice.'

And those times had been completely unsuccessful, he thought ruefully.

Rowenna raised her eyebrow and laughed gently. 'Robbie, I do love you, but you're a fool. Very well, continue.'

He wrinkled his brow. 'How would you begin to tell a man you like him? This man you would coo at?'

'I wouldn't! That is, it would be frowned upon for a woman to be forward enough to begin such a conversation. All I can do is make my eyes large and hope I am noticed.'

She made them as wide as possible and gazed at him from beneath her lashes in illustration.

'You can't possibly go unnoticed,' Robbie exclaimed. His eyes roved over her, from the dark curls and flashing eyes to her full, soft breasts and slender waist. He slid on to the bench beside her, twisting round so they were close. 'You must turn heads whenever you enter a room.'

'Oh, yes. All the rooms in Ravenscrag,' she said drily. 'If only they were occupied with more than kitchen cats or my mother, I might find a husband in no time at all. As you will surely win your woman. Now, start again.'

Their eyes met and they exchanged a smile. Robbie's chest grew warm at the confidence she showed.

'You fill my heart with hope whenever I look at you,' he said.

'Does she? I mean, do I?' Rowenna said, gazing away modestly and fluttering her hand over her heart.

'Yes,' Robbie said. 'I love you.'

Rowenna gave him a sweet smile and put her hand to his cheek.

'Why do you love me?' she purred.

Robbie opened his mouth to speak just as Rowenna began to stroke her fingertips down towards his jaw, brushing lightly against the corner of his open lips. Robbie's stomach rolled over, his cock jerked awake and his mind emptied. He gave a strangled gasp that was no word at all. Rowenna drew her hand away as if his skin were molten iron. Robbie rubbed his eyes and looked at her bleakly.

'I'm useless.'

Rowenna sat back with her arms folded and gave him a critical look. 'Well, you didn't sound convincing. Or convinced. If you can't tell Mary why you love her, are you so sure you do?'

Robbie didn't answer. Beyond describing her beauty or grace, he couldn't. It shocked him. He pushed himself to his feet and paced around the garden, frustration making him restless. He leaned against the fountain and peered into the bowl, head bent, the sore muscles in his back and shoulders tensing.

'I didn't mean to offend or distress you.'

Rowenna's whisper made him start. He hadn't realised she had followed him across the garden. He dropped one arm and faced her.

'You did neither. It's myself I'm annoyed with for suggesting something so foolish.'

'Why was it foolish?' Rowenna leaned against the fountain beside him and gave him another wide-eyed look that was so provocative it caused his head to swim.

'I can't pretend you are Mary. Everything

about you is different. It must seem ridiculous to you that I even have to do this.'

'No, it isn't. Nothing you do is ridiculous. You're the most serious person I know.'

It was intended as a compliment, but her words punched his guts. He reached for her hand and pressed it, drawing strength from the pressure she returned.

'You're the most vivid woman *I* know.'

Her face was grave, her eyes large and solemn. He wanted to make them dance again. Robbie released her hand and ran his fingertips up her arm to her shoulder. She blinked, black lashes beating rapidly like trapped moths in a lantern.

'You're witty and quick-tongued and clever,' he said. 'You make me laugh and perplex me— oh, you perplex me at times more than is good for my presence of mind.'

She slid her eyes to his and gave him a smile that managed to be simultaneously innocent and provocative. It sent chills racing up and down Robbie's spine, tightening the muscles in his chest. Mary had never looked at him with an expression of such wanton interest and he almost forgot to breathe. The words spilled from him with an ease he could not have imagined.

'A woman like you will never find a man lost for words unless he is in awe of your beauty.'

He let his hands travel from her shoulder to

her collarbone, his fingertips tingling when they shifted from the fabric of her dress to her bare skin. He slid them to the silken hollow of her neck and up further to rest against her cheek. Still, she said nothing, did nothing, remained perfectly still and silent. She could have been a statue. Only the hint of pink that was starting to blossom on each cheek suggested his words were having the desired effect. He stepped a little closer, not breaking the gaze between them.

'I could spend my life examining the colours in your eyes and never grow tired of them,' he breathed.

Rowenna bit her bottom lip, trapping it between small, even teeth and causing it to redden. She tilted her head on one side, her eyes never leaving his. She licked her lips, tongue skimming slowly over the full pinkness that Robbie ached to taste. He reached a hand to gently cup her chin, tilting her head up and bringing his lips close to hers. He leaned in towards her and brushed his lips briefly over her cheek, close enough to the corner of her mouth that he could feel the slight indentation that appeared whenever she smiled.

She gave a faint, breathy sigh. The sound caused blood to stampede through Robbie's veins, simultaneously awakening the part of his body that he had succeeded so far in ignoring. The words that he had held back burst forth.

'I love you.'

'What?'

Rowenna stiffened. She pulled out of his arms. She raked her fingers through her hair, lifting it and letting it fall. When she turned back to him, the pink that had coloured her cheeks had deepened to scarlet. She exhaled and tugged her neckline into place, giving him a flustered smile. He felt equally addled.

'Well, Robbie! That was much better. Very convincing. If you speak like that to… Any woman would… If you tell Mary, she's bound to—'

Mary?

Robbie slumped on to the bench Rowenna had vacated. He picked at a few stray stalks of hyssop, unsettled by how easily the words had come to venerate Rowenna and the effect they had on him. He couldn't place exactly when he had stopped thinking of Mary, and guilt riddled him.

'I have to go back,' Rowenna said. 'I'm sure you're busy, too.'

Robbie reached for her hand, but she skipped lightly out of reach. 'Your mother is upstairs scouring the house for anything she might have missed and your father is off searching for a bootmaker before he leaves. I must take my records to Father. I will see you at the Common Hall on Midsummer's Night.'

She swept out of the square, leaving Robbie wondering what had just happened.

Chapter Eight

Rowenna stayed at the forge until she was sure Robbie would have left the house, though the streets were starting to fill with rowdy towns-people again. She wished Robbie was at her side to keep her safe, but she was glad not to be in his presence. Her cheeks flamed whenever she remembered the way he had spoken to her. Seductive and captivating with no trace of his usual shyness. If he spoke like that to Mary, she would surely fall in love in an instant.

She divided the afternoon between playing card games with Lisbet and Ralf, reading to Anne and Joan, and peering from the window to try discovering what was happening outside. To her annoyance, Joanna, anxious about the noise from the streets, would not permit her to work down-stairs alone again. If Robbie returned to discuss Sir John's commission, he would not find her there.

* * *

Hal returned at sunset, looking more satisfied than when he had left Rowenna at noon. Rowenna served her father with hot bread softened in honey and milk and listened to his tale of what had occurred.

'Simon de Quixlay and the bailiffs have imposed a fine of forty pounds on any man who attempts to overrule the jurisdiction of the city,' Hal said. 'Thank goodness we have a sensible man in power now, not that corrupt cur Gisbourne.'

'The riot is over?' Joanna asked.

'I think there will be some trouble still from those too thickheaded to realise there is no purpose to it...' Hal grunted '...but, yes, I believe the walls of York will stand.'

'So I can go to the feast on Midsummer's Eve!' Rowenna blurted out.

Hal dropped his napkin on to the table and gave her a stern look.

'You'll be going nowhere! After the revolt in the city last year I didn't want you to come to York at all, Rowenna. The Common Hall was well guarded, but the rebels still managed to breach it.'

Rowenna gave a moan of disappointment and looked to her mother and aunt in appeal. 'I've barely left the house all the time I've been in York. I might as well have stayed in Ravenscrag.

Everyone of importance in York will be there. All the knights and squires taking part in the tournament will be there. You do want me to meet someone before I'm too old, don't you?'

'We want you to marry well, but not every knight is honourable,' Joanna said. 'If you—if you put yourself in harm's way while trying to do so, that will accomplish nothing.'

'Mother! I'm not planning to have my back against the wall while someone fills my belly!' Rowenna exclaimed with a shocked laugh.

Aunt Lucy coughed. Her face was dark and Rowenna found it hard to believe she had not heard language like that running the inn at Wharram. Joanna exchanged a glance with her and Lucy gave a tight smile.

'Intent does not always come into it.'

Rowenna sat beside her father and wrapped her arms about him. She gave him a wide-eyed look of appeal. It usually worked, but he had been hard to persuade to let her leave Ravenscrag on this occasion.

'There are still two days before the feast and you'll be there to see I come to no harm.'

Hal shook his head. 'Your mother and I are now engaged to dine with the burgomasters. Lucy and Roger are returning to Wharram Danby tomorrow and don't have time to take you. You cannot go alone, Rowenna.'

Rowenna could have wept with disappointment, but she kept her voice steady. 'If you're worried I'll come to harm, don't be. I'll stay in the Hall or grounds, I promise. Robbie will be there. He won't let anything happen to me. He always looks after me.'

Her mother and Aunt Lucy exchanged a smile that Rowenna pretended not to see. She had always suspected they hoped a deeper bond than friendship would develop between their children. Her stomach twisted at the thought that before long they would discover Robbie had other ideas.

'Let Rowenna have her fun. She's a sensible girl. Robbie will watch over her and her cousin Geoffrey will be there to act as her guardian,' Lucy said, bustling around and refilling Hal's cup with ale.

'Geoff is not my guardian!' Rowenna exclaimed. Nor would be if she had the choice.

'The guilds are paying for the feast,' Joanna said. 'It will be expected that someone from our family attends.'

'Ha! They'll take a bastard's money when it suits, but I'll never become the Master of the Guild.' Hal shook his head ruefully. 'I'm sorry, Rowenna, my birth dooms you to the lower tiers of society.'

The old, familiar self-reproach. Hal looked so downcast that a lump filled Rowenna's throat.

If she had her way, she would scorn everyone in turn who ignored her.

'Let me go and try to make my own luck,' she coaxed. 'If I have so few opportunities, it would be foolish to turn down the ones I have. I've seen so little of the city since I've been here.'

'You won't deny her the fun of a dance, surely?' Joanna asked, leaning over her husband's shoulders from behind and taking hold of his hands. 'Remember the dance we met at.'

Hal snorted. 'Perhaps you had better not remind me of that night, my dear, or I will decide not to let our daughter go to any gathering at all!'

Joanna swatted him playfully and Rowenna knew she had won. She raced upstairs to lay her gowns out, whispering silent thanks to her mother and aunt for their intervention. She would have the opportunity to dance with Robbie.

She bit her lip. Robbie had shocked her when he had said the word *love*. The more time she spent in his company, the deeper she was caring for him and that would only lead to heartbreak. She didn't think he was truly in love with Mary, but wasn't certain his feelings for her were beyond cousinly affection. The most sensible thing to do at the feast would be to try to find someone who was unattached, try to fall in love with him instead and forget all about Robbie.

* * *

The Common Hall looked lovelier that Rowenna could ever remember it being when her father escorted her there the following evening. A troupe of musicians were playing a lively tune that could be heard from outside. Rowenna's feet began to tap as she walked and she hummed along.

Hal pulled her close, smiling. 'You look so excited. I'm sorry I nearly didn't let you come to York. Can you forgive a father's caution?'

'Of course I can.' She kissed his cheek, thinking he might not say that if he knew what trouble Robbie had saved her from. A tremor of anticipation ran from the nape of her neck down the length of her back as she remembered her cousin's strong arms around her body. She had to bite her lip as it formed a smile of its own doing. Why must her mind continue to torment her with desires that were neither appropriate nor likely to be satisfied? Her expression must have betrayed the longing she felt because Hal's face became serious.

'Don't let your head get turned by any charming, feckless men,' Hal said sternly.

'Father! I'm here to dance, that's all. I'll do nothing you or Mother could possibly upbraid me for. I shall behave exactly as she would herself.'

Hal did not look reassured. 'I should have

stayed to chaperone you. Your mother or aunt should be here with you. Stay inside the hall. If you need to take the air, stay within the porch of the garden. Your mother's cousin Geoffrey will escort you home. I doubt Sir John will be attending, but if you need aid, ask him or his wife.'

'My cousin Robbie will also be here,' Rowenna pointed out. 'I will be perfectly safe in his company.'

'Of course you will. But Robbie will no doubt have duties to carry out and people he must see. You can't rely on him. Geoffrey knows to watch out for you. He's a good man, Rowenna.'

Rowenna bit her lip, her mood dropping. Of course Robbie had people to see. Or one person, at least. She kissed her father on the cheek and ushered him out firmly before he had her betrothed to Geoff before the dance had even begun.

She paused in the doorway to the great chamber, giving a sigh of pleasure. The guildsmen had worked hard to ensure no man or woman attending the events during the tournament would leave York with a less-than-favourable impression of the city. There was no indication that York had been subjected to terrible scenes only the day before. Servants in rich livery attended to tables laid with meats and pastries, savoury and sweet puddings. She looked for Robbie, but could not see him among the couples or groups already dancing.

Rowenna made her way to the meeting chamber that had been set aside for women to make adjustments to their outfits. The chamber was full of women, young and old, busy smoothing their hair, rebraiding ribbons, adjusting petticoats. Rowenna paused in the doorway, nerves rearing up as she gazed on the faces of women who had rebuffed her family in the past. It shouldn't matter to her that the noble wives and daughters ignored her. She had told Robbie the truth when she said that court life looked dull. She didn't crave their company, but walking in and standing alone was daunting and each rejection reminded her of the frustration her father tried to hide that he could only climb so high.

She almost turned and left, but then spotted one or two women who she could speak with, confident they would not snub her. She caught the eye of a spice merchant's wife and curtsied, receiving a cheery nod of the head in return. Her confidence fortified, she passed her cloak to an attendant and began to lace her bodice tighter. Despite her promise to her father—and she really did intend to make sure she did nothing to ruin her name—she wasn't going to keep her gown as loose as she had tied it before leaving the house when she could draw the waist in to emphasise her figure.

Her eye fell on two faces she had briefly seen sitting with Sir John's wife on the stands. Lady Isobel's attendants were sitting on low stools at the furthest end of a long table with refreshments on it. Rowenna moved closer, wondering which one of them was Robbie's love. They were discussing the knights, listing names Rowenna had seen on the board of victory and dividing them into those worthy of notice and those not. Rowenna took a honey cake and nibbled it while she listened, faintly bored.

'I shall kiss Lord Dunhelm's squire if he asks me to,' said the girl with crinkly red hair.

'Amy, you wouldn't!' the other said coldly. 'Then I shall dance with the Earl himself!'

'Will you dance with Master Danby if he asks you?' asked Amy.

Rowenna jerked her head up, interested now. She finished the cake and licked her fingers. So this was Mary. Rowenna examined her closely. She had a straight nose and bright blue eyes, and was small and slender. Her hair was golden and fell from a silver coif down the back of her pale blue cote-hardie. To Rowenna's eyes the colour was too bright to be natural.

'There are lots of handsome knights I might dance with,' Mary said primly, waving a heavily ringed hand. 'Why should I content myself with someone who is still a squire, however handsome he is?'

'Master Danby won't be a squire forever. He will be knighted before too long I expect,' Amy pointed out, quite reasonably in Rowenna's opinion. Rowenna decided she liked Amy better. What a pity Robbie hadn't fallen in love with her, if he must love anyone beside Rowenna.

'True. He dances well from what I've seen and he *is* very handsome,' Mary said wistfully.

Rowenna found herself nodding in agreement. She stopped and sipped her drink, which turned out to be a sickly nectar made of wine and honey. It was far too spice laden for her liking.

'He will inherit a title, too, won't he?' Amy said. 'A baronage, I believe.'

'I suppose so.' Mary's face brightened, then dropped into a pout. 'But he has illegitimate connections, I believe. The uncle I saw.'

Amy waved a hand. 'I doubt he has much to do with them. Any time the subject of bastardy is raised he goes so stiff and quiet. He looked furious when they interrupted Sir John's party at the tournament.'

Rowenna froze. Robbie had always assured her it didn't matter, but now she thought of it, he did become more solemn when she mentioned it. Did he secretly despise Hal's state and by definition her own? She felt sick at the thought.

Mary smoothed her skirts. 'Whether or not he disapproves of his relatives, I'm not sure Master Danby's father is rich enough to please my uncle. Uncle John insists I marry well.'

Though it pained Rowenna to admit it, Mary had a point. Rowenna's father had worked for years so that she had a handsome dowry to take to any man who could see past the fact he was marrying into illegitimacy and common birth. For the first time she saw Roger as slightly shiftless—content to live in peace on the moors. He had ensured Robbie would inherit a respectable but small property and an even smaller fortune, but did nothing to draw attention to himself or his son.

Robbie seemed content with that himself, content to fire arrows at silly straw targets, but not joust, and to be Sir John's Squire of the Body, not his personal squire. He did nothing to draw attention to himself where an ambitious young nobleman might seek to have his face and name known around the kingdom. And now he had decided he was in love with this woman who mocked him behind his back!

Deep in thought, she took another cup and reached for the flagon of water to dilute it.

'Well, it isn't your uncle Master Danby has

to please tonight.' Amy laughed. 'You make no commitment by dancing with Master Danby unless you choose to do so. He's probably too honourable to even try to kiss you.'

Rowenna drank her nectar in one gulp. Robbie had come very close to kissing her on the lips and she wondered if he would have carried it through if she had not pulled away at the last moment. Her face grew hot. How could he love someone as unkind and superior as Mary? And if Mary, with her jewels and ambition, was the sort of woman he wanted, why would he ever consider marrying a bastard's daughter?

'That settles it—I shall dance with him *and* I shall get him to kiss me, too,' Mary said. 'But he'll have to manage to ask me first. He speaks so poorly. Truly I could grow fond of him, but it makes my head ache listening to him. Who w-w-would w-w-want a husband who couldn't s-s-say his w-w-wife's n-n-name?'

Rowenna's fist clenched at hearing such cruel words from the woman Robbie adored. Almost physical pain gripped her stomach. Mary could not know Robbie in the slightest if she was mocking the one thing that had the power to hurt him more than any other.

Mary was in peals of laughter now. 'His mother has the most exquisite sapphires I've ever seen that would match my eyes perfectly. Perhaps

I could endure listening to him trying to talk to me in return for those.'

This woman did not deserve sapphires. She did not deserve Robbie. She didn't even deserve a lowly gong-farmer. She deserved...

Rowenna realised she was gripping the handle of the water flagon tightly. She grinned. Mary deserved a soaking.

Rowenna put the flagon carefully back on the very edge of the table and drained her second cup of wine. She moved away, then returned to the far side of the table, selected a third cup and leaned over the table precariously.

'Excuse me, is there water in that flagon?' she asked Mary.

Mary turned to see who had addressed her, just as Rowenna contrived to knock her hand against the flagon and send it spilling over. Water poured across the table, over the edge, and down the side of Mary's gown. Mary jumped to her feet with a shriek, ignoring the effusive apologies that Rowenna uttered.

'Can someone bring a cloth?' Rowenna called out.

A servant and other women crowded round to help. Mary gave Rowenna a look that was pure poison and rushed to the fireside, spreading the folds of her gown out in her hands. Rowenna righted the empty flagon, finished her third drink and left the room with the air of a king leading his army home from victory. Mary had been swifter to her feet than Rowenna had expected and most of the water had missed, but with any luck Mary would spend enough time drying herself that she would be absent for long enough that Rowenna could speak to Robbie.

She sighed in exasperation. How blindly in love was Robbie if he thought that woman was the best he had ever met?

'He needs his head boxed, not sympathetic hints,' she muttered, stalking away.

The centre of the Great Hall was filled with dancers now, their feet causing the scent of thyme and meadowsweet to rise from the rush floors. Beeswax candles in the sconces along the walls gave a soft light and sweet smell to the high-ceilinged room. A fire was blazing in the great fireplace at the furthest end of the room, taking the chill off the stone walls, but adding to the overpowering mixture of fragrances. Rowenna's head spun a little and she leaned against the wall, her anger at Mary's unkindness searing her heart.

'Do you need assistance?' A voice in her ear made her start. She turned to face a young blond man who was staring down at her with concern on his face.

'I'm not sure,' she said. She needed to think, more than anything. Somehow she would have to tell Robbie what she had overheard and he would be devastated. A small, selfish part of her whispered she might be the one to console him as well as bearing the unhappy news. This man couldn't help with that.

'Forgive my impudence for approaching you, but you look a little lost,' he said, smiling. 'My name is Master Hugone.'

That name was familiar. This was Sir John's other squire. Robbie's friend. She could talk to him safely.

'I'm Rowenna.' She fanned her neck with her hand. 'It's much hotter in here than I was expecting. I'm looking for my cousin, but I can't see him. I'm a little thirsty, too.'

'A lady without a drink is a sorry sight,' Master Hugone said. 'A lady without a partner even more so. May I accompany you to the table to find a cup of wine and then, if you are feeling better, we might dance?'

Rowenna smiled uncertainly. She had to find Robbie and tell him what Mary had said as soon as possible, but there was no sign of him anywhere. It was overpoweringly hot and she was thirsty and the sticky wine had done nothing to quench her thirst. A drink would help clear her thoughts and get her temper back under control. Her father had said to be careful of feckless men but she could trust Robbie's friend.

Rowenna took Master Hugone's arm and walked to the refreshment table. She accepted a cup of thin wine that was much more refreshing than the sickly nectar provided to the women. Master Hugone gave her a wide smile as she drank deeply.

'You really were thirsty! I believe you could match me cup for cup.'

Rowenna beamed back. 'I don't intend to try doing that!'

'Very wise. But perhaps the dance I mentioned?'

He left the question hanging, but held out a hand and raised an eyebrow invitingly. Rowenna smiled. Robbie hadn't told her his friend was so charming, or so blond and handsome. She looked across the room at the couples dancing and thought how many of them might reject her company. She would have too few dances and Robbie was not apparently here. There was no reason not to dance with Master Hugone while she waited for him to arrive.

What harm could that do after all?

Robbie was mildly surprised that the unrest had not stopped the celebrations from going ahead. Even though the riot has seemingly been suppressed, the city rumbled with discontent. Three days ago this building had closed the doors and barred them to keep rioters from breaking them down. Now they were wide open. To men of his supposed status, at least.

Hearing the sounds of laughter and music coming from within the Common Hall, he almost turned away at the door. He would dearly have liked to spend a quiet night sitting somewhere peaceful rather than surrounded by merrymaking. He unbuckled his cloak, noting how his ribs and belly muscles protested where they had been elbowed roughly the day before, compounding the bruising from his bout with the swords during the *bohort*. He made his way into the hall, but did not feel like dancing immediately so made his way to the benches at the back of the room and watched.

Mary was dancing with Lord Dunhelm, her head high and back straight. Every move was graceful and a studied perfection of the form she had learned. She wore pale blue that rippled like waves. Her beautiful face was serene and if she was aware of the attention her movements were drawing, she gave no sign. Robbie's heart thudded and he wished he had plucked up the courage to approach her himself.

He let his attention wander from one side of the hall to the other, idly observing the couples. He recognised Cecil in the most distant line partnered with a short, shapely woman dressed in

wine-coloured silk with a sheen to it that caught
the light when her skirts swayed. Her hair was
captured in fine ribbons of gold at each side of
her head, looped up to reveal a slender neck and
pinned beneath a gold caul at the back that glinted
in the candlelight.

As Robbie watched, Cecil's hand slipped from
her shoulder down the curve of her spine and his
fingers spread wide over her buttocks to draw her
close. Robbie grimaced, seeing his rival chanc-
ing his luck so blatantly in public. They skipped
a measure towards the far wall, then Cecil turned
and spun his partner around. For the first time
Robbie saw the woman's face and the sight made
him sit bolt upright and almost spill his wine.

The woman dancing so intimately in the arms
of Cecil was Rowenna.

Robbie's scalp prickled. The smile fell from his
face. Rowenna had her back against Cecil's chest
now, leaning her body against his as he held her
left arm outwards and rested his cheek against
hers. Robbie glared in outrage at the hand that
Cecil still had on Rowenna's waist. It was part
of the dance, but he did not have to hold her so
close and it was not necessary for the fingertips
that were curved over her hip bone to caress her
waist quite so intimately. A waist so shapely cried
out to be caressed, though.

Nor did they have to lace their fingers together in the hand they were required to hold.

Cecil said something to her, putting his lips close to her ear, and Rowenna laughed gaily, craning her head round so that she could reply. Her lips brushed against Cecil's jaw and Cecil grinned, before licking his lips and replying. Rowenna tossed her head with a merry laugh, causing her fine nets of gold thread to glint in the light. Cecil looked ecstatic at the effect he was having on her.

Robbie became aware he was gripping his goblet tightly. Dancing didn't require anyone to talk, much less to speak so intimately that they were close to kissing. He should not allow her to behave so freely with a man she barely knew, but short of striding through the crowd and separating them Robbie could do nothing. He sat and watched, seething inwardly at the sight of such shameless flirting.

Chapter Nine

As he watched Rowenna dancing, Robbie's anger was replaced with grudging admiration. Rowenna was an excellent dancer, light on her feet and in perfect time with the rhythm. She was clearly enjoying herself immensely and was lost within the music and steps. Robbie smiled, despite his instinct to disapprove, envious that Rowenna could behave with a sense of abandon that he could never permit himself to indulge.

Every move of her hand was flamboyant. Every graceful twirl of her skirt sent the fabric rippling. Her lips were parted in a wide smile and her dark eyes gleamed. She and Cecil were performing the same steps as Mary and Lord Dunhelm, but even from this distance Robbie could see the suppressed energy in Rowenna that seemed almost certain to burst out at any moment. Robbie's feet began to tap along with the rhythm and he suppressed a treacherous and completely unexpected thought—that dancing with Rowenna looked much more fun than dancing with Mary.

If only it had not been Cecil, with his charismatic manner, she had been bestowing her attention on. He drummed his fingers on the table and tried to convince himself that Rowenna would display the same pleasure in the dance, no matter who her partner was. It grew on him with rising outrage that he was not the only man in the room whose attention she had caught and that around the outside of the room other men besides him were watching her with interest. He had recognised since meeting her again that she had grown into a very beautiful woman and the effect had not been lost on him. Now he witnessed that the effect was equally alluring to other men and he wasn't sure whether he liked that realisation.

The lines of dancers threaded through each other, bringing Rowenna and Cecil closer to Robbie. Rowenna caught Robbie's eye as she crossed behind Cecil, skirts lifted gracefully to one side. Her step faltered for the first time and she paused. Her eyes widened as they fixed on Robbie until Cecil gently tugged her arm and she disappeared back into the dance with a laugh and not as much as a backward glance in Robbie's direction. His stomach knotted and he sat poised on the edge of his stool, determined to be the first to reach her and ask her to accompany him in the next dance. He would advise her to behave with more caution.

When the music came to an end Rowenna was at the other end of the room, and before Robbie had reached her another young man was intent on claiming her attention, bowing and holding out a cup of wine, which she took with enthusiasm. Writhing in frustration, Robbie turned away and noticed Mary was curtsying farewell to Lord Dunhelm. Robbie caught himself guiltily, remembering that he had intended to ask Mary to dance. He had completely forgotten to watch her since noticing Rowenna.

He could do nothing to prevent Rowenna disgracing herself without pulling her away and causing more of a scene, so he made his way swiftly to Mary. Remembering how speech had come so easily when he play-acted with Rowenna, he took a deep breath and, without too many hesitant words, asked Mary to dance. She gazed at him appraisingly before inclining her head in agreement.

Mary moved elegantly, never missing a step, her head erect and her body held as rigidly as a dancing master instructing a pupil. Robbie briefly wondered if perhaps he should risk a hand on her waist as Cecil had done with Rowenna. At once his mind filled with thoughts of his cousin that he could not suppress and he almost forgot the steps. He began to scan the dancers and discovered she was not among them, but was instead sitting on a bench between Cecil and the other man, raising a goblet to her lips.

'You dance well, Master Danby.'

He barely noticed he was being addressed at first, but Mary's soft voice burrowed into his brain and he dragged his eyes back to his partner. Her blue eyes were watching him closely as she waited for his response.

'With a partner as graceful as you, any man would d-dance as if his feet had w-wings.'

She gave a rippling laugh. Robbie forced a laugh, too, and for the rest of the dance he almost succeeded in forgetting to watch what Rowenna was doing and whom she was with. This was what he had dreamed of for so long after all, and the fact it made him feel like he had placed second in an event was hardly Mary's fault.

'M-may I dance with you again?' he asked when the dance ended.

'I promised my aunt I would not dance with anyone twice in succession,' Mary answered. 'Ask me again in two dances' time.'

Robbie looked for Rowenna and discovered she was dancing once more with Cecil, who had a gleam in his eye that Robbie recognised all too well. Robbie's mood darkened again. Two dances and the intervening time spent sitting with Cecil. Either Aunt Joanna had not given her daughter the same instruction as Mary's aunt had or, more likely, Rowenna had chosen to ignore the advice. Cecil caught his eye and gave him a wicked grin. This time Robbie was prepared and plunged through the company to be beside Rowenna and Cecil before the final notes of the lute had died away.

'Why, Master Danby, are you hoping to claim my partner?' Cecil asked in surprise. 'Have you been introduced?'

'W-w-we—' Robbie felt his throat tightening in frustration as the words would not come.

'Yes, we have,' Rowenna broke in. She giggled loudly and Robbie wondered how much wine she had drunk before he had noticed her.

'Would *you* like to dance with me, Robbie?'

She stepped towards him, raising her face in the manner she had gazed at Cecil. She bit her lip and turned her dark eyes on him, batting her long lashes in a coquettish manner that set his pulse unaccountably racing. His impulse was to agree that, yes, he very much did want to dance with her, but he reminded himself why he had sought her out.

'No. Let's talk.'

He took hold of her arm, slipped it through his and escorted her to his bench.

Rowenna shivered with exaggeration. 'You still always insist on sitting so far away from the fire. I wondered if you would have grown out of that. Never mind. I'm warm enough from dancing.'

She spun around in a whirl of skirts and threw herself on to the bench beside him. Tendrils of hair had come loose from her gold wire caul and were plastered to her cheeks and forehead. She blew upward to loosen them, taking deep breaths that lifted her breasts high in a manner Robbie found distracting. It was as if unseen hands had taken her body and sculpted it into something entirely new since he had parted from her the day before. Something fascinating and attractive and very, very desirable. Her eyes were bright and her cheeks were flushed, deepening her beauty. Robbie said nothing.

'That was fun, but I have such a thirst now. Fetch me another cup of wine please, Robbie,' she asked breathlessly, leaning close to him. He caught the scent of wine on her breath. Another? He wondered how many she'd drunk already.

'I think you've had enough,' he said sharply. 'You'll be tipsy.'

'No, I won't!' She hiccoughed and put her hand hastily over her mouth with a giggle. 'Perhaps you're right, but even if I am, why is that your business? You aren't my guardian.'

'Apparently tonight no one is,' Robbie muttered.

Rowenna pouted. 'Why are you being so sullen?'

She put her hand on his forearm, but he shrugged her off. He folded his arms and glared at her.

'Because when I should have been enjoying finally getting to dance with Mary I was instead concentrating on making sure you weren't ruining your reputation by behaving in such a flighty manner for half of York to see!'

'Flighty?' Her jaw dropped and her eyes blazed. 'I was only dancing, just the same as everyone else in the room. Why do you have to be so staid?'

He regarded her sternly.

'You can do as you please, of course, but I'm not going to stand by and watch you ruin your reputation and bring shame on our family.'

She glared at him. 'How can you be so unfair? You have no right to be so judgemental! You know I rarely get the chance to meet people and how I'll struggle to find a husband.'

She looked mutinous and he sensed they were on the verge of a quarrel. Nevertheless, he set his jaw.

'That's all the more reason to be discreet, I would have thought. I thought you were learning to behave as a lady.'

'I am! I haven't disgraced myself and I wasn't indiscreet.' She swept an arm around. 'There is not a woman here who hasn't danced with at least five men.'

'You need to curb your passion,' Robbie warned, catching her hand as it narrowly missed his head. 'Your eyes and manner give too much away. It isn't seemly. Or safe.'

'Mother talked about safety, too, as if I were about to offer myself to half the city!' Rowenna rolled her eyes, pique filling them. Robbie wished he had a mirror to show her how clearly her thoughts could be read. 'Is that what you think I'll do, too?'

He assumed she was still a virgin like him and therefore had no idea of the urges that assailed men. Were women immune to such hot, desperate hungers or did Rowenna crave the experience of lovemaking, too? The image of Rowenna offering herself to *him* thumped Robbie in the groin like the impact of a lance. Would Rowenna make love with as much abandonment and passion as she showed when dancing? Unbidden comparisons between Rowenna and Mary reared up inside him, turning his flesh hot and prickly as once again the balance tipped in favour of Rowenna. He pushed such coarse thoughts from his mind and took a deep breath.

'Of course not! But not all men would wait

to be offered. You need to show more caution,' he muttered. 'I might not be there to protect you next time.'

'Protect me from what? Rowenna pointed a finger at him and raised an eyebrow, giving him a wanton smile. 'Don't blame me because you didn't like what you saw and don't dare to do the same. If you had half the boldness to go ask your Lady Mary to dance as you did in dragging me away, you'd have spent less time sitting alone in the corner. Cecil told me you intended to ask her. Though on that subject—'

Robbie scowled and cut her off midsentence. Rowenna apparently hadn't even noticed that he had plucked up the courage to ask Mary. 'I was watching Cecil and he seemed to tell you a lot of things. He never appeared to stop whispering in your ear.'

She gave an indignant gasp, starting to her feet, then sat back. She arched her brow and pouted. 'Well, perhaps whispering with Cecil is more fun that sitting while you glare at me in silence. At least he's exciting.'

'Excitement is overrated. You need someone you can depend on.'

'Dependable is dull,' Rowenna snapped.

'Is it?' Robbie winced. She'd called him that before now. The urge to be impulsive began to bud inside him.

Rowenna stood and turned to him. 'Marriage is my only chance of escape from Ravenscrag and it is going to be hard enough to find a husband. I won't sit in a corner watching while the world dances around me!'

'Goodnight, Rowenna,' Robbie said curtly, standing. 'I'll get you your wine, then you can go back to your dancing. I think I shall leave. I've lost the taste for company, it appears.'

He bowed stiffly and walked away.

He half expected her to follow, but she didn't. He stormed across the hall, where the dancing couples had joined in a circle. Men and women—most likely strangers before this evening—were laughing, with arms about each other or hands linked. Robbie ground his teeth as he watched.

Had Rowenna been acting worse than any other woman, or was Robbie being unfair because watching her dancing with Cecil had created such a surge of unexpected jealousy it had made him lose all rationality? He looked back at her. She was sitting now, alone in the chilly corner with her head bowed, and he felt a rush of guilt. He had ruined her enjoyment and he was no longer convinced he had been justified in his accusations. He wasn't sure about anything any more and was beginning to fear he could no longer trust his judgement where Rowenna was concerned.

* * *

Rowenna watched Robbie cross the room until the crowd of dancers swallowed him. He didn't look back. Nor did he make his way to the table where the wine was. Instead he stood alone at the furthest end of the hall with his head turned away. She leaned back against the table with an angry exhalation. His company was no loss, not when he had been so cold and disapproving. It would almost serve him right to marry Mary and discover her contempt for him when it was too late.

She sat still for the remainder of the dance that was being played. Robbie did not return with her wine and she assumed he had left the Common Hall, but then caught sight of him. He was being introduced to one of the guildsmen who would not give Rowenna's family the time of day. Resentment bubbled inside her. It was well enough to chastise her, but if she didn't speak to the men who acknowledged her, how would she find one?

As she watched, Robbie took to the floor with a handsome, richly dressed matron who must have been forty or more. His head turned in Rowenna's direction and she whipped hers down so he could not see she had been looking. Tears sprang to her eyes and she blinked them clear. An insistent throbbing in each temple was beginning to plague her. She twisted on her bench to face the table and rested her chin on her elbows, taking deep breaths. If he did return, she was determined he would not know that their quarrel had upset her. She began to draw spirals in a puddle of spilled wine.

'You've been abandoned. I could scarcely believe what I saw when Danby walked away, but it is true.'

Cecil Hugone slipped smoothly on to the bench at Rowenna's side. She opened her mouth to pour out her woes but bit the words back. Robbie was family. Cecil was not. Oh, she would eviscerate her cousin's character to her mother when she returned home, but despite Robbie's accusations, she did care about her family's reputation and would not share a private matter with someone she didn't know.

'I'm weary of dancing,' she said curtly. 'I sent him away.'

'And he followed your instruction? I admire his obedience, but clearly my friend Danby doesn't know treasure when he has it in his hands because there isn't a woman to match you in the whole of York.'

Rowenna gave him a hard stare. The flattery wasn't true and Rowenna was beginning to doubt Robbie had any sense in his head. She risked a glance over Cecil's shoulder. Robbie was still dancing, his body stiff and his face expression-less. She took consolation in the fact he had not found Mary, who Rowenna spotted standing with her friend Amy looking aloof. She added a squiggle to the biggest spiral in the wine, hoping that if she continued to remain silent Cecil might leave her in peace, but instead he rested his hand on the table, disconcertingly close to Rowenna's, and looked deep into her eyes.

'Compliments have no effect on you. A rare woman indeed,' he breathed. 'I meant no offence, but I hate to see you looking so downcast. Perhaps I could offer you a drink?'

Rowenna's stomach rolled over as the remembrance of strong wine filled her mouth.

'Thank you, but I have had my fill of wine.'

Her conscience gave her stomach another prod. Robbie had been right to refuse her more wine when she had demanded it. Had he been right in what else he had said? Was she behaving badly?

'Then another dance, perhaps?'

Cecil reached for her hand and Rowenna allowed him to take it, her worries melting away. If Robbie was dancing, why shouldn't she? He helped her rise and they threaded their way into the throng. From the corner of her eye she saw Robbie's head jerk in her direction. He grimaced and stared pointedly at her, but she gave no indication she had noticed him.

* * *

For the remainder of the dance Rowenna ignored Robbie. He did not exist for her. If they drew near to him, Cecil whisked her away. When they had no choice but to pass in the line, her eye slid over him, past him or remained fixed on Cecil's, though she could see that Robbie's expression was dark. Cecil moved as well as he had before as he led her through the steps, but this dance held no joy for Rowenna.

It was not Cecil's fault. He smiled and joked, but the lips that obsessed her weren't his, and the arms she wanted to be in were lightly on the waist of another woman. Sitting in the dark corner alone was preferable to dancing close to Robbie and having to pretend their falling-out did not make her want to weep.

When the music ended, she thanked Cecil politely but brushed away his request for a second dance, explaining she was feeling breathless and faint. His expression of concern was so sincere and instant she felt guilty for deceiving him.

'In that case, why don't we take a walk into the garden?' he suggested, leaning close to whisper into her ear. 'It's cool and quiet. We could find a bench to rest on until you are feeling more active. We could get to know one another a little better.'

His voice was playful and Rowenna hesitated. She knew well enough why some couples took walks into the garden and it was a tempting thought. Cecil was a fine-looking man and was a good dancer. Rowenna couldn't deny that her heart raced a little when his hand strayed to her waist. Cecil was surely trustworthy otherwise Robbie would not be friends with him, but she recalled her father's words as he had left her at the door and the jest she had made to her mother and aunt. Even if she and Cecil sat side by side without as much as touching—which she was certain he did not intend to do—tongues might wag and she would be hard-pressed to deny any rumours. Robbie would have further reason to chastise her and, in that case, he would be right.

Regretfully, she must decline.

She was saved from having to refuse him by the master of musicians calling everyone to attention and announcing there would be a short break from dancing while the minstrels performed. Servants placed benches and stools in a semicircle before the dais where the musicians were arranged. Rowenna saw the wife and daughter of a silversmith her parents knew.

'Excuse me, I must relay a message from my father to Mistress Ashe.'

She curtsied to Cecil before he had time to protest at her leaving and joined the two women, finding a place on the bench towards the rear as the first notes began. She saw Robbie standing to her right, leaning on a pillar. Cecil had taken a place between Mary and Amy. Rowenna wondered if her cousin had not noticed. There was room on the bench beside Mary, but Robbie remained where he was. She tried to concentrate on the playing, which was accomplished, but her eye was obstinately drawn back to Robbie. His gaze wavered back and forth between the minstrels and the line of women and Rowenna realised his attention was on her, not the recital.

He looked miserable and the final traces of anger melted in Rowenna's heart. How could she have been so foolish as to fight with him? She had the urge to go to him and mend their quarrel, but she was careful that whenever his eyes slid to her she was looking elsewhere. If she allowed herself to meet his eyes, she doubted she would be able to control the emotion that welled up inside her.

The piece ended and polite applause flitted round the chamber. Now it was acceptable to turn her head slightly and meet Robbie's eyes. He inclined his head respectfully, but his eyes were wary after their quarrel and he did not smile. Waves of misery washed over Rowenna, making her shudder. She stood and began to move towards him, eager to share her thoughts until it struck her this was perhaps too forward. That he might not welcome her company. That he might prefer to search out Mary.

While she wavered, the decision was taken out of her hands as she saw Cecil sweep across the room and appear by Robbie's side. He had acquired a goblet of wine for each of them. Robbie gave one backward glance at Rowenna before following Cecil. She sat back down and made conversation with Mistress Ashe and her daughter for the bare minimum amount of time courtesy allowed. As soon as she was at liberty, she began her search for Robbie.

He was standing beside Cecil, close by the large stone fireplace, at the centre of a group of women. Cecil was speaking, waving his arms wildly as he described a joust or something. Robbie was silent. Mary had managed to manoeuvre close, weaving her way through the huddle until she was standing at Robbie's elbow, turning an innocent expression on him and talking rapidly. She had clearly decided to show interest in him as she had promised Amy. Rowenna's cheeks began to flame, remembering the callous way Mary had mocked Robbie. In all the commotion she hadn't told Robbie what she had overheard and now it was too late. She could not intrude upon the group without knowing how Robbie would react.

She was forced to watch impotently from a distance. Robbie was nodding and giving every appearance of listening attentively to each woman who spoke to him. His face bore a smile, but his shoulders were tense and there were small lines at the side of each eye. When he lifted his wine cup his knuckles were pale from gripping it. She recalled he had hated open flames when he was younger. A stranger might not notice his unease, but Rowenna had known him for so long. She knew what every tilt of his head meant, every twitch of his lips. He was nervous and the air of shyness that surrounded him only made him more endearing. How could someone so fearless and capable with a weapon retain the unassuming nature Robbie possessed?

Her scalp prickled as she watched the group of women, oblivious to his emotions but enthralled by his fine figure and handsome face, cooing and preening like a flock of peahens around a pair of cocks. Or geese around a pear tree. The memory flashed into her mind and, despite her anxiety, she giggled. She and Robbie had been friends for too long to let a few harsh words come between them. He would not turn away from her in front of everyone.

Emboldened, she wove her way through the crowd to stand within Robbie's eyeline. He looked in her direction and stiffened, the laugh freezing on his face, then vanishing. She almost turned away, but then the smile returned, became genuine, softer and moved to his eyes as well as his lips.

'My apologies for intruding, Master Danby,' Rowenna said, walking towards him and noting with pleasure that the women moved aside like the Red Sea parting before her. 'I have a message from a family member.'

'Of course. I'll come immediately.'

His reply was out of his mouth almost before she had finished and he was moving, muttering apologies to the group as he left them to follow Rowenna. She slipped behind a pillar to a quieter area of the hall.

'Who sends a message? What is wrong?' Robbie asked.

'The message is from your cousin.' Rowenna bit her lip. 'She said some things she regrets. She wishes to apologise for them.'

She looked at the ground. Robbie took hold of her hand and lifted it. Instead of kissing it, he placed it within his hand against his chest.

'You sent me for wine, but I failed my duty,' he remarked.

'I don't need any wine,' Rowenna muttered. 'You were right. Let's not argue any more.'

'I was unfair,' Robbie said.

'You have your opinions. I dare say some of them were right.' Rowenna affected a smile. 'You can't go through your whole life being wrong.'

He graced her with a slight smile and her spirits lifted a little. They stood in silence, watching the dancing. Men and women stood around in groups, flirting and laughing. Geoffrey caught her eye and she waved, though with little enthusiasm. Mary was dancing with an unknown nobleman, her blond hair gleaming.

'I'll wager she washes it with saffron water,' Rowenna muttered under her breath. She pushed a stray strand of her own dark locks back into their golden net, conscious of Robbie watching her with an odd expression on his face. She hoped he hadn't heard her comment.

'I thought this would be more fun,' she admitted. 'I love dancing, but the chatter and gossip bores me. How can you stand to be around such empty-headed frivolity?'

'I sometimes wish I could leave all this behind me, too,' Robbie admitted. He held his arm out.

'Would you like to take a w-walk outside? It will be cooler and quieter. I don't want to dance.'

This was the second time a man had suggested they venture out into the garden and now there was no hesitation or reservation in Rowenna's mind, only an all-consuming urge to be alone with Robbie.

'I don't want to dance any more, either,' she agreed. 'I see you so rarely and you'll be gone before long.'

She did not know if he had the same purpose in mind as Cecil had, but she knew without question that she would not refuse if he did.

Chapter Ten

Arm in arm, Robbie and Rowenna made their way to the courtyard. Torches burned in sconces set into the walls where insects buzzed frantically around the flames. A rowdy group of youths sat drinking on the closest wall, and somewhere behind them young couples were giggling together at some private amusement. Robbie instinctively shied away from both groups. Rowenna had called him staid and perhaps she was right. He escorted Rowenna away from the bustle and they wove through the low hedges to the opposite side of the square where it was darker and quieter.

'Mmm…' Rowenna tipped her head back, closing her eyes and inhaling deeply. 'That *is* better. The air smells lovely.'

Robbie bent and plucked a handful of lavender from the closest bush, rubbing it to release the scent. He held it out to Rowenna. She put her hand on Robbie's to hold it steady as she buried her nose deep into the leaves, drawing in the scent. Her fingers were warm and Robbie felt the heat from them spreading down his arm.

'I'm sorry I tricked you into leaving the group, but you looked so uncomfortable by the fire.'

'I don't mind,' Robbie said. It was true. At no point had he resented Rowenna enticing him away from the company. He had simply been relieved they were no longer quarrelling.

She giggled. 'Do you remember when I was surrounded by geese and you came to my rescue? I thought of that when I saw you there.'

They sat on the steps of a small fountain. Rowenna tilted her head back and stared at the sky, which was clear and star filled. The moon cast light on her bare throat, illuminating the curves of her collarbones and drawing Robbie's eye to the contrast between the creamy naked skin and deep red silk that concealed her bosom.

His tongue became unaccountably, insufferably dry and he found himself craving water or, better still, the wine he had denied Rowenna. He dragged his eyes from her neck and reached into the fountain for the cup on a long chain. He drank deeply, then passed it to Rowenna, who did likewise. She dropped the cup back into the fountain bowl.

'I really was thirsty. The wine was stronger than I realised! Thank you for bringing me out here,' Rowenna said with a smile that was slightly too wide. 'You don't mind that I took you away from your friends, do you?'

Rowenna dipped her fingers in the water and trailed them from behind her ears down her creamy neck. The gesture must have been unconscious, but it sent prickles down Robbie's spine and at that moment he would have forgiven her anything up to and including murder.

'I don't m-mind in the s-slightest,' he stammered.

He concentrated on a droplet that had caught in the curve of Rowenna's collarbone. Would a single drop of liquid stolen from Rowenna quench the thirst that was burning him inside? He wondered how it would feel to lean over and lick it away before letting his tongue explore further up or down her body. A shiver ran down his spine, as the image of himself doing just that exploded in his mind.

Confusion addled his brain. This was not right. It was Mary he wanted, yet he'd never imagined such outrageous thoughts about her, or craved acting on them so desperately.

'You're a good friend to look after me,' Rowenna said. 'I'm sorry you didn't get to dance more with your Mary.'

The words doused his rising passion more than a thousand pails of water hurled at him could do.

The corner of his mouth twitched. He hadn't been feeling very friendly towards her for one reason or another all evening.

'It isn't any fun drinking too much,' he said. 'I remember when I was twelve and first made myself sick by helping myself to an unready batch of Mother's ale without her knowing. I half believed I was going to die and wasn't sure that would have been a bad thing!'

Rowenna laughed, a merry peal that lightened Robbie's mood.

'I'm glad I didn't do that. I bet Aunt Lucy was furious. Did she whip you?'

'No. For once she and Lady Stick were in agreement that I deserved it, but Father said it was punishment enough to make me get up at dawn and tend to the sheep as usual. He was right, too. I had to dunk my head in the beck a dozen times before it stopped spinning.'

Robbie stretched his legs out and leaned back. They sat in companionable silence and it struck Robbie that he rarely saw Rowenna still and tranquil. She was usually darting about, laughing and active. The serene woman at his side was an alluring creature and one Robbie could happily spend the rest of the evening with. He felt a pang of homesickness for the quiet moorland village he hadn't seen for so long.

'Travelling round England and to France with

Sir John's retinue was exciting, but it feels good to talk of home,' Robbie said. Mary had talked only of her clothing and whether sapphires or diamonds would match her eyes best. It had become a little boring.

Rowenna flung her arms around his neck in an unexpected hug that almost knocked him off the edge of the step. He caught her around the waist to steady them both. Rowenna leaned against him so that her cheek rested on his shoulder, one arm still around him.

'I'm so pleased you've come back, I've missed you so much. I always wished I had a brother my own age, but I didn't need one really. You're almost a brother to me.'

'Am I?' He found himself unaccountably aghast at the thought.

Rowenna was still leaning into him, but now she twisted her body, inadvertently grinding her breasts against his chest, so that her face was turned to his. Her eyes had been sparkling, but now they grew serious.

'No. I don't think you are really.'

She was close enough that he caught the scent of wine that still lingered on her lips. It mingled with the cinnamon-scented oil she had dressed her hair with and the lavender he had given her in an intoxicating mix of scents. Robbie's head was muddled and his thoughts were anything but brotherly.

Rowenna withdrew her arm from around his shoulder and let it fall into her lap, brushing against his thigh as she did. She looked thoughtful, her eyes flickering over Robbie's face.

He held his breath, feeling as though someone was brushing fingers across the inside of his chest. He hadn't released Rowenna when he had the opportunity and he was content to keep his arm around her for as long as possible to prolong the feeling. He had the overpowering urge to kiss her to see what she would do in return.

'Robbie, is something wrong?'

Nothing other than the fact that his heart was ravaged and his flesh was on fire with the thought of kissing Rowenna. His cousin. His closest friend, whose familiar eyes looked out of a face he only half recognised and whose body was that of a woman, not a child any longer. He was more confused than he had ever been.

Rowenna's words pulled him back from the unexpected snicket his fantasies were leading him down.

'No. Nothing is wrong.' He smiled and shook his head. 'I was just remembering Wharram. The last time we sat together like this was the night before I left.'

'I remember.' She twirled her fingers in her hair. 'I gave you a ribbon as a favour.'

'I still have it,' he admitted.

She was looking at him solemnly, her eyes no longer gleaming. 'You told me you would see me before you left, but I woke late and you'd already gone.'

Robbie stretched out, digging his heels into the dirt. The truth swelled inside him, longing to burst out, but he refused to let it. Rejection from Rowenna was too terrible to contemplate.

'I quarrelled with Roger when I w-went home. Leaving w-was best for everyone.' It was the closest to the truth he dared confess.

'I've seen how uneasy you are around him. It's sad. Will you tell me what happened?' Rowenna stuck her legs out alongside his, feet pointed together, and leaned against him. Robbie became acutely conscious of where their bodies pressed and the gaps where they did not.

He drew a long breath, wishing more than ever he could share his secret. 'Things I considered important, he assumed could be stamped beneath fresh rushes and forgotten.'

He started to tell her how Roger had tried to commandeer the men during the riot, but fairness made him recall that Roger had backed down and let Robbie lead. 'You know him. He sweeps everyone up in his belief that he knows best. He has a long shadow I do not wish to live beneath.'

'You'll leave again soon, won't you?' Rowenna said. 'Will you make your peace with Roger before you do?'

'Perhaps. I'm in no hurry to return to Wharram.' Robbie examined his hands.

'I don't blame you.' Rowenna's voice was wistful. 'I wish I could see what you've seen. My father travelled the country during his apprenticeship. Your father spent years fighting in France and Italy.' She gestured towards Robbie, skimming his chest with her fingertips and causing his heart to beat double time. 'You've seen London. I've never been more than a day's travel from York.'

Robbie took a deep breath, catching the scent of the lavender again, and something else on the air behind it.

'Roses,' he murmured.

He stood and walked to the back of the garden until he found the trailing bushes that had been trained to climb around a small gateway. They were large blossoms, deep red and almost overpowering in the richness of their perfume. He twisted the fullest bloom from the stem, taking care to avoid the thorns. Rowenna had followed him.

'It smells wonderful,' he said, cupping the rose in the palm of his hand and bringing it to his nose.

'May I?' Rowenna asked.

This time Robbie did not hold the flower out at arm's length, but kept it where it was so he could smell it at the same time. Rowenna leaned in towards him. She rested one hand on Robbie's shoulder. The other took hold of his wrist to steady it as she had done when she smelled the lavender. She buried her nose in the petals and took a slow, deep breath, then sighed with pleasure, closing her eyes and inhaling again. Her face was close to Robbie's, tilted a little to one side, with only the flower between them. He could count the individual eyelashes that seemed to reach all the way up to her arched brows. Her lips were the same deep shade as the rose he held, almost as soft as the velvety petals, but much fuller and more enticing.

'Beautiful.' He sighed.

'It's so strong it makes me feel light-headed,' Rowenna said.

She opened her eyes and looked at him over the top of the flower, the long lashes widening to frame eyes that were now heavy with sensuality. Her lips curved into a wide smile and Robbie's heart began to beat faster. He was starting to feel light-headed himself, but that was nothing to do with the scent of the rose. Light-headed and more than a little reckless.

'I don't mean the flower,' he murmured.

He folded his hand over the rose and lowered it, noticing in the back of his mind that his hand was trembling. He bent his head down a little more until he was close enough that his mouth was next to Rowenna's. Close enough that he could feel the softness of her cheek against his. Close enough to whisper and be perfectly certain that no one else who might venture to this part of the garden would be able to hear the words that were meant only for her ears.

'I mean you.'

And he kissed her.

Rowenna gave a small squeak of surprise and her eyes widened. Her mouth hardened, but before Robbie pulled away, conscious that he had forced himself on her, they became soft again and Rowenna was kissing him back with a sensuous slowness, letting her eyes fall shut as she slid her hands around Robbie's waist to rest in the middle of his back. Her lips were as warm and eager as Robbie had dreamed they would be. He raised his hand, still clutching the rose, and rested it at the nape of her neck to draw her closer. The perfume of the bloom mingled with the scent from Rowenna's hair in an intoxicating manner, pulling

Robbie into a whirlpool of ecstasy that he would gladly drown in.

It was not Robbie's first kiss, but as Rowenna's lips moved with a gentle pressure that indicated she was far from unwilling, he realised with a jolt of jealousy that neither was it hers. Someone else had taught her to match the rhythm and pressure of her partner and respond in kind. Someone else had claimed her before him. He lowered his arm and slowly withdrew his lips from hers. Rowenna opened her eyes leisurely as if she was waking after a heavy sleep. Robbie wished he could be at her side to see if she looked as alluring then as she did now. Her lips were still slightly parted. Robbie shivered at the idea of returning to the kiss, but she took a step backwards and another, keeping her eyes fixed on Robbie.

'That was the first impetuous thing I can remember you doing!' she said. 'I should never have called you staid.'

She raised her hand and ran her fingertips over her lips. Shadows played across her face and Robbie couldn't tell if she was angry, disappointed or consumed with the same desire that riddled his body.

'I'm sorry,' Robbie muttered.

'Why? It was only a kiss! There was no harm in it.'

No harm. She seemed unaffected.

'I didn't ask.'

He was as shameful as the men he had warned her against, but even as he denied it, he drew closer, leaning in towards her so that their faces were close and he could lose himself in her eyes.

'Oh, but you did,' Rowenna assured him. She licked her lips with the tip of her tongue and Robbie's legs threatened to give way. He could still taste her on his own lips. 'You've been asking ever since we came outside, only not with words. With your eyes.'

'But you're my friend,' he said, edging closer.

'Well, that was very friendly indeed!' She gave a merry, rippling laugh, then looked at him coyly. 'Did you like it?'

Certain parts of Robbie's anatomy were threatening to demonstrate their approval whether he willed it or not. He could feel himself swelling, acutely conscious of the uncomfortable shifting and hardening taking place inside his breeches. He hoped to all the saints that Rowenna was not aware of the bulge that was growing firmer and more commanding of his attention with every moment. Had his body so obviously betrayed the urges he felt? It had been intoxicating. So exquisitely good. Jealousy coursed through him once more.

'You've done that before,' he said.

She lifted her jaw, unabashed but with a hint of defensiveness in her voice. 'So have you.'

'Who? Was it Cecil?' If she said yes, Robbie was sure he would explode with jealousy.

'I only met your friend today. Credit me with some discretion!' Rowenna's brows knotted. She twisted the end of her ribbon around her finger-tip and gave him a sidelong glance.

'I kissed Tom the fuller's son on May Day three years past, and Matthew Esmond kissed me at Ralf's last birthday feast. Oh, and on Twelfth Night just gone I kissed Wat Corridge.'

Nothing more recent than six months. Wat was a friend of her older brother who Robbie remembered, probably unfairly, as a dull-witted lout, not remotely worthy of her notice. Better than kissing Cecil, but even so, Robbie couldn't keep the surprise out of his voice.

'Why them?'

'Because I wanted to see what it was like, of course.'

She sighed and her shoulder dropped with an unwittingly seductive ripple. 'It wasn't very inter-esting kissing Tom or Matthew and I think Wat was too nervous of me. I wouldn't want a man who jumped when I entered the room.'

Robbie sniggered.

'I'm not surprised you scared Wat. He would

flee from a sheep if it started unexpectedly. You must have terrified him!'

'It isn't funny.'

Rowenna glared and Robbie bit his lip to keep from laughing further. He might have been scared himself if he had been planning to kiss her all along, but it had been a complete impulse, the desire overwhelming any sense he possessed and surprising him as much as it had surprised her.

Rowenna tilted her head and looked at him with catlike eyes, her full lips curling into a beguiling smile that caused his heart to thump.

'*You* weren't too scared to kiss me.'

Was she implying the kiss was better? Her voice held the same tone of challenge that in their childhood had seen Robbie drawn into some reckless escapade or other that usually ended in a whipping or loss of sweetmeats. He refused to rise to it now. Still, he felt back on familiar ground with easy playful teasing.

Yes, better to keep jesting. Anything to distract him from what he would rather be doing with her. He stepped closer, swaggering a little, and bent his head over hers. He put two fingers under her chin and tilted her head up.

'Nothing you could do would scare me, Rowenna Danby.'

Madden, certainly. Infuriate, definitely. Arouse, disconcertingly yes. But not scare him.

'And would you be too scared to kiss me again?'

She dipped her head and looked at him through her eyelashes. If she was aiming for a demure expression, she was failing utterly. She giggled suddenly. A bubbling sound that made Robbie want to join in. She was being playful now, with no trace in her eyes of the unsettling sensuality that had knocked Robbie off his feet, but with a devilry that was just as enticing in its own way. Rowenna in a playful mood might be just as fun to kiss, if not more, but now Robbie was in full command of his body and had no intention of trying to find out. Clearly the kiss had been nothing more than an amusing diversion for Rowenna. Robbie was uncomfortably aware of the feelings that were budding within him and he was not going to risk further awakening them and repeating the desperate, unrequited longing that had plagued him over Mary.

Mary!

Robbie writhed with shame. He been planning to spend as much of the evening as possible with Mary with the aim of declaring his love for her, but instead he had brought another woman to a concealed part of the gardens, sat intimately on the bench and kissed her. He was behaving like a complete rogue. He was not sure whom he had betrayed more. Then again, Rowenna knew he loved Mary and had kissed him back anyway.

'It shouldn't have happened,' he said firmly.

He glanced back to the Common Hall, guilt prickling up and down his spine once again. Rowenna followed his gaze, then looked at Robbie, all merriness gone from her eyes.

'You're right. I thank you for a particularly interesting evening. I think I shall go home now.' She adjusted the neck of her gown, which had become pushed askew, and began to walk away.

'You can't go alone!' Robbie called in alarm.

She smiled back at him over one shoulder. 'I won't. My father arranged for Geoffrey to escort me. There are people you'd rather be with.'

She had hesitated before she said *people* and Robbie knew exactly whom she referred to. No barb could have wounded him more than the look of resignation in her eyes.

'No, there aren't.'

As he spoke, he realised he meant it. No one mattered as much as she did. His devotion to her intensified, blossoming into something deeper and altogether more terrifying. How had he not seen before how deeply he cared for her?

He rushed to her side, but the stiffening of her whole frame as he approached brought him up short. He held himself rigid because the alternative was to take hold of her again and demonstrate how much he wanted to hold her, touch her and keep her close. To do much, much more than kiss her. If Sir John himself had asked Robbie to make his oath of chastity, he would have laughed in his master's face. If the Bishop of York had appeared, he would have married her on the spot.

'Rowenna, I—'

Robbie had never been grateful for his difficult tongue, but now he blessed it for preventing him declaring he loved her and making a fool of himself. 'If you truly wish to go, then *I* will take you home,' he said.

'Thank you.'

She broke into a smile and before Robbie could catch a breath, she put her hand to his jaw and kissed him once again, taking her time to pull her lips from his. The world felt like a frozen pond with cracks beginning to appear beneath Robbie's feet. One false step would see him plunge beneath the waters. He escorted Rowenna to a seat in the hall and explained he would retrieve her cloak. He had taken no more than five paces further when Cecil barred his way.

'You stole my partner, Rob. Twice!'

'You mean liberated!'

Rowenna hadn't been an unwilling partner to Cecil, though. The unpleasant thought occurred to him that she might have been equally happy to go outside if Cecil had asked her. If she was free with her kisses, she might not care whom she gave them to. It made Robbie writhe in misery to think that what they had done might have meant little to her.

'She looks good in red,' Cecil mused. 'If you're not intending to make use of her, perhaps I'll see if I can persuade her to come out with me and I'll see if I can give her a green gown instead. She seems the kind of girl who wouldn't take much coaxing to gratify a man.'

Robbie's temper flared, both at the dreadful pun and the act Cecil's euphemism referred to.

'She's my cousin,' he snarled, bunching his fist. 'And you're asking for a beating!'

He would have gladly administered it, but at that moment the music died away.

'Ah,' Cecil murmured. 'She mentioned a cousin, but I didn't know it was you or I'd have been a little more prudent. I must beg your forgiveness. I was jesting, of course.'

Robbie smiled tightly. He felt again the protective instinct that had made him so determined to warn Rowenna away from Cecil.

'Excuse me, I have left Rowenna waiting for too long.'

He bowed his head stiffly and turned to leave, but a single trumpet sounded a lone note, indicating something was about to happen. The Lord Mayor of York, Simon de Quixlay, appeared from a small antechamber and stepped on to the raised dais at the end of the room. Simon de Quixlay waited for silence before he spoke, describing the carnage and violence that had taken place, praising the city militia and the knights, nobles and squires who had come to the aid of the city.

'As Mayor of York, I intend to remind the citizens that our country is well defended from such untoward attempts at wresting control from their betters,' said de Quixlay. With a smile and arms wide to demonstrate his largesse, he announced the forthcoming ceremony of knighthood and the names of those who were to be honoured. Robbie's name was among them. He could not join Rowenna now. With a sinking heart, he stepped forward to the dais to stand with four other squires he did not know.

Mayor de Quixlay addressed him. 'You acquitted yourself well over the past two days, I'm told, Master Danby. The city should not have been subjected to such turmoil. The peasantry are in danger of forgetting their place and the mood is still volatile.'

Robbie bowed. There had been peasants and beggars, but Robbie had also seen shopkeepers, tradesmen and labourers taking the opportunity to vent their frustrations at the elite who squeezed them more and more.

He scanned the room as thunderous applause

filled the air. Mary was standing with Amy Mortimer, Lady Isobel's maid. She wore a serene smile on her face. Robbie met her eye briefly and moved on, searching for Rowenna. He spotted her beside the door, her smile ecstatic. The two women could not have been more different. Rowenna clad in scarlet and glowing, Mary in palest blue, shimmering. Fire and ice. The sun and moon. Robbie was conscious that the balance of his affections had tipped firmly in Rowenna's direction. How fortunate he had never declared his infatuation openly to Mary.

'You're supposed to be happy, not staring at the wall,' Cecil hissed in his ear.

Robbie smiled, though he did not feel it. As the musicians started again he turned to receive the congratulations of the men and women who clustered around him. Mary was among them. He murmured pleasantries, eyes returning to the spot where Rowenna stood. He began to edge through the crowd towards her, but a hand on his sleeve made him pause. Mary was at his side. Robbie bit back the frustration that filled him at being prevented from joining Rowenna. Mary turned her watery blue eyes on him.

'I never saw you again after you left to take your message. Someone as dashing as you should have been easy to spot.'

'I… M-my cousin,' Robbie murmured, taken

aback at being called dashing. 'W-we went to the garden to take the air. She was feeling faint.'

He glanced across in time to see Geoffrey Vernon appear at Rowenna's side. Rowenna spoke briefly and Geoffrey scuttled away, leaving her alone again.

'How unfortunate!' Irritation flashed across Mary's face. It was the first time Robbie had seen the emotion there and it was startling to see how her features turned from serene to icy. He blinked in surprise, wondering if he had been mistaken. Mary followed Robbie's gaze and her eyes hardened.

'Is that woman your cousin? I have heard about her father and pity the poor girl. To be stained with illegitimacy is a trial.'

Mary's nose wrinkled in obvious distaste and, for all her beauty and charm, Robbie despised her at that moment.

'Excuse me. Rowenna is waiting for me.' He took a step towards Rowenna, but Mary held his sleeve. He could not physically shake her off without appearing rude.

'She seems to have recovered from her swoon. And appears to be leaving with someone else.'

Geoffrey had reappeared, bearing Rowenna's cloak. A chill passed over Robbie as Rowenna turned one way, then the other, smiling at him as he passed it around her shoulders. Geoffrey held out an arm. Before she took it, Rowenna's eyes roved around the room once more. They landed on Robbie, then on Mary at his side. She raised her hand and gave a gentle wave of farewell before placing it on Geoffrey's arm. She might as well have stuck a hook into Robbie's chest and pulled his intestines out as she walked away. His stomach filled with bile. She had given up waiting for Robbie to find her and, worse, had seen him with Mary. No wonder she accepted Geoffrey's company. Remembering that Hal hoped for a marriage between them, Robbie hoped desperately that was all she would accept that night.

'I have seen you looking at me, Master Danby, but naturally modesty has forbidden me from talking to you until tonight,' Mary murmured in a manner that did not seem modest to Robbie. 'Perhaps I might allow you to call on me tomorrow and we can become better acquainted. I am sure my uncle would allow it.'

She lifted her face, pushing her lips into a bud, clearly hoping to be kissed. Caught by surprise, Robbie dipped his head but regained his presence of mind and did not let his lips meet hers. Instead, he lifted her hand and brushed his lips across the back of it.

'Master Danby, you promised me a second dance, but you broke your oath,' Mary said, her voice smooth as cream. 'A knight would not do that, would he?'

Her implication was clear and he felt a ripple of disdain. She had shown no interest in him before, but a future baron who had been brought to the attention of the assembled nobility and influential citizens of York was not beneath her notice.

He would have excused himself, but the other four knights-in-waiting were standing with their partners and Robbie was expected to lead the measure. With everyone watching it was impossible to decline without causing Mary offence. Robbie bowed with a flourish and led Mary to the centre of the floor.

Chapter Eleven

Daylight exploded into the room. Rowenna woke with a jolt in a tangle of sheets and a consciousness of Robbie's lips on hers. They had been kissing with frantic passion, bodies pressing close while their hands stroked and explored each other in increasingly intimate ways. The sensations had been so realistic that she pulled her coverlet up high to conceal him from discovery, but she was alone in her bed. It had been a dream.

'Good morning, Lady Layabed. Time to rise.'

Rowenna's mother was bustling around the room with her customary briskness, chiding her daughter for leaving the new gown on the floor where she had stepped out of it, rearranging trinkets on the dresser and gathering discarded ribbons. Rowenna let the monologue wash over her and avoided eye contact until her breath came more easily and the feelings of excitement subsided. There was no way Joanna could guess what

Rowenna had been dreaming of, but all the same, Rowenna felt a pang of shame that she had been interrupted in the middle of such sensual acts.

She sat up and hugged her knees before she recalled it had not only been a dream but a glorious reality. The night before she had abandoned all decorum and encouraged Robbie to kiss her and he had responded eagerly and expertly. It had been the most enthralling moment of Rowenna's life, the shiver down her spine and surging of her blood far surpassing all her previous kisses rolled into one. They had been enjoyable and diverting, but nothing more than that—pleasant while they lasted, but leaving her untouched. When Robbie had kissed her, the minutes had stretched into hours and shrunk to the blink of an eye at the same time. Her body had come alive and she could not have told what day it was from the overpowering confusion that filled her mind. She must have sighed aloud because her mother stopped folding blankets and came to the bed.

'Did you enjoy yourself? I heard the door last night. Did Geoffrey stop to take a cup of wine with Hal?'

Geoffrey! Who cared what he had done? Rowenna shrugged. She had evaded her father, leaving the two men alone, and gone directly to her room where she had been able to vent her frustration and relive her delights in privacy.

Joanna indicated a cup of milk and honey on the table. 'You should drink that. You look pale. Are you feeling ill? Did you drink more wine than was wise last night?'

Rowenna shook her head to all questions, but Joanna did not look convinced. She sat on the edge of the mattress, held her daughter's hands tightly and raised her eyebrows. Rowenna realised she was trembling, but her cheeks were hot enough to be scarlet. The flames continued down her throat, between her breasts and ended in the centre of her belly. Her nightshift clung to her skin, damp and sticky in places and she wanted to tear it off and plunge into ice water to quench the fires that made her weak and restless.

'Are you sickening for a fever?' Joanna asked anxiously.

The ache for Robbie's lips and hands on her body caused Rowenna such dramatic symptoms that fever was a good description. It was not a fever in the sense that everyone in the city dreaded—a sickness caused by the bad air or vapours from the river that left the strongest of men weak and dying, but something far more deadly from which there was no chance of recovery.

She knew now what she had suspected for years and which their kiss had confirmed. She was hopelessly in love with Robbie.

'Did anyone—did any harm befall you?' Joanna asked, anxiously peering at Rowenna.

Not intentionally, at least. Robbie could not possibly have suspected what his kiss would do to her or he would never have inflicted such sweet pain on her. When he had ended the kiss she had felt as if her heart was being dragged from her body.

'I spent most of the evening with Robbie,' Rowenna said quietly. 'No one harmed me.'

'So you didn't manage to find yourself a knight to marry?'

Rowenna chewed her fingernail. She knew who she wanted to marry. She recognised what desire looked like and had seen it clearly in Robbie's eyes. Hadn't she longed to see such an expression for so many years that she had pictured it perfectly? But then after the announcement Robbie had stayed with Mary and had clearly abandoned Rowenna to Geoffrey's company, despite his insistence he would take her home himself. His preference was clear. Rowenna could only torture herself by imagining what had occurred between Robbie and Mary after Geoffrey had taken her home. Even if Robbie found Rowenna attractive, desire was not the same as love. The short, stolen moment of joy in the gardens would be all Rowenna could claim from Robbie. Thank goodness she had not humiliated herself by admitting the effect his kiss had had on her.

'Robbie is to be knighted very soon,' Rowenna told her mother.

'So we have heard this morning,' Joanna said. 'Did you know?'

Rowenna flung herself back on to the pillows. The joy she had felt at hearing Simon de Quixlay's announcement had been the perfect end to the evening. Now she understood why Robbie had been dwelling on his vows of knighthood and asked her to help him rehearse them. He had already known when the ceremony was to take place, but hadn't told her.

She flushed with indignation, but sadness mingled with it. Once she and Robbie had been so close that he would never have kept something so important from her. The only thing that made it better was knowing that he had clearly kept the secret from Mary, as well.

And Mary had lost no time in capturing Robbie as soon as he stepped from the dais, gazing up at him like a newborn calf. It was obvious even to the slowest thinker that she would be happy for him to court her now.

'Drink your milk,' Joanna urged.

Rowenna drained the cup listlessly, conscious of her mother studying her.

'I should not have let you go last night if this

is how you return home!' Joanna gave her a maddening smile that Rowenna recognised as the one
she wore herself when she intended to vex people and Rowenna wondered what conclusions her
mother had drawn. 'I shall have to have words
with Robbie about how he takes care of you.'

'He took care of me wonderfully,' Rowenna
exclaimed.

'Did he now! I hope you didn't disgrace yourself!' Joanna's sharp look left Rowenna under
no illusion that her mother had read the situation
correctly. Joanna relieved her of the cup. 'It's like
that, is it?'

Rowenna bit her lip to stop it trembling. How
could her mother possibly understand the pain
of loving someone who she could not have? She
sniffed and wiped her eyes on her sleeve, turning away.

'Does Robbie know you feel this way?' Joanna asked.

'No, and he loves someone else who is not
worth his love. I have to tell him what I feel. I'll
go to Sir John's stand at the tournament today.'

'You'd humiliate yourself if you did. Can you
imagine what would happen if you appeared at
the lists and started declaring love?' She reached
for Rowenna's hand. 'Remember, sometimes a
person you are fond of is not the person you

should be with. There might be someone better waiting that you haven't even considered.'

'You don't know what you're talking about.' Rowenna scowled.

'Of course not. I'm far too old to know anything about anything,' Joanna said, folding her arms. 'I do know your father is leaving the house shortly. You can help clean the pantry with me or act as his clerk, but I want you out of bed!'

Rowenna's mood improved slightly when she went into the workshop and discovered a list of orders to be written up and bills issued. At least she would be occupied. Never one to enjoy idleness, she set about arranging the disordered piles.

'I will do half now and half later. I have a fancy to go watch the jousting this afternoon,' she told her father.

'Not today,' Hal said. 'The streets are still not safe. I fear trouble is still brewing. I hope you shook off your restlessness enough through dancing last night and don't feel the need to go running all over the city this morning.'

He chucked her under the chin and told her to stay in the house. Rowenna could barely contain her frustration. She had hoped to visit the tournament grounds now that the riots had ceased. Most of her visit to York had been spent trapped inside the house. Soon her parents would return to Ravenscrag and her life would become dull and quiet again. It was easy for Joanna to tell her to look elsewhere for a husband, but when she was doomed to spend her life in Ravenscrag, where might she look and who might she look to? Only Geoff or one of the village men.

No more dancing. No more bustling streets and interesting fair stalls.

No more Robbie.

She swallowed back bitter tears and set to work, and immediately came across the bill her father had written for Sir John's commission of a pair of daggers. Robbie had brought the original message.

Her usual optimism returned. Last night she had missed the opportunity to tell Robbie what she had overheard Mary saying, but it was not too late to tell Robbie how cruelly Mary had spoken of him and prevent him hurting himself by continuing to moon after her. Even if she said nothing of her feelings, she had to tell him the truth before it was too late.

Her intentions to stay in the house melted. Despite Joanna's advice, she would borrow her mother's maid and take the estimate to Sir John's lodgings herself once she had finished her tasks, rather than trusting it to Hal's runabout boy. She wanted to congratulate Robbie in person as she had been unable to do so at the dance.

Perhaps she would see in his face some of the affection she had seen the previous night. She wouldn't be so foolish as to declare her feelings openly, but if she could steer the conversation around to the matter of Mary, she could tell him what she had overheard. It would hurt Robbie to learn of Mary's opinion, but better now than if he spent more time in her company and believed she cared for him. Rowenna knew herself how painful it was to hope for a kind glance from someone who did not realise the significance.

She was thwarted in this plan, because before noon a knock on the door brought Cecil Hugone into her presence, requesting the invoice. She tried to hide her disappointment that Robbie had not come and admitted the handsome squire.

'I had hoped to dance with you again last night,' Cecil said with a disarming smile. 'I was doubly pleased to be asked to perform Sir John's errand.'

He looked round the workshop, clearly interested, before sitting, uninvited, on the bench beside Rowenna. She smiled uncertainly. He had flattered and flirted the night before when they had danced together. He had made his interest in her clear, but the memory of that did not stir her.

'Let me find the message for your master.' She rummaged through the box of papers to find the bill she had seen. If Robbie had come, she would have taken longer and chatted, but she was in no mood for Cecil's company. He took it from her with both hands and extended his fingers so they brushed hers.

'I will see you tonight, I hope.'

He gazed at her earnestly. Rowenna frowned at this display of forwardness, wondering what impression she had given and whether she had rashly promised him a tryst she had forgotten. 'I don't—'

'Oh, my pardon. Sir John is bidding Master Danby's family to join him this evening in celebration of Rob's successes.' Cecil looked embarrassed. 'I assumed the invitation included you. It was delivered early this morning.'

'Did my cousin bring it?' Rowenna asked, trying not to sound too eager. She could scarcely believe neither parent had seen fit to tell her of something so important. Why had Joanna not woken her?

'No, he was busy with other matters. He escorted Sir John's party to the last day of the tournament.'

Cecil's smile was impenetrable, but if he hoped Rowenna would try wheedling the meaning out of him, she determined he was to be disappointed.

'I did not know about the message,' she admitted, glad, at least, that she had not missed Robbie. 'I stayed late in bed this morning.'

Cecil's eyes flickered hungrily. Rowenna wondered if he was picturing her in her bed and wished she had not mentioned it.

'The dancing exhausted you that much! Tonight you will have to find a less strenuous way of amusing yourself. I shall have to put my mind to some diverting games.'

He bowed over her hand and Rowenna walked with him to the door before rushing back to the bench in excitement and burying herself in her work. The day would pass slowly. She would see Robbie tonight and this time there would be nothing to prevent her doing what she must to save him from heartbreak.

Robbie's day had started equally abruptly. Once again he had awoken to discover Cecil standing over him.

He'd been dreaming of dancing again, but this time he knew who had been his companion. Rowenna's sweet laugh and sweeter lips had filled his night, but the dream had turned sour as she laughingly danced from his arms to Cecil, to Geoffrey and on to faceless others while Robbie was forced to watch, his tongue transformed to stone and unable to call her back to him.

'What do you want?' He glowered, not quite

shaking off the animosity the dream had caused towards Cecil.

'Sir John wants to speak to you before you leave for the tournament. Again.'

Cecil loitered while Robbie dunked his face in the bowl of water and rubbed his teeth clean.

'You played me false with your description of your cousin, Robbie. You told me she was a scholarly girl, but she's far prettier than I would have imagined. Nothing like you at all.'

'She's not to be played with. You won't use and discard her.' Heat rose to Robbie's cheeks. He pulled on his clothes and ran his comb through the tangles of his hair.

Cecil affected a look of shock. 'Who says I mean to discard her? She's a rare creature. The way she stalked up like an avenging angel and stole you from beneath Mary's nose last night was enchanting. *She* is enchanting. I never thought I'd see Mary so furious.'

Robbie winced. Mary had indeed glared at Rowenna in the most alarming manner. It had been unpleasant to see. To think he had once imagined the two women could be friends.

Cecil's eyes took on a dreamlike expression and he sighed. 'I can imagine some merry battles of will with fair Rowenna. There's a woman a man could really fall in love with.'

Robbie's jaw tightened at the casual mention

of the emotion he was battling with himself. He had told her after the kiss that nothing she did would scare him, but he had lied. The emotions that were roiling in his brain and belly and heart were beginning to scare him very much indeed.

'You don't fall in love,' he said.

'Perhaps I might this time,' Cecil replied.

Cecil genuinely caring about Rowenna might be almost as bad as Cecil behaving in his usual way.

'Rowenna is the daughter of a bastard. You wouldn't wish to m-marry into a family with such a dubious pedigree. We're only half cousins really,' he said. It occurred to him as he said it that it was wrong. Rowenna was not of his blood at all.

Cecil gave him a penetrating look. 'You seem very keen to dissuade me. Do you have designs on her yourself? I thought you disapproved of illegitimacy.'

'No!' The answer came too quick, too harsh on Robbie's lips to sound convincing. He wrinkled his brow in astonishment. 'I seem disapproving?'

'A little. I know how principled your morals are.' Cecil leered. 'Would you prefer me to keep out of your way? Perhaps if my attentions were elsewhere engaged. Our lovely Mary, for instance...'

He let the suggestion hang. Robbie's belly twisted at this blatant attempt at bartering Rowenna in return for a clear path to Mary. Oddly, the idea of Cecil and Mary no longer filled him with the despair it once had. It did not fill him with any emotion, if he was perfectly honest, but the idea of Cecil and Rowenna made him want to reach for the nearest bottle of wine to drown his misery.

'You are assuming neither Rowenna nor Mary would have opinions on the m-matter,' he said tersely.

Cecil grinned again. 'You make a fair point. Perchance I'll try finding out what they are.'

Robbie marched downstairs ahead of Cecil and greeted his master. To his satisfaction, Cecil was dismissed, leaving Robbie alone with Sir John.

'You have brought honour on my household and your knighthood is well-deserved. Your parents will surely delay their departure until after your ceremony. I would like to invite your family to dine here tonight in celebration.'

He steepled his fingers and looked at Robbie over the top. 'I hope we may be celebrating more than one event.'

'Is Cecil also to be knighted?'

'Not that.' Sir John indicated the stool at his feet. Robbie sat, wondering where the interview would lead. 'Everyone in my household is aware you have a certain interest in my niece.'

Robbie considered it fortunate he was already

seated, because he might have staggered at such an abrupt start to the interview. He opened his mouth to deny it, but Sir John raised a hand.

'Watching you dance together last night, I think she has a liking for you, too. Or at least for your future title and rank.'

Sir John permitted himself a laugh that Robbie did not join in. Of course it was his knighthood that had caught Mary's eye. Robbie understood that, however much he wished otherwise. A stuttering, shy man held little attraction in himself.

'I consider it my responsibility to find a suitable husband for Mary now she is in my household. I am in mind to grant permission for you to marry.'

A week earlier Robbie would have leapt from the stool and prostrated himself at Sir John's feet in thanks. Now he felt sick at the thought.

'I have not asked her.'

'You do not need to. I am her guardian and I have decided.'

'My lord, I must apologise. If I have m-m-m—' Robbie could not speak. He shook his head in agitation. Marrying Mary was abhorrent now he knew who commanded his heart. It would be a grave injustice to her, to Rowenna and to himself.

'I did not intend to mislead the lady,' he managed in a rush. 'I may have hoped once, but I know I will not make her happy. We will not make each other happy.'

Robbie looked up into Sir John's eyes and found them full of kindness and a little confusion. Robbie was caught in a net of his own weaving that Sir John honestly believed was to his liking. And until Rowenna had swept back into his life and beguiled him, it had been. It would be the height of ingratitude and stupidity to reject Sir John's kindness and patronage over the years. And why? Because the infatuation for Mary— as he now knew it had been—had cooled in the flame of his sudden passion for Rowenna.

'This is a very sudden change of heart, Master Danby. Last night you danced with Mary in front of the assembly. Before that you clearly hankered after her. This morning she came to us and told my wife you asked her to dance twice in a row. Your attentions touched her deeply. She believes you will make her happy.'

Robbie couldn't help himself and raised an eyebrow. Mary had scorned his offer of a second dance and shown no interest before Simon de Quixlay's announcement. The difference towards him then had been quite marked.

'Her affection towards me is very sudden. I need time to think.'

Sir John looked severely at him. He leaned forward in his chair and spoke in a whisper. 'I know about your family, Master Danby. Your father appraised me of it before I took you into my household.'

The blood chilled in Robbie's veins. Had Sir John been party to the deception all along? 'My lord, what do you mean?'

'Your father's reputation was always questionable, to say the least. Roger Danby was known as a rogue and a mercenary with a string of unsuitable affairs across Europe and England. I believe there was some scandal even here in York at one time. Your family was poor before he reappeared with a sudden fortune and family. As your mother was a common alewife before your father married her, it is highly unlikely she was the source of his wealth.'

Robbie's head jerked upward. He flushed with anger, the impulse to rant strong in him, but somehow he managed to remain calm enough to stay seated. The picture Sir John painted of his stepfather was damning. Acid filled his belly and he clenched his fists.

'My mother ran the finest inn in Cheshire and Father's honour has never been called into question by his liege lord. He treats his tenants fairly and performs all his duties.' He stopped, a little surprised at the vehemence with which he defended his stepfather. He writhed internally, thinking of the way he had rejected all Roger's overtures of reconciliation since learning the secret.

Sir John smiled frostily. 'You are a fine young man who has the potential to rise high. If you don't take Mary's hand, then you will lose your chance of a secure and prosperous future. You will be knighted, but how many noblemen who remember the young Roger Danby will leap forward to have you marry his daughter?'

Was this a threat? A chill raced down Robbie's spine, filling him with dread. He looked his master in the eye. 'I am not ashamed of my parents,' he said. 'Nor would I wish to marry anyone who despises my kin.'

'Your loyalty gives you credit, but be warned, my niece would be unlikely to excuse scandal. Mary is a proud girl. Too proud, if truth be told. But what a woman does not know will not trouble her.'

Robbie gaped. 'I would want to share everything with the woman I love,' he said.

'Then you're naive.' Sir John shook his head reproachfully. 'Are we now getting to the truth of the matter? Has another woman given you hope of marriage?'

Robbie dropped his head. Despite the warmth of her kiss and her pleasure in his company, Rowenna had given him quite the opposite. He had been left not with hope, but with a sense of de-

spair greater than he had felt when he believed
he loved Mary. Rowenna loved him as a friend,
but it had been clear the kiss was nothing more
than fun for her, like dancing with different men,
like kissing Wat or the village boys. He raked
his memory of their encounter for any sign her
feelings ran as deeply as his, but each indication could be explained away and every flicker of
hope was quenched. Even her misunderstanding
in thinking he was asking for her hand in marriage had been met with amusement rather than
eagerness.

'No one has given me her heart,' he said, his
face twisting.

'You are far too unworldly, Master Danby.
Now, you are expected at the tournament grounds
this morning. Do well in your events and think
on what I have said. If you choose to reject my
offer, you will be rejecting everything I have
given you.'

The tournament was not as well attended as
before. The riots and days of delay meant people had either lost interest or could not spare the
time and the audience consisted mainly of the
parties who had a personal interest: squires and
their lords, wives and lovers. Robbie looked for
Rowenna in the crowded stands, but could not
see her and came to the conclusion she had not

attended. He missed the sound of her laughter and the sight of her bright eyes gleaming with excitement. He missed the feel of her in his arms as she embraced him enthusiastically. The kiss he dropped on to Mary's hand left him unmoved. He vented his frustration with his sword and was placed third in the contest. He achieved greater success with his bow, as each arrow found the centre of the target. Perhaps imagining it was his heart they pierced helped.

He received his prize to great applause, conscious of Mary's eyes on him. As he bowed before Sir John, she beckoned him over. Aware of being watched, he could not refuse. To slight her in public would be the height of rudeness, especially given that everyone seemed to know of his interest. He made sure his conversation was politely formal. It would not be fair to continue with the warmth he had tried to show now that he knew he was not in love with her, but as he did his best to ignore the barely masked irritation he saw in her eyes when he stumbled over his words, he wondered why she had set her cap at him at all.

He studied her placid expression—an unkind observer might call it vacuous—and concentrated on the way she spoke with visitors to their stand easily, making perfectly judged observations and compliments. She was elegant and well connected, accomplished and wealthy. There was no doubt she would make an excellent wife for an ambitious knight. Sir John was quite right; Robbie would be a fool to turn down the chance of advancement such a connection would bring. He had longed for Mary's affection and she was still the beautiful woman who had caught his eye. No doubt they would be happy enough together.

But as he contemplated it, his stomach grew heavy with an aching he could barely withstand. If there was the slightest chance Rowenna could learn to return his feelings, he could not throw that away.

Before he gathered his bow to return to the butts, he spoke in a low voice to Sir John.

'I have been thinking about your offer. You are being generous in allowing me to celebrate my knighthood with my family,' he said. 'I will receive them and I will make my decision tonight.'

Tonight he would speak with Rowenna. The right word or a significant look would tell him if there was any hope for him and see his life set down one path or another.

Chapter Twelve

The wine-coloured surcoat seemed too extrav-
agant to wear for a private dinner and still bore
creases from a night on the bedroom floor, so
Rowenna dressed in her favourite blue gown
and bound her hair with the pale ribbons she
had bought at the market. She was halfway to
the inn before she recalled that Mary had worn
a similar blue.

Hal walked between his wife and daughter,
an arm for each woman. He must have sensed
Rowenna's change of mood because he paused.

'What is wrong?'

'Nothing. I was just wishing I had worn a different gown.'

'This is a small gathering of family and
friends. There is no need for ceremony,' Joanna
said. 'Besides, you look beautiful in that one. Any
man who could not see that would be a fool.'

'Who said anything about a man?'

Her parents exchanged knowing looks. Rowenna did her best to ignore them.

'This one is so simple.' Rowenna sighed, tweaking the neck into place so that it rested on the edges of her collarbones.

'You look as fine as any lady of court. You would shine in any company,' Hal said.

'Any company that would admit a bastard's daughter,' Rowenna muttered beneath her breath. 'No gown in the world would help me otherwise.'

Joanna elbowed her sharply and Rowenna glanced at Hal, hoping he had not overheard her. She had heard the hint of bitterness in his laugh and did not want to add to her beloved father's frustration at something that was not his fault.

She quickened her step. Sir John, at least, was one nobleman who did not think their family was beneath his notice. No doubt Mary would be wearing a fresh gown of a different colour, and Robbie would not compare them anyway.

Roger and Lucy had already arrived with their daughters. Rowenna's party was the last to arrive at the inn and were admitted by the innkeeper himself. The man must have been overjoyed at the unanticipated size of the party and had filled the room with lamps. Even though it was a hot night, a fire burned fiercely in the hearth and the air was stifling. The tempting smell of roasting pig wafted through the room, mingling with the scent of beeswax, and a pair of musicians played soft airs from the corner of the room.

Rowenna's foot began to tap and she hoped that there would be more dancing. She would show Cecil Hugone that it took more than one evening of dancing to tire her. She was glad of the loose sleeves of her underkirtle that billowed freely and would cool her as she moved. She paused. Dancing with Cecil had caused the argument with Robbie. It was not worth her pride to risk another argument. Cecil's opinion could go unchallenged.

The dividing doors were open between Sir John's private chamber and the communal room. There was still an invisible division between master and household, Rowenna noticed, as he and his wife sat at their fireplace in the recess on comfortable cushioned chairs, while his retinue kept to the long table and wooden stools in the larger part of the inn. Cecil was sitting on the end closest to the nobleman, but Rowenna was pleased to see Robbie was actually sitting with Sir John's party. Now he was a knight-in-waiting he had been elevated to a superior position.

He wore his finest livery, his dark hair brushing the collar of the high-necked tabard. Rowenna remembered the way her fingers had played with the soft curls the night before and a shudder of longing rippled over her.

Her pleasure was dampened by the sight of Mary sitting beside Robbie, with her low-backed seat pulled close to his. Of course Sir John's niece would be included, but it irked Rowenna to see she was sitting beside Robbie rather than at her mistress's side. They had their heads together and Mary was talking rapidly while Robbie listened with a polite smile. Mary was wearing another gown of blue, this time edged with a trim of pale fur. In June, Rowenna thought with contempt. She must be far too hot to be comfortable. Nevertheless, it was laced tight and pushed her small breasts high up her narrow torso, giving her a slender and elegant profile.

Robbie looked up and smiled towards the visitors. Mary was still talking and had either not noticed their arrival or, more likely, did not care. Robbie put his hand on her arm to pause her as his family arrived, and cocked his head towards them. It was an oddly proprietorial gesture. Rowenna felt her jaw clench and forced herself to smile as she followed her parents to greet Sir John and Lady Isobel. She waited while Hal and Joanna presented themselves and Hal spoke briefly about the matter of the swords before they moved to join Roger and Lucy. She avoided looking at Robbie and Mary, who waited in turn to receive the guests. There was something about the way they sat that caused a sense of foreboding in Rowenna. When it was her turn to move forward, she dropped into a deep curtsy and made her greetings to Robbie's master and mistress.

'I remember you, young woman,' Sir John said. He gave her a penetrating look. 'You claimed Master Danby from me the first night we arrived. I trust you don't intend to steal him away from us tonight?'

Rowenna felt herself blushing to the roots of her hair. The way Sir John spoke implied she had all manner of indiscretions planned. The fact that her mind had been full of outrageous daydreams was best kept to herself. She lowered her eyes demurely.

'Oh, no, my lord. I would not be so greedy as to take him from his duty or family tonight. I have no wish to claim my cousin for myself.'

She stammered her answer with difficulty, half expecting to be struck dead on the spot for such falsehoods, and wondering if this was how Robbie felt when called on to talk. She glanced at Robbie and caught his eye. She expected him to be laughing at her discomfiture but his face was alarmingly solemn. He should be happy on such a night and her stomach plummeted with a sense that something was amiss.

'Good evening, Cousin Robbie,' she said formally. 'May I offer my congratulations on your happy news? No one is more deserving.'

Robbie's expression grew warmer, but his posture remained stiff. 'Good evening to you, Cousin. M-my thanks for your w-w-words of kindness.'

He pressed his lips together. Mary's lips had twitched at his struggle and Rowenna felt her jaw tighten in response. Her heart swelled with pity that he was forced to speak so publicly and her stomach burned with anger that Mary clearly found it so tiresome. She wished she had another water jug at hand to wash away the woman's cruel expression, and resolved to speak to Robbie alone as soon as she could.

'I remember you also,' Mary said, peering at Rowenna. 'You knocked water over me last night.'

Rowenna no longer felt like laughing at the memory. Robbie blinked rapidly and looked between them. Rowenna could not tell if he was amused or angry at what he was hearing.

'I do hope you weren't too inconvenienced,' she said as sincerely as she could manage, wishing now it had been wine, not water.

'It dried,' Mary said.

Lucy and Joanna were quietly talking, but stopped as soon as Rowenna arrived. They began asking her in detail to tell them what had happened at the feast until she became so tangled in trying to make sure she did not reveal what had happened in the garden that she became quite confused. Robbie left Sir John's side, so she made her excuse and followed him to the table, where he was arranging cups on a tray. He moved over to allow her space at his side.

'Hello, Rowenna.' His voice was low and private. It reached inside her and sent ripples through her body, setting her skin buzzing like a cat that had been stroked the wrong way.

'Hello, Robbie.' To her dismay her voice shook. She caught a breath, unaccountably nervous in his presence.

Robbie seemed nervous, too. His hand shook as he meticulously lined up the goblets on the tray. He looked at her from the side of his eyes.

'Did you really knock a w-water jug over Mary?' Robbie's tone gave nothing away, but as she met his eyes, she saw a brief flicker of amusement that he blinked away.

'I was so busy concentrating on an interesting conversation I became clumsy. Fortunately Mary seems to have suffered no ill effects.'

'Yes, fortunate indeed.'

Now was the chance she had been waiting for to tell him why she had done it, but she would have to admit to eavesdropping, which Robbie would, quite rightly, take a dislike to. It could lead to another argument, which she was determined to avoid.

'I'm glad to see you. I wanted to congratulate you last night, but you were busy once the announcement had been made and Geoff insisted on taking me home.'

'I'm sorry I couldn't take you,' he said, dropping his voice even lower so she had to concentrate to hear it. He looked so concerned and sounded so earnest. 'Believe that I would have if the choice had been mine.'

He moved his fingers in slow circles over the back of her hand. Rowenna's heart melted with affection, but her resolve to declare her feelings wavered. He'd warned her to hide her emotions and there had never been a greater need than now. She must not let slip the desires he caused to blossom within her. If she could draw him away to somewhere private, the words would spill from her lips easily enough, but here was too public.

'Oh, Robbie, it doesn't matter.' She laughed, squeezing his hand. 'I reached home safely and it was sweet of you to worry, but I was happy to go with Geoffrey.'

'Do you m-mean that?' He sounded so serious, as if he had received a mortal wound. Rowenna tossed her head airily, determined to stop him feeling guilty.

'Of course. It was of no consequence who took me. I would not have torn you away at such a time for all the world.'

'You wouldn't have been tearing me away. I told you I wanted to take you.' He leaned in close and took her hand. Flames danced up and down her arm. She wanted to tell him that she had lied and it mattered very much, but the thought of admitting her feelings was worrying.

She put her hand on his arm, speaking playfully. 'I'm so pleased for you, but you do vex me. Why didn't you tell me before when you came to the house that you were to be knighted? You did know, didn't you?'

His grin transformed from shy to broad and his entire face lit with pride. Rowenna tilted her head to one side and gave him a mock-stern glare.

'You made me play-act with you and I teased you horribly. I would have been more serious had I known.'

She paused, recalling the other pretence they had done and the words of love she had wished were for her. Robbie had sounded so convincing that it had been hard for her to believe he was not in love with her. What a fool she had been to turn away from his kiss then. The gentle endearments echoed in her memory and made her want to sob at the missed opportunity. It was not too late.

'I can be serious, you know,' she said. 'When there are things that matter. You believe that, don't you?'

'I do.' Robbie spoke quietly and his voice was

grave. His eyes looked sad and it tore her heart. She reached a hand to his cheek and turned his face to hers. His slight beard was soft beneath her fingertips. She remembered the way it had prickled against her lips and became distracted by the memory for a moment. He must think her mad to be daydreaming. She lifted her eyes to apologise, but found he was staring past her with an unfathomable expression. He looked over her shoulder to where their parents were standing and his expression grew dark.

'Is Roger angry that you kept your knighthood secret from him?' she asked.

Robbie's lips twitched. 'No. He approves of keeping secrets.'

They were standing in shadows, half-hidden from the room. Rowenna reached for his hand again and laced her fingers through his.

'I looked for you at the tournament ground today, but I couldn't see you,' Robbie said. His eyes flickered, roving up and down her face, and she felt the sense he was searching for something she did not understand.

'I did want to talk to you, but Father wouldn't let me go,' she said irritably. 'I have barely any time left in York and I had to spend it in the house. Thank goodness Cecil came to visit. He was the only company I had all day.'

'Cecil visited you?' The corner of Robbie's

eyes tightened. Jealousy? Not enough to give her hope.

'Yes, regarding Sir John's commission. I would rather it had been you who had come, of course. Mother has designed the most intricate hilt for the daggers. They're beautiful. They have leaves and acorns and...' She bit her lip and left her description unfinished. Everything she uttered sounded so foolish that, if he had not guessed how she felt, Robbie must think her weak-minded.

'You would rather I had come than Cecil?' Robbie leaned towards her, lips parting slightly, and for one wonderful moment she thought he might be about to kiss her. Her heart began to beat rapidly and she felt breathless at the thought. The temptation to give in to her desire was so fervent it took her a great deal of strength to keep from reaching out to him and pouring out the way her heart burned. Though it pained her, she affected a wide smile.

'Of course. I'm always happy to see you. I rarely see my friends as often as I'd like.'

He looked at her sharply. 'We are friends, as well as cousins? You see me as a friend? And there is nothing that could alter that?'

He was talking in riddles. What did he fear would happen between them to break that bond? Not a half hour conversing with Cecil. Not even a dance.

She fixed her gaze on him and studied the thickly lashed, dark pools of brown that were burning with an intensity she could not explain. A little closer and she would be able to kiss him. His mouth was set in an uncertain line and she longed to press her lips to them and feel them yield to the gentle pressure of hers. She remembered Joanna's warning. She spoke in a cheerful voice.

'Robbie, you have always been—and always will be—my dearest friend. No secrets, no knighthood, no illicit kisses can change that.'

For a moment there was stillness. Silence surrounding them. Robbie's pupils flared, but the skin around his eyes tightened. His mouth curled slowly into a gentle smile.

'Then we shall always be friends.'

For some reason his tone made her want to sob. From the corner of her eye Rowenna saw Mary walking towards them.

'Robbie, my uncle is waiting for his drink,' she called. 'May I claim your attention on his behalf?'

Robbie dropped Rowenna's hand and gave her a smile that she could almost convince herself was one of regret. 'We must talk soon.'

She nodded dumbly, heart too full of words to be capable of speaking any of them before Mary was with them, sliding herself in between Robbie and Rowenna. She bestowed a serene smile on Robbie and gestured to the table beside them.

'Robbie, you should advise my uncle's servants to take care where to place the jugs on the table, unless we all might be awash again.'

Wine was too good to waste tipping over her. Pig's grease. Boiling pitch. Goose muck. Rowenna seethed silently while affecting a smile.

Robbie picked up the tray. Rowenna straightened the goblets and turned the handle of the jug to face him, giving him a defiant grin. She was pleased to see a flicker of amusement in his eyes.

'Perfectly safe from spilling. You'd best go and do as you are bidden.' Robbie held her gaze, looking doubtful. Rowenna slid her eyes meaningfully to Mary. 'Go. I promised Cecil earlier that I would say hello to him and I really should. I'll speak again with you later,' she called as Robbie made his way slickly through the gathering.

'Your cousin is fond of you, I see,' Mary said. 'I wish I had known beforehand of your existence. A female companion in the city would have been pleasant, but he never spoke of you.'

Mary gave a sly smile. She implied they shared confidences, but Rowenna knew Robbie had barely spoken with her. She ached to tell Mary what she had overheard, but settled for returning the smile.

'I can imagine how lonely it could be without a

companion to share confidences, but you seemed to have a friend last night from what I recall.' She looked past Mary to where Robbie was attending Sir John. He stood straight backed with his head inclined deferentially towards his master, but their eyes met briefly. He wrinkled his forehead and his expression clouded. Rowenna winked at him and he looked away quickly. Rowenna fixed Mary with a stern look.

'As for Robbie, he does not speak much to anyone unless he has something worth saying. Or someone worth saying it to.'

Mary's smile froze and her lips turned into a sharp pout. 'Then I shall have to learn to coax words from him. We shall have plenty of time.'

She curtsied and made her way across the room to Robbie, leaving Rowenna to ponder her words in misery. Mary would have all the time she wished to spend with Robbie, while Rowenna would be forced to return to Ravenscrag and solitude.

Cecil was talking with one of Sir John's servants but, seeing Rowenna standing alone, walked over to join her. They stood together, talking of nothing, which Rowenna was glad of as it gave her the chance to watch Robbie. She glanced once more at him. He was standing with his parents and Mary, but watching her and Cecil. She waved and gave him a beaming smile that hurt the muscles in her face. He leaned over to Mary and whispered something. They walked to where Sir John was seated and spoke. Cecil's words turned to wool in Rowenna's ears as she tried in vain to make out what they were saying.

She did not have to wait long to discover it, because Sir John stood and raised his hand. The effect was almost immediate as the guests ceased speaking and turned to face him.

'My friends, we are gathered to honour Robbie for his success in the tournament, for his part in quelling the riots and for his impending advancement to the position of knight.' He waited while everyone roared in approval. Rowenna dabbed the tears that had sprung to her eyes at the sight of her beloved cousin standing proudly before them all. Sir John had not finished, however. He looked between Robbie and Mary.

'Before we are seated to dine, I am also pleased to announce that the connection with Master Danby, my most favoured squire, will be further secured by the marriage between him and my niece, Mary.'

A high-pitched whine filled Rowenna's skull and she felt her skin grow cold and clammy. Inside she began to scream, *Too late… Too late*, and had to bite down on her tongue to reassure herself she was not doing it out loud. Was this what Robbie had been trying to tell her? At her side Cecil stood rigid. The tendons in his jaw were tight.

'Did you know?' Rowenna muttered to him.

'Not I. I am not favoured with Rob's confidence. You look surprised, too. I thought he would have told you,' Cecil said.

'I don't think I gave him the chance,' Rowenna whispered. She leaned against the table for support and realised she was half resting against Cecil. He looked down at her and she saw pity etched on his face. Were her emotions so clearly written that he could read her distress? He reached for her hand and pressed it gently without speaking. It was a kind gesture that at any other time would reach her heart, but now she was too numb to appreciate it. She stared around the room, barely making out the faces of the people who were beginning to cluster around Robbie and Mary, offering congratulations. Joanna caught Rowenna's eye. She spoke to Hal and made her way back to her daughter. Cecil retreated as Joanna approached.

'Don't say anything,' Rowenna said tightly before her mother could speak. Sympathy now would end what little composure she was retaining. She felt her bottom lip start to tremble and bit it hard. Joanna hugged her, then poured them both wine.

Rowenna took the cup. 'You were wrong. I have to tell Robbie how I feel.'

'What good could come of it?' Joanna said, pursing her lips.

'Better now than after he is married.'

'Better not at all! He is engaged to be married, which is close enough that it would cause a scene,' Joanna said sharply. She took Rowenna by the shoulders.

'I told you before. A sensible woman would not dwell on what she cannot have, but look for what else there might be available.'

Rowenna pushed the empty cup back towards Joanna, thinking that if she could not have Robbie, she would rather have no one at all, for who could make her laugh and love and quiver inside as much as her friend? 'I'm going home.'

'You have to stay,' Joanna said. 'What would Robbie think if you left now? Go congratulate them.'

On leaden feet Rowenna joined the cluster around the couple. She watched as they spoke to everyone. Or rather, as Mary spoke. Robbie stood at her side silently. His smile seemed forced and didn't reach his eyes, while Mary's was full of glee. He looked more like a man being led to the scaffold than one who had achieved everything he dreamed of. A lump filled Rowenna's throat and she could feel the prickle at her eyes that warned tears would form before long. She blinked furiously and took a deep breath, pinning a smile to her face before stepping forward.

'Do we have your congratulations, Cousin?' Robbie asked. His eyes bored into her and Rowenna couldn't believe Mary was not aware of the intensity of his look. She leaned forward to kiss Mary's cheek, then turned to Robbie. He made a move towards her, but she stepped back before he could embrace her. She longed to feel his arms around her, warm and tender as he had been the previous night, but he belonged to Mary now and Rowenna had no right to touch him. He froze and his eyes filled with hurt before he reached for her hand and pressed it tightly. Rowenna touched his hand as briefly as politeness would allow before withdrawing it. Somehow she found her voice to congratulate them before stepping away. His look of anguish as she departed was another wound inflicted on her already ruined heart.

She wanted to run from the inn and cry out her pain, but servants were starting to appear with platters of food and she was ushered to the table. She watched in despair as Mary took her place at Robbie's side, giving him a brilliant smile. Rowenna had to console herself with knowing that Robbie had achieved his heart's desire. Mary might prove to be a good wife and, if he never knew what she had said, he would surely be happily married.

The meal was a trial. Rowenna barely tasted the food that was put before her, finding it sticking in her throat. Anne and Lisbet talked around her, planning how to best approach their new sister, and she was content to let them. Roger and Lucy sat at Sir John's table. Rowenna gained some satisfaction from watching Mary try and fail to charm Lucy, who seemed utterly unimpressed with her new daughter-in-law. She tried not to watch Robbie, who sat at his bride-to-be's side, filling her goblet. His mouth was fixed in a smile, but it did not reach his eyes. As he looked at Rowenna he became solemn once again. She forced herself not to look at him, unable to bear the thought she was making him uncomfortable.

Had he proposed marriage to Mary before he had taken Rowenna into the garden and kissed her? She doubted it. Honour and fairness ran through Robbie as if it was welded to his bones and she was sure he would not have played either of them so ill.

In which case, it must have happened after Rowenna had left with Geoffrey. And after Mayor de Quixlay's announcement of Robbie's knighthood. Of course, that was the source of Mary's interest. That and the sapphires Lucy wore.

When the meal had finished and the guests moved once more around the room, Rowenna found Mary. Robbie was speaking to Cecil and the two women stood side by side, watching the squires.

'How long have you been in love with my cousin?' Rowenna asked, annoyed at how wobbly her voice was.

'In love?' Mary put her hand on her heart and blinked in surprise. Rowenna did not believe her astonishment was real. 'Oh, perhaps in the society you move in love is a consideration. How I wish sometimes I had the luxury of not having to consider my fortune or connections.'

Rowenna's jaw tightened. What chance did she have to marry for love now that the man who owned her heart was engaged to this woman? She leaned in a little closer to Mary. 'I told Robbie I had been engrossed in a conversation when I spilled water over you. It was yours I overheard. Shall I tell Robbie what you said and how you mocked him? Would he want to marry you then?'

'Only if you wish to hurt him,' Mary said. 'We will be married. He is too honourable to reject a woman he has publicly shown interest in.'

'You showed no interest in him last night,' Rowenna said. 'Why now?'

Mary's smile was serene. 'Robbie has shown he has excellent prospects and a bright future. He will be an excellent husband. My uncle was keen to make the match. It doesn't matter for Robbie's happiness whether I love him, only that he believes it and loves me in return. You do want him to be happy, don't you? I can tell you care for him a great deal.'

Rowenna bowed her head and said nothing, but she seethed inside. Mary moved away and Rowenna was unsurprised when Cecil came to sit by her side. She was aware from the corner of her eye of Robbie watching her. She knew he had disapproved of her conduct with Cecil the night before and almost turned him away, but her heart was heavy and he had been kind before.

She moved up and let him squeeze on to the end of the bench and listened to his tales of life in Sir John's household, affecting a smile and laugh when obliged to. She was not happy, but nor did she think she was about to burst into tears.

Her mother's words from earlier in the day rang in her head.

Robbie was lost to her. If she could not have him, perhaps Cecil would do as well as any man.

Chapter Thirteen

The word had been spoken and the deal done. Robbie ate and drank and listened and smiled, and no one would have suspected that, far from being the happiest man in York, his heart was a dried husk. Mary flitted from person to person, clearly delighted at being a bride-to-be. Robbie wryly wondered if she was happier at that state than the prospect of their life together. She was currently being assailed by Lisbet and Anne, who appeared as excited as she was.

Unlike his parents. They walked over, and before they spoke Robbie could tell they were furious.

'Come see us tomorrow,' Roger said, shaking his head.

'I'll attend on you tomorrow,' Robbie agreed.

Lucy turned back and snapped, 'What are you thinking?'

They couple walked away to join Hal and Joanna. Robbie gripped the stem of his goblet and took a deep swig. Seeing his mother so irate was unbearable and, to his surprise, he found Roger's obvious disappointment almost as hard to bear.

And then there was Rowenna.

Her dark curls and the blue gown that gave her figure such an arresting shape were easy to spot as she moved about the room. She was currently sitting with Cecil close to the open window. A light breeze lifted the strands of hair that had come loose from her ribbons as she tossed her head back and laughed.

Robbie's entire body convulsed with jealousy and anguish. He repeated her words over and over in his mind. She did not love him as he loved her. She was content to be his friend and seemed equally content to keep company with Cecil. There had been brief moments of their snatched, private conversation where his spirits had risen and he had believed her feelings ran as deep as his, but nothing had given him a strong enough reason to believe she loved him. He had wanted an answer and he had been granted it.

Cecil whispered in Rowenna's ear. She glanced over at Robbie and their eyes met. Her smile slid away and she pursed her lips, staring at him with eyes that were stripping him bare down to the bone and soul. Robbie knew her well enough to recognise her disapproval.

She had already hinted that she thought Mary frivolous and silly, and she was right. What a pity Robbie had been too infatuated to heed her words. Mary's spiteful comment about keeping the water jugs away from her must have annoyed her, so she had another reason to disapprove of Robbie's choice of bride.

Choice!

The more he thought about it, the less it seemed as if he had any alternative but to marry Mary. Weariness besieged him. He wanted to explain to Rowenna what had happened. It became the greatest importance to Robbie that she understood the marriage was not his choice.

He watched Rowenna keenly and noticed her eyes were startlingly bright and glossy. She looked fragile and it almost killed him to think Cecil was the one to comfort her. She blinked and the hint of tears was gone, replaced with a hardness he had never seen before. She nodded at him gravely, then turned back to Cecil, tilting her head and batting her eyelashes. Cecil stood and offered his hand to Rowenna. She paused momentarily before taking it and rising gracefully. She probably didn't notice the way Cecil licked his lips and straightened his jerkin, but Robbie had seen the expression on his friend's face a dozen times. If he wasn't mistaken, Cecil was laying the foundations for a seduction and his earlier remarks about falling in love weren't enough to ease Robbie's mind.

Robbie eased his way through the people, praying no one would claim his attention. He reached them as Cecil was about to put his arm through Rowenna's and called her name. She craned her head to look over her shoulder. Cecil gave him a stare that was a mixture of triumph and malevolence.

'Can I help you, Rob?' he said. 'I'll be back shortly. I've offered to escort Rowenna and her mother back home.'

'I was hoping to speak to Rowenna.'

'Shall I wait while you speak to your cousin?' Cecil asked her. 'We can continue our conversation as we walk home.'

She gave Robbie a penetrating stare that somehow communicated disdain and sorrow at the same time.

'There is no need. I am tired. I would rather wait until I possess a little more strength.'

Rowenna didn't tire after an evening of eating and mingling in a room. She was too vital, always strong, and he knew how she treasured every moment she was not isolated in Ravenscrag. It was a clear rejection. He had lost the friendship he had treasured. Robbie forced an easy smile on to his face, though inside he felt close to weeping.

'It can wait,' he said.

He watched the couple gather Joanna and leave. Robbie released his breath. If Aunt Joanna was there, Rowenna would be safe from Cecil's advances. He would have years to explain the sad circumstances of his marriage to Mary, if she allowed him to explain. He returned to his seat and listened to Mary talk of dresses and gossip, and discovered that now he was no longer blinded in the light of her beauty, they had little to say to each other. He missed Rowenna's quick wit and wished he had been bold enough to take her from Cecil and explain his mistake.

The following morning Robbie visited his parents as early as his duties would permit him to escape. He had hoped to see Rowenna, but she had left the house early to go to the market with Joanna and his sisters, who were taking advantage of an extra day in the city.

His mother hugged him, then glared. 'Why in the name of all that is good are you marrying that insipid little piece of work? Has the thought of knighthood addled your brains?'

'Can you be happy for me, Mother?' Robbie asked, taking her hand.

Lucy sniffed. 'If you can be happy, then I expect I can. I hope you've told her my sapphires will be Lisbet's and Anne's dowries when they marry. She couldn't tear her eyes from them at the tournament.'

Robbie looked at the ring with the gem glinting in the sunlight. Of course Mary hoped it would be hers one day. She probably thought there would be caskets full. He'd exaggerated their wealth to impress her as they spoke at the tournament. It was something in her favour that Mary had obviously not thought to ask Sir John how accurate Robbie's claims had been, otherwise she would not have been so keen.

Lucy pecked his cheek. 'I'm going to market to join Joanna and the girls, and that poor young man they've doubtless charmed into acting as a packhorse.'

She swept from the room, leaving Robbie and Roger alone. Roger waited until her footsteps died away, then unearthed a bottle of wine from Hal's pantry and poured two large measures.

'A toast?' he suggested, offering Robbie a cup. 'To a knighthood well-deserved.'

Robbie gave a tight smile and accepted it. The wine was better than such an occasion warranted.

'Mother isn't happy.'

'No, she isn't. This betrothal is unexpected,' Roger said. 'I'm not sure I agree with her description of Mary, but she is a better judge of character than I am. Why did you do it, lad?'

Robbie's hackles rose at the patronising tone.

'You told me you approved when we spoke before.'

'I said no such thing!' Roger exclaimed.

Robbie drained his cup and refilled it. He glared over the top at his stepfather.

'You said the whole family would approve after you had seen us together. That my eyes were expressive, or some such rot.'

'When did I see you together?' Roger's face creased, then he frowned and threw his hands out wide. 'Not Mary! I was talking about Rowenna after you rescued her from being crushed. If I didn't know it was impossible, I'd have sworn the pair of you were already lovers, the way you held each other.'

Hot fire raced across Robbie's throat and down his belly. He swallowed, remembering the great rush of protectiveness as he had held Rowenna and the way his senses had flared like kindling struck with a flint as she embraced him. Had that been the first step on the road to loving her? He ran his hands through his hair, pulling at it, and gave Roger an incredulous look.

'Why didn't you say who you meant?'

Roger rolled his eyes. 'I didn't think I had to. No one who had seen you two together would suspect you could be thinking of anyone else. It's been clear to all of us the poor girl has been half in love with you for years. Why do you think she cajoled Hal into inviting you over as soon as you arrived?'

'Rowenna loves me?' Robbie's heart had barely beaten since what he considered her rejection. Now it began thumping hard enough to burst free and fly around the room.

'I didn't know. I thought I had no hope.'

'Did you ever ask her?'

Robbie shook his head, feeling like the greatest dullard in history. There was no point having hope now. His jaw tightened and he met Roger's eye, expecting to see pity or, worse, amusement. Roger merely shrugged in the same careless manner he always did and took another drink.

'Tell Mary you cannot marry her. I'll gladly swear you and Rowenna have been betrothed since childhood if you wish.'

'I don't wish!' Robbie exclaimed. 'That is, I could never deceive Mary in such a manner. It's a coward's way. No one honourable could reject a woman once he had publicly accepted her.'

Roger's mouth twitched. 'No one honourable, but many sensible men have.'

'Is that what you would have done?' He eyed Roger coldly, remembering Sir John's words. 'I've heard about the women you seduced, then abandoned. How many women did you leave because it didn't suit you?'

'Too many, and I lost a good woman because

of it.' Roger narrowed his eyes, then his face softened. 'Fortunately I found your mother and not a day goes past when I don't treasure that. Will you be as happy with your Mary?' He waited, arms folded and a smug grin on his face that made Robbie bristle. 'The choice is yours, naturally, and if you choose to continue your engagement I'm sure you will find happiness.'

Roger filled his cup and offered the bottle to Robbie, who shook his head. Any more to drink would be unwise, given his current state of mind.

'I'm not like you. While Mary wishes to be my wife, I am honour-bound to be her husband.'

Roger ran his hand through his hair. 'Then perhaps you should consider what might change her mind so that she releases you.'

Robbie ground his teeth.

'You don't have to take my advice,' Roger said. 'When do you ever? If you choose to make yourself unhappy, that is your choice, but it isn't just your happiness at stake.'

Robbie bowed and picked up his cloak. Roger called his name as he reached the door and he turned.

'What?'

'Joanna said Rowenna cried all night.'

Robbie's stomach twisted with guilt that he had caused her pain. Roger's comment had been unnecessary. He left before his carefully controlled anger erupted. He emerged into bright sunshine, blinking to clear his vision, and while he stood in the doorway of Hal's house, he heard Rowenna's familiar laugh floating from across the street. At least she appeared to be having a good day.

She was not alone. Cecil walked beside her. He carried a basket on one arm and a wrapped parcel beneath the other. This was the young man Lucy had referred to. Robbie had assumed it would be Geoffrey, but this was an entirely more unwelcome escort.

Rowenna held Simon the puppy on a leash and had her light cloak thrown back to cool her. They had not noticed him and he watched Rowenna and Cecil talking with an ease that implied they had known each other for years, not days. Robbie's breath caught. Was it any wonder he had dismissed Rowenna's affection for him when she seemed happy to be in anyone's company?

He walked towards them. Simon spotted him first and began to pull on the leash towards him. Rowenna tore her attention from Cecil to see why and met Robbie's eyes. The easy smile fell from her face and her mouth jerked down, but not before Robbie noticed the softening in her eyes as she had looked at him. She bent to pull Simon back under control. Robbie knelt to stroke the puppy so they were both low while Cecil stood upright, holding Rowenna's shopping.

'Good d-d-day, Ro,' he murmured. He fondled Simon's ears, wishing he could be running his fingers over Rowenna's hair instead, tugging the ribbons loose until her curls fell free.

Her cheeks coloured. She stood, tugging the leash so Simon came to heel, and relieved Cecil of the basket. Cecil showed no signs of leaving. Remembering how Rowenna had claimed him the night of the ball and whisked him away from the company, Robbie imposed himself between them.

'Cousin, I need to speak to you on a private family matter. Cecil, will you excuse us?'

It was only as he finished speaking that he realised he had not stammered at all. Rowenna raised her eyebrows and looked about to refuse, but when Robbie gave her an earnest look she extracted her other parcel from Cecil's hand.

'Of course. Excuse me, please, Master Hugone. Thank you for your assistance. I may see you again soon and I will consider your offer.'

Robbie's stomach lurched, wondering what dark intrigue Cecil had suggested. Rowenna wanted a husband and Cecil must seem a more appealing prospect than Geoffrey. Cecil had suggested he might actually care for Rowenna, but Robbie had seen too many women fall under his spell to believe him.

They stood in silence until he had left and Robbie watched Rowenna from the corner of his eye.

She looked solemn. When she glanced his direction, he held her gaze, hoping to see any sign that Roger had spoken the truth.

'Let's walk to the garden,' he said. He offered her his arm, but Rowenna shook her head slightly and walked stiffly at his side.

'You won't take my arm?'

She tilted her head and looked at him with bright, dark eyes.

'I doubt your future wife would appreciate that, don't you?' Her mouth twitched downward and she stopped walking. They stopped beside the fountain. The garden was busier today. Children raced about and a large grey dog threatened to show interest in Simon. Robbie would have preferred somewhere more private for their conversation. He walked towards the shade of the trees, trusting she would follow.

Sunlight and shadow played chase across Rowenna's face, dancing over her cheeks and neck. Her eyes were ringed with purple.

'You look tired,' Robbie said, recalling Roger's words. 'Did you sleep badly?'

'A little. It is of no consequence.'

Robbie stepped close to Rowenna, drawn by the need to touch her, but she took a step back.

'Tell me what you want quickly,' she said. 'I was enjoying myself with Cecil.'

Robbie's jaw clenched. 'I could see that. What was his offer?'

'He pointed out to me that once Mary is married, Lady Isobel would need a new attendant. He suggested I petition to be allowed to join Sir John's household. I could finally travel and see something of England!'

Rowenna's eyes grew bright and she looked happier than he had seen her for days, but the idea was monstrous.

'And more of Cecil?'

Rowenna tipped her head on one side, eyes sharp. 'And what is wrong with that? Cecil likes me, I can tell. Women can tell when a man is interested. At least, I thought I could tell.'

Her voice tailed off quietly, thoughtfully. Her lip was starting to quiver. She looked about to cry and he would not be able to bear it. She blinked and turned her gaze to him, eyes sharp and clear.

'On the night of the ball, if I *had* said Cecil had been the one to kiss me, what would you have done?'

'Nothing. You can choose who you kiss.' *Liar*, a voice whispered in his heart. At the very least he would have crumbled to dust.

She gave him a withering look. 'Why did you ask me to come here with you, Robbie? Was it to ask how I slept or to upbraid me for my choice of company?'

He took her hand and drew her further into the shadows of the trees, acutely aware of how risky his behaviour was. He gestured to the bench and they both sat side by side. Rowenna arranged her skirts, taking care not to touch Robbie. He trembled with the need to touch her and seeing her so clearly creating a barrier was close to destroying him.

'I wanted to explain about M-Mary,' he said. 'About our engagement.'

'What is there to explain?' Rowenna sighed. 'I have heard nothing from you but your love for her since you arrived in York. I am overjoyed you have won the heart of the woman you want. A triumph greater than any in the tournament and an exploit as daring, no doubt.'

Her tone was as carefree as ever, but there was the glint in her eye again. A trace of pink in her cheeks that hinted at heightened feelings. If only she realised how far from the truth it was.

'You disapprove,' Robbie said.

'I was only surprised at how quickly you must have asked her. You cannot have had long together at the ball after we—' She lowered her eyes and bit her lip, which had started to quiver. 'After I went home.'

She turned away, but Robbie took hold of her shoulders and gently twisted her to face him. Her expression had changed and her eyes were hard.

'Had you already asked for her hand before we kissed in the garden?'

Robbie's breath quickened. He felt his blood racing through the heart that grieved for the loss of her love.

'No! I am not so dishonourable.' He flushed. 'M-Mary's uncle, my m-master, spoke with me yesterday morning and told me it was his wish that we marry.'

Rowenna's face was serious. 'Then you are fortunate indeed to have such a good master whose wishes coincide with yours. What has this to do with me?'

'I feel lessened in your eyes,' Robbie admitted.

'Robbie, no!' She shook her head, but stopped and pulled away from him, folding her arms and raising her eyes to the sky. 'Yes. Forgive me. I said only last night that I would always be your friend, whatever you did, and I have already broken this vow. I cannot be happy for you.'

'I asked for your congratulations and you gave them,' Robbie pointed out.

Rowenna began petting the puppy that lay at their feet, avoiding looking at Robbie.

'I congratulated you on achieving what you wanted,' she said crisply. 'I did not say I approve of your bride. I hope you will find the happiness with her you're seeking, though I very much doubt it.'

'Why do you doubt it?' Robbie asked.

Rowenna opened her mouth, then closed it firmly and shook her head. She began gathering the leash and pulling Simon close.

'I should go. No good can come of this conversation.'

'Ro,' Robbie said firmly. He put a hand on her wrist, feeling the steady rhythm of her pulse. His own began to race at the touch. She bit her lip, looking uncertain. Robbie ran his other hand up her arm, tracing his way over the tight sleeve, intensely aware of her form beneath the fabric.

'W-we don't keep secrets from each other. Not us.'

'You do.'

He dipped his head so she would not see the shame in his eyes as he thought of the secret he carried, in the process bringing it close to hers. Her eyes widened and he hoped she was remembering the time they had kissed and times they almost had.

'Please.'

'She doesn't love you,' Rowenna whispered.

Was that all? He'd hoped for a reason to end his entanglement. Robbie rubbed his eyes with the heel of his hand. 'I know that.'

Rowenna's expression was incredulous. 'But you're going to marry her anyway? Does she mean that much to you that you would demean yourself so thoroughly?'

He saw distaste clear in her eyes. Mingled with the disbelief in her voice it stoked fires of shame in the pit of his belly.

'My lord wishes it. And I have given my word to Mary,' Robbie said firmly. 'And now I must marry her. I led her to believe I cared.'

'You don't?' Rowenna raised her head sharply. Robbie studied his hands, unwilling to meet her eyes.

'I believed I did, for a while. But now I think what was love was simply infatuation.'

He expected scorn, but she gave him the first genuine smile since their meeting, tinged with the air of exasperation he remembered from childhood. 'I could have told you that the first time you spoke of her.'

'I wish you had,' Robbie said fervently. 'So to do you the kindness you didn't do for me, let me warn you of something. Don't enter Sir John's household. Don't get too fond of Cecil.'

'Why not? He's charming and entertaining.'

'I don't want you to get hurt.'

Rowenna rolled her eyes expressively and Robbie's stomach somersaulted in response.

'How considerate of you. But you see, my heart is not your responsibility to safeguard. You have another's heart to own now.'

Robbie ignored the barb that stabbed his guts. 'Perhaps not. I will do it anyway. Cecil has a habit of making women fall in love with him, then abandoning them when he is bored.'

He bit his tongue, thinking of how that charge could be levelled against him for transferring his love from Mary to Rowenna so quickly. He was the worst hypocrite. He ran them both through his mind, testing whether the emotions he felt were what he believed them to be and found them unchanged. Thoughts of his impending marriage wound around him like chains he was incapable of breaking, constricting the breath in his chest.

'Fortunately I'm not in love with Cecil,' Rowenna said. 'I dare say I could be if I tried hard enough to be. More than I might be with Geoff, in any case.'

Instinctively Robbie reached out to her, but she pulled away and set her jaw. 'You don't approve of the company I keep and I dislike your bride, so we are both equally disappointed in each other.'

His heart swelled to the point of bursting with the need to declare his love. He bit back the words he had no right to say. 'You could never disappoint me, Ro. I care for you too much.'

He took hold of her hands, drawing her towards him before looking up at her shyly. He saw uncertainty in her eyes and a flash of the need that had flared when they had kissed in the garden, but she drew her hands away and her expression hardened.

'Perhaps Cecil wouldn't abandon me and we wouldn't get bored of each other.'

'He won't m-make you happy. He won't make you laugh and he won't appreciate who you are. He won't marry you.' Robbie spoke with complete certainty.

'You don't know that.'

'I do know.' Robbie almost shouted the words. Rowenna's head jerked up. Their eyes met with the violence of a lance splitting a shield.

'How can you be so certain? What is wrong with me?'

She put her hands on her hips and jutted her chin high, as if daring him to list her faults. He stared at her, captivated by the curves of her breasts and waist, the slender line of her neck from ear to collarbone. All called out to be caressed and explored and worshipped. His body answered with a silent yet unmistakable response that caused him to shudder with lust. Her defiant response claimed his soul.

'Nothing is wrong with you, but Cecil is ambitious,' he said. 'He intends to marry well.'

'I have wealth. My father is rich. He's richer than *your* father,' Rowenna pointed out, gesturing towards Hal's house.

'He intends to marry someone of noble birth,' Robbie muttered.

'Not the daughter of a bastard.' Understanding flashed across Rowenna's face.

'I'm sorry.'

'Don't be.' She cut him off with an abrupt wave of her hand. She gave a sob, swallowed it, then forced a brave smile on to her lips. 'My father has worked so hard to overcome his past, but it isn't enough. My birth means I'm not good enough for Cecil, or anyone like him, and I never will be, with good reason. Who would want to marry anyone with such low connections? You wouldn't.'

She turned away and hugged herself. Robbie slid his arms around her shoulders. She did not resist his touch, but he felt stiffness in her shoulders. A barrier between them.

'Someone who truly loves you won't care for your background,' he said, drawing her closer than he had anticipated she would permit.

'You think I am worth so much, yet you take pains to remind me of my background. I overheard Mary saying you are repelled by the mere mention of illegitimacy. I know what you must think of my family and our station.'

'I have never thought anything less of you or your father. You know that I do not see your father's illegitimacy as shameful. How can I when…?'

Robbie caught his words and pulled them back. It was true, though not for the reason she believed and he had come so close to revealing his secret. If Mary knew the pedigree of the man she was marrying, would she be so eager to claim him? He unwound his arms and clutched Rowenna's hand for emphasis, his voice low.

'You have a good dowry and a fine family. Even without those, you'd be worth a dozen simpering ladies. You must believe that.'

He placed a hand on either side of her face and tilted her face up, thumbs caressing the arches of her cheekbones and fingertips buried in the soft rolls of hair at her temple. His flesh seemed to sing where his fingers brushed her skin. She closed her eyes and he saw the fluttering of her eyelashes.

'You are beautiful,' he murmured. 'You're perfect. So beautiful. No man could wish for a woman better. If it comes to it, Cecil is not good enough for *you*! I meant every word I said in the workshop the other day.'

'Pretty words, very capable of stirring a heart, but they were meant for Mary.'

A bolt of lightning speared Robbie. A heart that was stirred. Was that an admission of love?

'They were meant for you.'

She made an explosive sound of disgust. Her eyes hardened. Robbie pulled his hands back as if he had been burned and saw they were shaking. He hoped Rowenna had not noticed. He balled his fists and drove them against his sides.

'Don't do this to me. It isn't fair. Don't torment me with the promise of something you would not give me.'

Her lips were trembling and her eyes bright with fury. She spun on her heel with an angry cry, tugging Simon with her. Robbie caught her in three paces.

'Don't go.'

She faced him and he was appalled to see her eyes were moist.

'We should not be seen together like this, otherwise people will talk, and neither of us would want scandal, would we?' she snapped.

Robbie didn't answer. He was more than half-tempted to kiss Rowenna despite her warnings. A scandal like that would bring disgrace on him and would most likely put a swift end to his engagement. He could bear that for himself, but not for Rowenna, who had so precisely explained the odds that were already stacked against her.

'I will bid you good day and leave you to return to your bride.'

Rowenna began to walk away, head high and shoulders set back, leaving Robbie weaker than a day in the melee could have left him and with a mind in turmoil.

He stood rooted to the spot, watching her walk out of his life and realising he had made the biggest mistake possible. She had only reached the corner before he began to run after her.

Chapter Fourteen

Rowenna kept her tears under control by sheer willpower, channelling her sorrow into anger. Robbie was a fool. She was a fool for loving him.

He cared for her. Her spirits soared.

He knew Mary didn't love him but he was going to marry her anyway. Her spirits plummeted again.

She would marry Geoff or Cecil. It scarcely mattered who.

She scooped up Simon and buried her head in his soft fur, stumbling away from the town house. She could not return home in such a state or questions would be asked.

Before she had reached the end of her street Robbie had caught up with her. He tugged her sleeve.

'Let me go!' she snarled. A couple of women walking on the other side of the road stopped and looked over, concern on their faces in case she was being assaulted.

'S-stop. I have to—I need to—'

Robbie's forehead creased with the effort of trying to force out his words. He looked more distraught than she had ever seen him and her fury melted away. Her body tingled with the impulse to throw herself into his arms, but that was not her right.

'I'm all right,' she called to the women. They shot Robbie an evil look, but carried on walking.

Robbie released her sleeve, still looking uncertain that she would not run. He was out of breath, though he had hardly run any distance and his tangle of curls flopped across his face. Rowenna controlled the urge to reach out and push them back out of his eyes.

'What now? Haven't you said enough to wound me? Have you come to lecture me further about whom I should fall in love with? Show me the man you approve of. Tell me who you will allow to love me,' Rowenna said, her voice rising. Her face grew hot.

'I do not need your approval, Robbie Danby. Of my behaviour or my position or myself! I'm not the one who promises marriage to one woman while kissing another. To do that, then to have the impudence to pretend you care for me!'

'You are right,' Robbie muttered. 'I have no

right to control you or command you. But never believe I don't care, or that it did not kill me to watch you flit between Cecil and Geoffrey and me at the banquet.'

'Is that how you see me?' Rowenna felt as if she had been stabbed through the chest. She leaned against the wall. 'You think I am so flighty I could be happy with any man who crosses my path?'

'Am I wrong?' Robbie was very still and his voice was so quiet she could barely hear it. He lifted his head and gave her a look that reached inside her, stroking her belly and rousing the flames that danced within.

'I did not flit! I danced with different partners and so did you. Should I accuse you of trifling with the matron you danced with?'

She was so furious her hand trembled as she pointed at him.

'Show me how can I distinguish between your kisses with Wat Corridge or your fancy for Cecil, and our kiss,' Robbie said scornfully.

If he only knew what those words did to her, how they sent a tingle through every limb, he would surely not speak so cruelly. She blinked away her tears and dipped her head, fearful that he would see the effect on her written on her face.

'Do not demand I justify myself to you,' she snapped. 'Oh, a man can speak words of love to

one woman and marry another without consequence, but for a woman to even spend time with
more than one man sees her branded as a harlot.
What else can I do? I need a husband, but must
wait to be asked and hope a man sees beyond my
shameful connections to want me.'

She put Simon down and stepped closer to
Robbie, lifting her chin and piercing him with
her gaze. He began to speak, but she cut him off
abruptly with an angry exhalation.

'You dare question my character when you are
going to marry Mary. You know she doesn't care
for you and you don't care for her.'

Robbie dropped his hands. He began pacing
back and forth, body held rigid. The tendons in
his neck were iron hard.

'I told you, my lord demands it. My situation
makes me despair, yet I cannot see my way clear
to freeing myself without bringing dishonour on
myself or shaming Mary.'

'So what if Sir John wishes you to marry her?
He does not own you body and soul. You will be
knighted within a week and your own man. Your
father is a baron, not a mere knight, and you will
be Lord Danby one day.'

Robbie paled before her eyes. His shoulders
tensed and he looked away.

'I cannot shame Mary when I have led her to
believe I would marry her.'

'You led her to believe no such thing!' Rowenna cried in exasperation. 'She knows it, too. Simply tell her you do not wish to marry her.'

'Roger said the same thing,' Robbie said. His lip jerked down to one side. 'I told him that I am honour-bound to marry her unless she releases me.'

'And of course, you will do anything other than listen to your father,' Rowenna snapped. 'An honourable man would tell her the truth. That you don't love her.'

Robbie tensed. He lifted his head slowly. His eyes bored into Rowenna. 'That I love you.'

'Don't say that!' Rowenna's heart seized.

'I do.' He held his hands out. Rowenna folded her arms.

'Really? Yesterday you loved Mary! How do I know you mean it? Who will you throw your heart to tomorrow?'

'No one but you.'

Wretchedness washed over her. She had longed to hear these words for so long, but not under these circumstances, when it was like a toy dandled to tease a cat, enticing but out of reach for ever. She covered her face with her hands and turned away. Robbie's hands slid round her and he leaned against her, his broad chest pressing against her back, warm and sturdy.

'Your love is more changeable than mine, Robbie. At least, I never professed to love the men I kissed. I don't want to hear such words from you, now or ever.'

Robbie rested his head on her shoulder, his lips close to her ear. The soft whisper of his breath against her neck was a torment.

'If I had believed then I might one day win your heart, I would never have accepted Mary,' Robbie said.

Their odd conversation flashed through her mind from the night before and she groaned. Robbie had been trying to discover if she cared and she had been so intent on not revealing her feelings she had even made him believe he was interchangeable with Geoffrey. She remembered his words at the banquet and how he had disliked Cecil paying her attention. At the time she had attributed it to his concern for their family's name, but now she was uncertain. What point was there in hurting him by admitting her love for him now when it was too late for either of them?

'But you did,' she said quietly. Her cheeks were damp and she wiped at them savagely with her sleeve. 'You were the one who told me to mask my feelings.'

'I was wrong to say that.'

Robbie stepped forward and in one fluid movement put his hands to her cheeks, wiping away the tears with his thumbs. He bent his head to hers, foreheads touching.

'When I kissed you...' he murmured, burying his face against her neck.

The scratch of his beard against her skin sent shivers over her. She moaned with desire. It must have triggered something inside Robbie because his arms snaked around her body, pulling her even closer, one reaching up to rest between her shoulder blades, the other around her waist.

'I meant the words for you, Ro,' he murmured, his lips close so that the warmth of his breath caressed her cheek. 'I didn't realise at the time, but I couldn't have spoken so easily if it wasn't the truth. I was blind not to see it before.'

Her memory flowed back to when they had play-acted in the herb garden. She pressed against his chest, feeling the strength in him. She should reject such intimacy with a man who was betrothed, but his touch weakened her resistance and she could do nothing but yield and try not to explode with the desire she felt. She could have stayed lost in his caress for a lifetime, but almost before they had begun, Robbie's hands moved from her waist to her arms and he firmly, yet gently, held her at arm's length. As always, he had more control and wisdom than she did.

'We mustn't! I am no longer a free man.'

'Dependable and sensible. And correct. How

I hate you for being so,' Rowenna said, trying to keep the sorrow from her voice.

Robbie shook his head, dragging the hair back from his cheeks. His face was contorted in a reflection of the misery she felt.

'Do you hate me?'

Rowenna looked into the eyes of her friend and saw the boy who had stood by her side through childhood in the man who had crossed crowds to rescue her and had kissed her with such fire. Her anger fled, leaving only sadness for them both. If he broke his engagement he would no longer be that man. So, though her heart was breaking, she smiled.

'No. I never could. You are a good man, Robbie Danby. The very best.' She touched his cheek, unable to ignore the way his skin tightened beneath her fingers. The tremor ran down her arm and through her until every nerve in her body was alight with longing. 'I shall say farewell now, because being in your presence can do neither of us any good.'

'You w-won't attend m-my d-dubbing ceremony?' His voice began to break. He looked dismayed and she recalled the promise she had made to be there as his encouragement.

'I will,' she agreed. 'But we should not meet again after that.'

Knowing it would be the last time she could,

she stood on tiptoe and left a kiss on his lips, committing the feel and taste of him to memory. She tugged Simon's leash and walked swiftly away and did not look back again as she returned home. Her own folly had led to this. If she had not been determined to show how little Robbie's attention affected her, she could have shown him how deeply she truly cared while there was a chance for her. Now it was too late and there was nothing to do about the situation unless Mary decided to break the engagement herself.

She smoothed her hair and steadied her nerve to speak to her parents. She would beg them to let her join Sir John's household. Given time, she might marry Cecil, whether he loved her or not.

What did it matter who she married when her heart belonged to someone she could not have?

Four days passed. Robbie did not see Rowenna again. His only contact with Hal's household was a scribbled note confirming attendance at the ceremony in St Peter's Church. Rowenna was not mentioned by name and Robbie was uncertain whether she would keep her word and attend.

He practised his vows repeatedly, but was unable to refrain from stumbling over the words. His voice was locked behind his teeth and would not break free, however much he tried. He performed his duties for Sir John with his usual efficiency, but took no joy in them.

Mary clamed much of his free time, inviting him to sit with her as she attended Lady Isobel or walk with him through the city. She gave every outward sign of being devoted to him, but her attentions left Robbie unmoved. He tried to summon the rapture that even the slightest glance had once raised but could not. He listened to her talk of what she would wear in church, of the feast they would share afterwards and of a date they would be able to be wed.

Finally unable to keep silent, he sought her out on the morning before his ceremony was due to take place. She was sewing alone in the antechamber and gave him a warm smile when he approached.

'Your final day as a squire, Master Danby.'

'I must speak. I d-d-do not believe w-we should m-m-m—' he said.

He watched, noticing how she was unable to hide the irritation that filled her eyes when he stumbled over words. She might not even be trying. She returned to her embroidery as if he had not spoken.

'I am bound by conscience to tell you I do not love you.'

'Nor I you,' she replied, setting down her frame

and finally giving him her full attention. 'That is of no consequence. You are handsome and I know you find me attractive. I believe we will grow fond of each other over time, otherwise I would not have agreed to the marriage.'

She sounded so cold. They might have been discussing the purchase of a horse.

'We cannot be happy. I love someone else,' Robbie said. 'I'm sorry.'

Fury flashed over Mary's beautiful face and she jabbed the needle through the cloth viciously. Her expression recovered so quickly Robbie half believed he had imagined it.

'Your clumsy dark-haired cousin? I suspected as much when I saw you together.' Mary folded her hands. 'Be sensible, Master Danby. She is the daughter of a bastard. No right-thinking person would willingly enter into an alliance with someone of such low birth.'

Robbie flushed. Rowenna had said the same. If Mary knew the truth about his own birth, she would scorn him as equally as she scorned Rowenna. He stood.

'Then you should not be so willing to marry me. Release me from our engagement.'

'There is no need. The connection is not so close as to matter,' Mary said. She held her hand for Robbie to help her rise. He kissed it dutifully and sat back on the settle, deep in thought after she had left.

A notion started to grow that would not be suppressed, but it filled Robbie with dread. With her spiteful comment about Rowenna, Mary had inadvertently shown him a path to his release. It would come at a great cost and he wondered if he were strong enough to bear it.

He begged an hour's leave and walked through the city, mind in turmoil, before he finally made his way to Hal's house. It might have been his mood, but the atmosphere on the streets seemed threatening once more. The riots had been quelled, but for how long?

He could hear Rowenna humming tunelessly to herself through the open door to the storeroom. Robbie's body jerked towards the sound, but she stopped as Robbie spoke to Hal. He hoped she would come out to greet him, but instead she pulled the door and resumed her song. Conscious of Hal's eyes narrowing, he dragged his attention away and requested an audience with Roger and Lucy.

'The workroom is empty,' Hal said.

Robbie led the way, palms growing damp from nerves.

'What's wrong?' Roger asked. 'I've heard rumours that Gisbourne is massing a mob in the countryside. Lucky we delayed returning home or we'd have run straight into them.'

'That's not why I'm here.' Before his parents could start questioning him he took a deep breath and spoke slowly. 'I cannot continue my engagement, but Mary will not release me.'

His mother hugged him. He patted her hand. In a few moments she would doubtless be furious with him.

'You told me to think of a way to make her break from me and I have.' He looked at Roger. The older man stared back at him, eyes watchful. If the truth had been known all along, the matter would never have arisen.

'Mary is proud. She would not marry a bastard. I plan to tell her the truth about my birth.'

The reaction was what he had predicted.

'What do you have to gain by admitting this now?' Lucy asked.

Roger's face was thunderous. 'Are you feeble-minded? Do you expect to be knighted as planned if this deception is revealed?'

'I understand the consequences.' Robbie folded his arms, swallowing down the fear.

Hearing the words spoken aloud was chilling. The deeds he had done during the riots should still be enough to see him knighted on his own merit, but the circumstances of his birth might outweigh them. At the very least there would be questions to answer and even a bastard of noble birth would risk being outcast.

'I'll gain my freedom from a match I cannot bear to take part in. If I lose my chance of knighthood, that is the price I must pay.'

'I would gladly see you end this reckless betrothal, but not at such a cost,' Lucy said. 'You've wanted this for so long.'

'There's something I want more.' Robbie couldn't stop himself from glancing upward.

'Rowenna?' Roger asked, rolling his eyes and following Robbie's look. 'Do you hope to win her?'

Had Rowenna heard them shouting? Robbie had burned for so long to share his burden with her, but would she have him once she knew the truth? Robbie lifted his chin and looked his stepfather in the eye. 'I have to try.'

'You are a romantic fool,' Roger said. There was a touch of humour in his voice and a hint of approval that gave Robbie the strength he needed to defy him.

'You do not need to reveal the truth,' Lucy said. 'We'll find another way to untangle you.'

The ire that Robbie had bottled for so many years burst free. 'What way? There is none and I have lived too long under a name I have no right to. It burns me to know the deception I commit every day. Whether or not I am engaged to Mary, I cannot live with this any longer.'

'I do not permit this. I won't let you ruin your life,' Roger said firmly. Robbie rounded on him.

'Permit? The choice should be mine to make, not yours! I'm done with following your orders.'

'You don't need to ruin your future by admitting to this,' Lucy said.

She rushed to Robbie and took him by the shoulders, trying to pull him to her breast as if he was still a child. Robbie recoiled and she dropped her hands. Her expression was of complete misery.

'Who is my father?' he asked. 'Why won't you tell me? Was it some tavern boy you took a fancy to?'

A backhanded blow to the face knocked him sideways. He snapped his head up, glaring at Roger whose face was furious.

'You will not speak to my wife in such a way if you want to ever set foot in my house again,' he growled.

'Why w-would I w-want to stay in a house full of deceptions?' Robbie yelled.

The two men squared their shoulders. Robbie's fists clenched and he snarled. Roger's eyes became slits.

'Is this what you want to do, lad?' Roger growled.

Roger was broader, but older. Robbie wasn't

certain he could best the man opposite him, even with youth on his side, but he jerked forward, determined that if he was to receive a beating he would go down fighting to the last. Lucy stepped between them, thrusting her hands against each man's chest.

'No! I will not have fighting between the two men I love most dearly.'

Her voice was sharp and reached into the part of Robbie's brain that had obeyed her since childhood. He dropped his fists and head. Out of the corner of his eye he saw Roger had done likewise. There was grey in his stepfather's black curls. Curls that were so like Robbie's own that they could have been kin. No wonder the deception had been so easy to carry out.

'If you won't think of yourself, think of your mother's shame,' Roger growled. 'Her reputation is at stake.'

Her reputation. Robbie drew a sharp breath. He had assumed Roger was concerned with his own reputation and not considered the effect the revelation would have on his mother.

Lucy shot her husband an angry look. 'I put my shame in the grave long ago and you know it.'

She put her hands on Robbie's shoulders. 'Your father was a man of noble birth, greater and wealthier than the Danbys, but he refused to acknowledge you. If I hadn't met Roger you'd have grown up in Tom's inn outside Mattonfield, scorned and poor. Is that what you want? The risk is too great.'

'Compared to the certainty of saying nothing? I know well how much my fortunes are at the whim of fate. What if Anne and Lisbet had been boys?' he asked. 'What if you'd birthed a son on the day I left instead of Joan? I'd have been disinherited while your legitimate son followed you as baron? What would you have done with me? Sent me to serve with Uncle Tom at the inn back in Cheshire or apprenticed me to Uncle Hal to learn a trade? Or should I have become my brother's squire and served him?'

'None of those things,' Lucy cried. Her eyes filled with tears that made Robbie's conscience cry out in anguish. 'We would have made a settlement for you. You are a Danby, and once you become a knight you will earn honour and titles of your own.'

'Then I shall do so under my own name, whatever that may be.'

'You could lose everything,' Roger warned. 'Think carefully about the consequences.'

Robbie ran his hands through his hair. The sacrifice of wealth and rank, of Sir John's patronage and of the name he had made were nothing compared to a life with Mary and without Rowenna.

'I will live with whatever the consequences are. If you do not forgive me, I shall bear that, too.'

He made a curt bow and left, but had taken no more than a dozen steps when Rowenna called his name from the upstairs window. He winced, closing his eyes and intending to carry on, but he could not deny her call any more than he could stop the sun circling the earth.

'I heard shouting. Robbie—what's wrong?' She was leaning out of the open window, shutter thrown wide. Her face was contorted with worry.

He lifted a hand up, as if hoping to touch her from where he stood, and she stretched down.

'Wait for me. I'll come down.'

The gulf between them was wider than worlds and filled with the secrets he'd kept. He longed to spill the truth out, but curbed his tongue. She would know soon enough and he had to hope she would not turn from him. Even if he had wanted to speak, the words filled his throat, threatening to choke him. If she came to him, he would not be able to resist embracing her or stealing one last kiss before he left.

'Don't. I have to go.'

Her eyes hardened with determination and her head vanished. The day was growing late and he had to prepare for his vigil, but he waited, knowing she would ignore his orders and appear. As he had predicted, the door opened and she slipped out.

'Why are you angry at Roger?' she demanded as she strode towards him. 'You were so close when you lived in Wharram as a child. What changed when you left?'

'Would you turn against me if you knew?' Robbie murmured, more to himself than Rowenna. His belly rolled with anxiety. Their friendship already seemed broken beyond repair.

'I would never turn against you! You can tell me anything and I would stand by your side.'

He took her hand and brought it briefly to his lips before lowering it. He could not ignore the way her skin fluttered at his kiss. If he were not bound by his engagement, he would have taken her in his arms and kissed her with the full force of all the pent-up longing that coursed through him, until she had no doubt how much he felt for her.

'I would not keep anything from you, my dear friend, if it were my choice, but there are promises I have sworn and there are some matters that cannot be shared, however much I wish I could.' His smile was sad. 'You will not resent me if I keep my word, will you? For the time being, at least.'

'Of course not!' Rowenna said. Her face contorted into a mask of misery. 'If you have given your word, I would not expect you to break it on my account, however strong our friendship was.'

Bile filled Robbie's stomach. *Was*, not *is*.

'The greatest tragedy is that I have lost my friend,' he said.

To his dismay, she burst into tears. Angry, gulping sobs racked her frame.

'Forgive me,' Robbie said. He tried to take her in his arms, but she wriggled free, glaring at him.

'Leave me alone. I hate that I cry so easily. I hate that you think it's anything you've done. That you think there is anything you can do to make me weep.' She wiped her eyes and swallowed. 'There's something you should know. My father has agreed I may speak to Lady Isobel. After your ceremony tomorrow I shall ask to become part of her household.'

'Don't do that,' Robbie said. Visions racked him of watching her grow close to Cecil and being hurt or ruined by his sweet words.

'Why not?' she asked, wiping away the tears. 'There is nothing for me here or at home.'

'Cecil will break your heart.'

'You assume it is intact!' Rowenna raised her voice, pain cracking it.

Robbie set his shoulders and turned away without answering. He returned to the inn and gathered what he needed before saying farewell to Sir John and his friends for what could be the last time. If he revealed the truth, he could no longer expect their friendship. He unlocked the small chest he kept beneath his bed and took out his money pouch and his eye fell on Rowenna's ribbon.

He made his preparations in a trance, bathing and dressing in his white vesture and red robe. No one would suspect that beneath his clothing and tied around his arm was a faded and blood-stained piece of ribbon. He knelt before the altar, hands clasped in silent prayer, but could not force his mind where it should be. He should be contemplating his future role with all the solemnity it demanded, but he could think of nothing beyond the turmoil in his heart and the decision he had to make. As he had jokingly predicted, he spent the night contemplating the loss of Rowenna and dreaming of a future together. How could he profess to purity when such profane thoughts ran through his mind?

Chapter Fifteen

Ten hours of stillness and fasting had left Robbie aching and weary. He would argue that any man who could endure such a feat uncomplaining deserved his *adoubement*, but Robbie felt no such right for himself. He had spent the night kneeling before the altar, but had seen no holy visions, nor felt the touch of the divine that a man worthy of knighthood would surely experience. He felt light-headed and sick, but knew in his heart that the cause was a lack of food and sleep.

As the congregation filed in for Mass, he searched for faces he knew and loved. His mother and Roger were sitting together with the girls. Roger was whispering to Joan to keep still. Hal and Joanna sat with the other guildsmen. Robbie's nerve strengthened at the sight of his uncle dressed in gold chains and velvet. If one bastard could rise high through effort and skill, why not another? After the ceremony he would be a knight, and before too long he would have a wife and the secured patronage of Sir John. A wife.

A wife he did not want. Even without the chance of Rowenna's love, he could not bear to spend his life with Mary.

Moving on, he spotted Sir John's retinue. Mary was sitting beside Lady Isobel, a serene smile on her face. Robbie felt none of the fire of adoration he once had, only a cold lump where his heart should be. Cecil was sitting a few seats along from Mary and beside him sat Rowenna. Their heads were bowed together and Cecil was whispering something in her ear that caused her to grin. As the lump in Robbie's heart exploded, she looked up and met his eye. Her smile became fixed and solemn as she held his gaze and Robbie's stomach plunged. He felt certain he had lost her friendship for ever. Then she gave him a slight smile that was lacking her customary merriness and mouthed something to him that might have been 'good luck'. Robbie dipped his head in acknowledgement, but try as he might, he could not force himself to return her smile when she was sitting so close to Cecil.

He faced the altar and sleepwalked through Mass until the lengthy service ended. Sir John, acting as Robbie's sponsor, joined him at the altar. He gave Robbie a solemn look, which Robbie returned. His master could not suspect the upheaval Robbie was about to unleash.

He spoke his vows clearly, with less hesitation than he had feared, his eyes fixed on Rowenna. *Imagine you are talking to me alone*, she had said. Her smile was a beacon in the crowd.

The time had come for his dubbing and he had made his decision. As Sir John took possession of the sword and shield, Robbie faced the congregation and prepared to destroy his future.

'Robert Danby, kneel.'

Robbie remained standing. He held his head high and spoke.

'I cannot claim this honour. I stand before you with no right to the name I bear.'

A ripple of astonishment passed through the church. Roger had leapt from his seat and was glaring at Robbie. Lucy shook her head. Robbie dared not look at Rowenna or Mary.

Sir John's face was white and he looked baffled. 'Is this an ill-thought-out jest?'

'I am afraid not, my lord. I do not know what name I can lay claim to, but I am not the son of Roger Danby and I cannot be knighted under this name.'

Uproar followed. The ripple became a rumble of voices echoing to the arched ceiling. Voices called out for Robbie's arrest for so grave a deception, others in his defence. A cloak of serenity seemed to fall over his shoulders, replacing the heaviness that he had carried for so long. He walked away from the altar. Roger blocked his way.

'You've made your choice, now you'll have to live with the consequences. I hope you think it was worth it.'

Robbie returned his gaze, unblinking. 'So do I.'

Roger held a hand out. After a moment of hesitation, Robbie shook it. Rowenna was standing at the end of a row of pews. As Robbie approached her, Cecil stalked towards him, but Robbie held a hand out and he fell back. Tears fell freely from Rowenna's eyes. She dragged a hand violently across her eyes to clear them and glared.

'Have you lost your mind?'

Behind the tears there was cold fury. Before Robbie could find his voice she bolted, running from the church with her head down. Robbie could have withstood anything else, but the rejection he had feared came close to unmanning him.

He walked slowly through the nave and stopped before Mary. She eyed him coldly and he wondered why he had ever thought her beautiful.

'Forgive me. I should have told you before.'

She raised her hand and delivered a ringing slap to his cheek.

'You vile, deceiving—'

She curled her lip with a cry of disgust and threw herself into Amy's arms.

Robbie walked on, relishing the pain in his jaw. It signified freedom.

Rowenna was not in the square outside the church when he emerged into the harsh sunlight and he had to trust that she had made her way home safely.

'Rob. Wait, Danby.'

Robbie stopped at the sound of Cecil's voice.

'Didn't you hear me? Not Danby,' he growled. 'Did you see where Rowenna went?'

'Home, surely. Was that true? You kept a secret like that?' Cecil shook his head incredulously. 'Can I help?'

'Why?' Robbie asked suspiciously. There had been enough competitiveness between the two men over the years.

Cecil laughed, but there was kindness in his eyes. 'Because I've never witnessed a man throw his entire world away in such dramatic a fashion. Besides, once you are gone, I can try taking your place. I'll be Sir John's favoured squire. I might even try for Mary's hand.'

Robbie looked him in the eye. 'You are welcome to.'

Cecil looked dumbfounded. 'What are you going to do now?'

Robbie straightened up. He could not return

to the inn and, though he wished more than anything to see Rowenna, could not face the angry response he would doubtless receive at Hal's house. It would be best to wait until the following day to beg an audience with his relatives.

'I plan firstly to get drunk. After that I'll consider my future.'

'You don't get drunk,' Cecil said.

'I intend to today.' He put a hand on Cecil's shoulder. 'There's a tavern near the Bootham Gate. Will you bring my belongings from the inn? I'll be there at dusk.'

'Willingly,' Cecil said.

He walked into the city, not caring where his feet took him.

There were signs that the anger that had been simmering under the surface was about to boil over. Shopfronts were being shuttered and already men were squaring their shoulders as they passed watchmen.

When he tired of walking and being jostled, Robbie found the tavern and bought a bottle of wine. He stared at it as he waited for Cecil to arrive, wondering what future there might be for a nameless, masterless squire. He was clearly free of Mary, but he feared that he had lost Rowenna, too.

A dozen emotions rolled inside Rowenna's belly as she ran for home. Guilt was foremost.

Robbie's revelation had hit her like a hammer on an anvil, and instead of offering her support she had run from him. She was the first to arrive and flung herself on to her bed, burying her face in the coverlet and sobbing. He had deceived her and the cold rage that had flooded her veins turned her limbs to water, but he was still the same Robbie she had loved for as long as she could remember.

Presently, the door slammed. Rowenna bolted downstairs. The four older Danbys had entered together, Joanna with her arm around a red-eyed Lucy.

'Where's Robbie?' Rowenna demanded.

Roger threw his arms wide. 'You expect us to know? The reckless fool ran off after you and hasn't been seen since.'

'Is it true?' she asked.

Their looks confirmed her question.

'How could you hide that from me? How could Robbie? Why would he reveal it at such an important moment?'

'You don't know?' her mother asked.

Rowenna shook her head. Roger unbuckled his cloak and hung it on the peg. He looked older and weary.

'Aren't you going out to search for him?' Rowenna exclaimed.

'Not today,' Roger said. 'I've spent all afternoon speaking with Sir John and trying to explain what I did.'

His face was pale and all his vitality seemed to have left him. Rowenna could scarcely believe they weren't father and son. If Robbie could see the love and pain in Roger's eyes, he would never have rejected the family who loved him so greatly.

'Robbie needs to decide what he wants to do. We'll be here when he wants to see us.' Lucy added. 'This has been a long time building.'

'Does he know that?'

Lucy's eyes filled with tears.

'He will not welcome my interference today,' Roger said, holding her tightly.

Rowenna froze. What if Robbie did not come? What if he did not want to see them? Did not want to see her? She folded her arms, glaring at them all.

'If you won't search for him, I will.'

Dodging her mother's attempts to seize her by the arm, Rowenna ducked past the adults and through the open door. She ran, ducking down an alley, and waited with a thumping heart in case they came after her. Hiding gave her time to clear her head. She had burst out of the house with no cloak, no money and no idea where to begin searching for Robbie. The city was huge and sprawling, but she had to begin somewhere.

She passed the garden where they had sat together and headed back towards St Peter's Church.

Things were very wrong. In the distance she could hear angry shouting coming from outside the walls. Members of the city watch were moving swiftly towards the city gates at Bootham Bar and, to Rowenna's alarm, there were gangs of roughly dressed men roaming the streets. She bunched her fists and realised her hands were clammy with nerves. She pressed herself against a wall as a pair of men holding staves ran past and began to think sensibly. She would never find Robbie by chance while walking about the city, so decided instead to go to the inn where Sir John was staying. Halfway there she encountered Cecil walking in the opposite direction.

She gave him no time to speak, but asked if he knew where Robbie was. In answer he held up a bulging leather bag and a case for a bow.

'I know where he will be soon. There's a tavern. I said I would take his belongings.'

'Can I come with you?' she asked.

Cecil grinned. 'If you prefer, you could deliver them. I don't want to spend the evening acting as a courier while there is fighting to be done.'

'Fighting?' The dreadful claustrophobia of the crush on tournament day grew fresh in Rowenna's mind. The shoves and crushing bodies. The way her breath had been forced from her lungs.

The helplessness as she had sprawled in the mud, unable to stand, believing she might die there. Leaving home had been unwise when the city was still teeming with discontent.

'John Gisbourne is outside the city, demanding to be admitted. This could be my chance to earn my spurs, especially as that dolt Robbie has passed up his.'

Rowenna ignored the insult to Robbie, feeling it well earned.

'Will you take these to Robbie?' Cecil held out the bow and bag.

Rowenna wrapped her arms tightly around herself, her lip twisting in anxiety. She didn't want to subject herself to that again. But Robbie…

Robbie had saved her from that horror. He had come to her aid, as he had so many times before, and she loved him as truly as ever. Now he was somewhere in the city, heartbroken and exiled from the family he had thought belonged to him. Alone and friendless.

She could not—would not—leave him to endure his misery alone.

'Tell me where he is,' she said, relieving Cecil of his burden.

The inn was close to Bootham Gate, the very direction where the loudest cries and thickest crowds were. With difficulty she squeezed her way through the mass of people, unable to work out if they were trying to aid or prevent the former Mayor and his mob entering the city. The door was closed and she hammered on it until her fist smarted and a frightened-looking boy admitted her.

'Is there a Master Danby here?' she asked breathlessly. 'I'm seeking my cousin.'

'Do I still own that name or connection?' Robbie was sitting in the darkest corner, arms folded around him over the red robe he had worn during his ceremony, and a wine bottle on the table in front of him. He looked weary, but his eyes crinkled as they met hers. 'How did you find me?'

'Cecil told me where you'd be.' She held out the bow and bag. Robbie made no move to take them, but his face twisted.

'You've been with Cecil?' His face collapsed. His fingers closed around the neck of the wine bottle, but he obviously thought better of it as he set it down and stood.

'Why did you come here, Ro? Are you here to announce an engagement to our friend M-Master Hugone and now you're entering Sir John's household? Or to judge me and reject me?'

'Stop being so ridiculous!' she snapped. She heard the very real anxiety in his voice and softened hers. 'You know I don't care for Cecil. I only said I'd ask Lady Isobel because I can see no other future beyond marrying Geoffrey. I came because I was worried about you. Everyone is. Will you come home with me?'

'Roger warned me not to reveal the truth and I defied him. I'm not sure I will be welcome.'

'You will be. I've seen him.' She folded her arms. 'But what do you care what he thinks? You always told me that you never intended to walk in his shadow and you've proved it. Turn your back on everything if you must, but know that you are not only leaving behind your parents. There are others who love you and would miss you.'

She crossed the room in a rush, desperate to throw herself into his arms and comfort him, to take comfort herself from the ordeal of her journey. Robbie held up a hand to ward her off and she stopped abruptly. The other occupants of the tavern, who had been drinking or clamouring round the window to watch events in the street, were now watching them with open interest. Robbie glanced towards the boy who had admitted Rowenna. 'Do you have a room upstairs? I want privacy.'

The boy pointed upward. Exactly where an upstairs room would be. Despite the situation, Rowenna grinned. Robbie met her eyes and the tightness around his mouth and eyes softened a little. He gestured and she led the way up the staircase into a small chamber at the front of the building sparsely furnished with a wobbly table, three-legged stool and a bed. She ignored the bed because the sight of it set every nerve in her being colliding with an insufferable intensity.

They faced each other, an arm's length apart, watchful and tense. A rhythmic pounding filled Rowenna's ears, mingling with the sound of thumping from the street below. She wanted to scream and rail at him, but reined in her fury.

'How long have you known?' Rowenna asked quietly.

Robbie clenched his jaw. 'Since the night Roger told me I was to be Sir John's squire. He was waiting for me when I went home after leaving you.'

Rowenna's mouth fell open. So much longer than she had imagined. She glared at him. 'All these years you've been hurting and you didn't tell me. You kept something so big from me. Don't you trust me enough to share your troubles with me?'

Robbie was beside her before she had finished speaking. He clasped her shoulders, holding her firmly, his eyes boring into her. 'I wanted to, believe me, but I swore to tell no one. Even if I had been allowed, it didn't seem the sort of news to share in a letter.'

Rowenna folded her arms, though the impulse to wrap them around Robbie was unbearably strong. 'No,' she said drily. 'Much better that I find out like that, in front of half the population of York and everyone who matters to us both.'

He looked guilty and a flicker of the same emotion ignited in Rowenna. When he had admitted it, instead of telling him it did not matter to her, she had shouted and run from him. No wonder he had not told her before, when she proved how unworthy she was of his trust.

'It wasn't like you at all to be so rash.'

'I'm not sure what I am like any longer,' Robbie said. He took a long swig from the bottle. 'I think now is the time I start to find out.'

Rowenna tugged the bottle from his hand. Surprisingly, it was almost full. 'How many bottles have you gone through?'

'This is the first. I planned to get very drunk, but I couldn't bring myself to. I'm not sure what is happening out there, but it sounds dangerous. A muddled head is not wise.'

'Oh, you do still have some sense! That's good to know.'

She swallowed a large mouthful, eyeing him defiantly. Robbie reached for the bottle, but instead of drinking, he set it on the table.

'Tell me why you did it. You know how hard my father's life is and how my prospects have suffered in consequence. We are ostracised by half of York.' The anger that Rowenna had been suppressing burst out. 'Why damn yourself to the same fate as me?'

'I only damn myself if the people I care about reject me in consequence,' he said grimly.

Rowenna put her hand to Robbie's chest as she had done when examining his bruise at the *bohort*. When she touched him the muscles in his neck tightened and he closed his eyes. His heart was beating fast through the fine wool tunic. He pinned her hand in place with his and stood, head bowed and silent for a long time. Rowenna waited patiently, sensing that to push him would see him close up completely.

He came back from wherever he had been travelling in his mind and his eyes were clearer and brighter than they had been before.

'While Mary chose to accept me, I was bound by my honour to become her husband. She will not ally herself to a bastard, no matter how many sapphires I could throw into her lap.'

'So you wilfully ruined your future in the knowledge she would refuse you?'

He gave her a slight smile that caused her legs to quiver.

'And now I am free and my future is what *I* will make it.' His voice did not waver and his eyes shone with a certainty that sharpened them.

He had not acted impulsively after all. But then, Robbie rarely did.

'And was it worth it?' Rowenna asked. Her heart sang. Free. No longer Mary's.

'I d-don't know. I know you intend to m-marry w-well and I'm not—'

The muscles in his throat were tightening and she could see how much he was struggling. He broke off, but his meaning was clear.

Rowenna's mouth fell open in astonishment. 'I care nothing for your status or that of your true father. I want you, whoever and whatever you are.'

Robbie gave her a look of pure anguish.

'You ran from me.'

'It was a shock. You destroyed everything you had with one word. I was angry at such stupidity. Furious you hadn't trusted me and told me years ago. You can't say that is unreasonable.'

He looked away.

'Nevertheless, it broke my heart.'

Rowenna could no longer deny her desire to hold him. She moved towards Robbie, arms opening, and found him halfway towards her. They fell on each other, clutching tight and staggering with the force of their meeting. Somehow they found the bed and sank on to the mattress, hands spreading out to grasp and pull at each other.

Robbie's mouth closed over hers and she tasted

the wine they had shared. He began to move his lips against hers, steadily and slowly. There was no hesitancy in his kiss this time, only fervour and a thoroughness that left her trembling and light-headed. She craned her head, hungrily parting her lips and brushing her tongue against the tip of his. His hand slid down, moving slowly with firm strokes over Rowenna's breasts and belly. His tongue eased inside her mouth, hot and deft. She thrust hers against it, revelling in the delicious taste of him. Her hand crept to his arm again. She could feel muscles beneath the thick tunic and her fingers began to curl round them.

She pulled at him, hands roving over the firm muscles in his back, pressing her body to his as she gave in to the desire she had mastered for so long. He turned his head as she moved so that he was still filling her vision. He leaned close to nibble at her ear. His breath, dancing lightly over her cheeks brought flames to them.

She pushed herself closer, tilting her hips up and feeling the excitement begin to rise inside her. A moan like that of an animal escaped Robbie as she scraped against his crotch. He bent over her, his eyes wide with the same fierce desire she burned with and ran his thumb from her ear to the hollow of her throat, setting her alight within. He gave a soft growl and slid his hand lower until it rested in the crook of her bent knee. She grabbed his buttocks and tugged so he settled himself between her legs.

His body stiffened, the arms that had held her so tenderly becoming stone.

'Rowenna, no.'

She unwrapped herself from around Robbie and looked into his eyes.

'I thought you wanted me as much as I want you.'

She ran her hands along his forearms. Excitement rose in her belly as her fingers brushed over the fine hairs and well-shaped muscles, and she saw the tightening of his throat. He took her face between his hands and brought it close to hers.

'Being with you and not touching you is torture. I want you so much it turns my limbs to straw at the very idea. But not here, not like this.'

Rowenna glanced towards the window. The sun was dipping below the houses opposite, casting an orange light over the room. He was, as always, more sensible than she was.

She sat up and straightened her dress, relacing the ribbon that Robbie had pulled free, aware how close to surrender she was. She had craved Robbie's touch and yearned for his love for so long, but if they did what they were close to doing, she would be ruined. She would have proved to Lady Stick she was the common, worthless chit she had tried so hard not to be.

'I should go home. Mother will be wondering where I am.'

'It's getting late and raucous out there.' Robbie jerked upright, his eyes alert. 'You should stay here tonight.'

She glanced at the bed. 'I think that would be highly unwise, don't you?'

He followed her gaze and gave a slow grin.

'I agree. I'll take you part of the way.'

But wouldn't come in and face Roger. At this rate the rift would never heal.

'Take me all the way or none.' She stroked his cheek. 'I won't ask you to come with me now. It isn't far. Stay and think about what you plan to do. You know where I will be when you decide.'

Rowenna swept from the room before he could object or she gave into her urges. The crowd had grown denser, surging towards the walls and she had to fight to make her way through towards home. She had not gone more than a dozen steps when there was a loud cheer. The gates that had been well defended opened with a crack loud enough to split the rumble of dissatisfaction. John Gisbourne's rebels, on foot and horseback, surged through the archway and the city became a battleground.

Chapter Sixteen

Robbie sprang from the bed as soon as Rowenna had left the room. How close they had come to sliding into bed together had left him shaken. He straightened his disordered clothes and leaned from the window, gulping pungent summer air into his lungs, determined to get another glimpse of her.

The narrow street was alarmingly busy. He saw Rowenna leave the tavern and try to push through the mass of bodies. He should have insisted on taking her, realising with a heart-stopping burst of fear that she would never reach home safely with such crowds. He was halfway towards the door when a splintering crack filled his ears, followed by a roar of triumph. He raced back in time to see the great doors of the Bootham Gate burst open and men dressed in the white hoods of Gisbourne's supporters surge through, spilling down the road in the direction Rowenna had taken.

Instinctively he reached for the sword at his waist, but it was not there. He swore and searched around frantically for something else he could use as a weapon and his eyes fell on the stool. He broke off one of the legs to use as a cudgel and remembered the bow Rowenna had brought him. He slung it over his back and ran outside, almost being trampled by men on horseback.

As he ran along Petergate, towards the church where he had made his announcement, Robbie relived the nightmare of the tournament day. Rowenna was ahead of him, somewhere, but this time the people preventing him reaching her were not confused and aimless, but a mob intent on destruction. Already buildings were on fire where flaming torches had been thrown through open doors. Sweat broke out over Robbie's entire body at the sound and smell. People were screaming and trying to extinguish flames or hurling belongings into the street and fighting with the gang who were intent on causing as much damage as possible.

He spotted Rowenna amid the crowds. She was edging along the row of houses, her back to the walls. He cried out, but she was too far away to hear him. She was so intent on getting through the rioters that she had not noticed the white-hooded man who had changed direction and was moving purposefully towards her. Robbie gripped his chair leg, but he knew he would not reach Rowenna in time, and sure enough, before he was halfway there, the man had grabbed hold of her arm and began dragging her towards an alley. She tugged against him, but was no match for his size.

Robbie leapt on to an upturned box, pulled his bow from his back and loosed an arrow. It caught the man straight between the shoulder blades. He staggered, his head lolled back and he fell, pulling Rowenna down with him. She looked in incomprehension at her would-be assailant and began frantically searching around for the bowman. Robbie yelled her name and elbowed his way towards her. She saw him at last and her face lit with relief. By the time he had reached her she had scrambled to her feet and Robbie was able to wrap his arms around her, crushing her to him with a force so great she squeaked in protest and he reluctantly loosened his embrace.

'I've come to take you home,' he murmured into Rowenna's hair.

He glanced over her head at the potential rapist who was slumped in a heap. Dead. It was the first time Robbie had killed. His throat filled with bitterness, but he pushed it to the back of his mind to think about later.

Rowenna clutched the sleeves of his tunic. 'Robbie, you have to tell the Mayor what is happening. The city needs defending.'

A spark ignited in Robbie's breast. He'd won recognition before in defending York. He could do it again and was minded to agree, but at the sound of breaking glass Rowenna flinched. She was worryingly pale and her clothes and hair were in disarray. The urge to protect her and keep her close to him was too powerful.

'It doesn't have to be me who tells him. I'm here to look after you.'

'I'm not hurt and there's no need to guard me,' she said, against all the evidence to the contrary. Her eyes glowed with determination. 'This could be your chance to redeem yourself. You can still become the knight you always dreamed of being.'

Robbie pulled her closer. After his fumbled attempt to seduce her at the tavern, he could barely contain himself when he was this close to her. He brushed the hair from her brow and kissed her forehead.

'If you were not safe, I would have no future worth speaking of.'

She was going to argue again. Before she had the chance, Robbie pulled her to him and kissed her. She held him tightly, clutching to him and kissing him back with an intensity that left him breathless and in ecstasy. If they were racing headlong into danger, he would do it with the memory of Rowenna's enthusiasm bolstering his courage. When he pulled away her eyes were brimming with surprise. Robbie took her face in his hands and gave her the most commanding look he could muster, given how deeply he wanted to embrace her.

'Rowenna Danby, do as I tell you, when I tell you, for the first time in your life.'

She nodded, silently. He did not believe her meekness would last, but while she seemed inclined to obey, he took her by the hand. The crowds were getting thicker and it was hard to determine who was part of the ex-Mayor's mob and who was simply taking the opportunity to resume rioting. If Simon de Quixlay did not know what was happening, he soon would hear of it as the violence was spreading towards the centre of the city and the Guild Hall. Together Robbie and Rowenna ran down the alleyway that led behind the church into the stonemason's yard. It would bring them out only a little way from Hal's house. Coming out the other side, they almost collided with a group of men and ducked swiftly through the open doorway of a workshop and into the safety of the furthest corner.

'We'll never make it home,' Rowenna groaned. 'It's too dangerous.'

She might well be right. It would be more sensible to stay in the workshop for the time being. Before he could console her as he wished to, a flaming torch sailed through the door. Sparks burst everywhere, catching on the rush matting that covered the floor. The rush mats in the doorway, dried and brittle from weeks of hot weather, began to burn.

Robbie recoiled. Panic closed over him, a fist squeezing his throat.

'We're going to die,' Rowenna cried.

Robbie fought the urge to join her cries. Trapped between flames and freedom, a cold sweat of terror covered his body.

'I won't let that happen,' he soothed. He hugged Rowenna to him, staring over her head at the fire with eyes that were blurring. Flames leaping higher than these filled his memory, though where such a demonic vision had sprung from, he could not tell. The furniture had not yet caught fire and the door was open.

'We'll run through the flames,' he said. 'Quickly, before they reach further into the room.'

Robbie fumbled for Rowenna's hand and clutched it tightly. The fire was spreading, but knowing it could be the last chance he had, he looked into her eyes. 'I love you.'

'I love you.' She curled her fingers into his palm.

'We go together.'

They exchanged a glance, then sprang towards the door. Hand in hand they leapt through the flames. Rowenna's skirt billowed and the hem caught. She screamed and as they tumbled out on to the road she began to beat frantically at the cloth. Robbie threw her to the ground and rolled her over. He gathered the folds of her skirt and ground them into the dusty street. He beat the flames until they were extinguished, ignoring the pain in his hands. They slumped together, legs sprawled and arms around each other, both weeping with relief and oblivious to the chaos around them.

Robbie stroked her face, brushing away the tears with his thumb. She loved him. He couldn't confront that knowledge now when they were not safe, but his entire body sang with glee.

'I think I preferred it when you were only trapped by geese,' he joked. Saying anything else would be too momentous. They both laughed, giggles bordering on mania, as they ran hand in hand for home.

Hal's house was close by, and as they rounded the final corner they almost ran face-to-face into Roger and Hal, both armed with swords, and working alongside neighbouring men to subdue a party of rioters. As they spotted Robbie and Rowenna, Hal ran forward and tore his daughter from Robbie, engulfing her in a hug, calling her name over and over as she sobbed. Robbie stood awkwardly by, trying to ignore the jealous urge to wrestle her back into his own embrace. He turned instead to Roger.

'The Mayor needs to know what is happening.'

'He already does,' Roger said. 'The militia are gathering.'

The silence that enclosed them after that could have lasted eternally but Hal broke the unease by thumping Robbie between the shoulder blades.

'You brought my daughter back safely. I can't repay that, but I'm for ever in your debt. Whatever obstacles you have to confront, you have me at your side.'

Rowenna beamed at him from her father's arms. Robbie studied her, taking in the singed hem, dishevelled hair and a bruise forming across the mound of her cheek that he could not explain.'

'Robbie saved my life. Twice. He shot someone, then we were trapped in a fire. I would have burned if it had not been for him.'

Robbie flexed his fingers, aware for the first time of stinging spots where the flames had licked the backs of his hands.

'A fire?'

Roger and Hal exchanged a look that meant nothing to Robbie. Roger held his hand out to Robbie: the pink, smooth one that had always puzzled Robbie.

'You were burned?' he asked.

'When you were a baby. One of the many

things Lucy and I should have told you about. It seems to be a tendency of Danby men to rush headlong into danger,' Roger remarked. 'And you *are* a Danby, make no mistake of that.'

'I stand by what I did,' Robbie said, drawing himself up tall. He found it hard to speak, but it was the lump that filled his throat, not his disobedient tongue that caused him difficulties.

Roger cocked his head to one side. 'I would expect nothing less. You may not be my blood, but you're my son as truly as any could be. Your recklessness and obstinacy is proof of that. The Mayor's men want every able man to defend the city. Will you join them? Will you join me?'

He held out his hand once more. After the briefest hesitation Robbie took it.

Rowenna broke free from her father's arms and into Robbie's. She held him tightly and buried her face against his chest.

'I'll be waiting for you.' Turning to Roger, she said, 'Bring him back to me safely.'

'I think Robbie is capable of ensuring his own safety.' Roger grinned.

'Especially when I have you waiting for me. How could I do otherwise?' Robbie asked Rowenna. He kissed her lightly on the cheek and felt her break into a smile as her cheek dimpled beneath his lips. It was nowhere near as passionate or thorough a kiss as he wanted to give her, but with their fathers watching it would have to suffice. He promised himself more of those later.

'Come back,' she whispered.

He watched as Rowenna slipped inside the house and the door closed. With Roger beside him, he walked out into the city.

He did return once it was clear the stirrings of violence were starting to be quelled. It was growing light and Robbie was bone-weary and aching everywhere from a night of fighting.

Two nights without sleep had left him uncertain what was real and what was his imagination. The soft mattress he slumped on to might have been real, but the gentle hands that helped ease the grime-and-sweat-matted tunic over his aching arms and pulled the light coverlet over him belonged in a dream. A sweet scent filled his nostrils and a kiss of such gentleness that it made him weak sent him off to sleep.

He awoke to full daylight. His fingers felt sticky and a pungent smell of salve reminded him he had been burned. They did not sting as much as they had the previous day. He opened his eyes and discovered Rowenna was sitting at the end of his bed, her head bowed and her hands moving rapidly over something she was sewing. He eased on to his elbows and she turned, her face breaking into a smile that heated Robbie's belly.

'Why are you in my room?' he asked, momentarily disoriented.

'You're in mine,' she said, her smile dimpling. 'In my bed.'

Robbie became aware he was naked to the waist. He jerked upward then winced as his ribs spasmed. Rowenna's eyes skimmed him anxiously. She laid her sewing down and shifted along the bed to sit beside him.

'You're hurt. Let me.' She squeezed a cloth out of a bowl of water and ran it over his chest, where fresh bruises had formed over old ones. Robbie closed his eyes as the cool water soothed his sore flesh, which immediately flamed as Rowenna's palms ran across his chest, tracing the contours of his muscles.

'I was so worried,' she said. 'I stayed awake all night. I don't think you even knew where you were when you returned.'

'I told you I would be back.' The thin sheet that covered his lower half did nothing to conceal the stirring that her touch was causing. He bunched the sheets into his lap and sat up. Resisting her was the hardest trial he had to overcome, up to and including subduing two drunken rioters intent on stealing a cart.

'Where did you sleep?' he asked. A blush was

rising to his cheeks and he wondered how much blood remained in his veins, given that most of it was centred in two very distinct areas of his body.

'On the pallet beside you.' Rowenna turned crimson as she indicated one of the thin mattresses that lay with a heap of crumpled blankets. 'I'm not so forward as to slip into bed with an unconscious man.'

'What about a conscious man?' Robbie asked daringly. He reached for her hand and slid his fingers over her wrist up beneath the wide sleeve, delighting in the way her bare skin shivered at his touch. She leaned in closer until the scent of her hair and skin filled his nostrils, intoxicating him.

'Perhaps once he's bathed.' She dropped a playful kiss on to his cheek that left him gasping for breath. 'I'll go tell everyone you're awake. Get dressed and make yourself presentable.'

She fled, leaving Robbie to dress in a borrowed tunic of Hal's and hose that were far too shabby for what he had planned.

Presently he walked uncertainly into the parlour. As on the first night of his arrival in York, his mother fell on him, weeping and chastising him, examining his burns and kissing him by turn.

'Can you forgive me?' he asked.

Lucy's tight embrace was answer enough to

know he had her pardon. He faced Roger. They had not spoken of the matter the night before.

'It isn't how I would have dealt with the matter, but I think you were right to do what you did. We should have been honest from the start. I will formally adopt and name you as my heir as I should have long ago,' Roger said. 'Titles can pass to adopted sons if there is no legitimate son. It has been known. I'll petition Horace of Pickering as I should have done so years ago. The estate is not entailed and with his clemency the estate and title may pass to you still. He is more charitable than his father would have been and I believe he will agree. You certainly have the courage and principles required of a knight.'

Robbie knelt. 'Sir, I cannot repay the debt I owe you for your kindness and understanding.'

'It is purely self-interest. Wharram needs a man like you to care for it.' Roger winked to show he was joking. He tugged Robbie upright with a smile and placed both hands on Robbie's shoulders.

'Thank you,' Robbie said. 'Father.'

Roger raised his brows, then grinned and clasped Robbie's wrist. He called for wine and the women rushed to fetch it. There was much that needed to be said, but for the time being Robbie was content to sit on the settle, surrounded by family with a cup of warm spiced wine in his hand.

Rowenna sat opposite Robbie at the other side of the fireplace and while in company they were content to simply stare at each other, smiling as their eyes met. Finally Robbie could wait no longer.

'I m-must go and seek an audience with Sir John. I have his forgiveness to beg more than any, perhaps. I do not expect him to take me back into his house and, truly, I will be glad to start afresh. Cecil deserves his place as Sir John's principal squire.'

Robbie walked to Hal, who was watching with a stern look in his brown eyes. The bastard who had made himself a life to be proud of. From the corner of his eye he noticed his mother starting to speak and Roger hushing her.

'Uncle Hal, I'm not a knight. I might never become one now, though I shall work my hardest to gain the status I gave up. I have no fortune to offer, but if you will allow me to love your daughter, the debt you say you owe me will be repaid in full, with more besides.'

'I think you're asking the wrong person, Robbie.'

Hal cocked his head towards Rowenna who bit her lip and looked as if she was about to cry. He walked over and sat beside Rowenna, taking her hand. She laced her fingers between his and gripped tightly.

'On the night of my engagement I asked if you would always be my friend, but I asked the wrong question,' Robbie said. 'What I should have asked was could you ever imagine we could be more than friends? That I could mean *more* to you?'

'You mean everything to me,' Rowenna said. 'No one else matters. No one else ever has.'

Robbie sank to his knee.

'Ro, you once asked if my love was changeable and I tell you it is not. I love you, but more than that, I am *in love* with you. M-more deeply than I dreamed was possible. You vex and infuriate me, inspire and sustain me. I would very much like to m-marry you, if you'll have me. I cannot guarantee you wealth or status, but I promise to love you every day until I die.'

He pulled the faded ribbon from his pouch and pressed it into her hand. 'I've kept this with me for years to remind me of you. Now I want to keep you as close.'

'Robbie, you're a fool.' Tears filled Rowenna's eyes, then spilled down her cheeks. She crumpled the ribbon in her hand.

'I don't care if you're a knight or a squire, or… or a tavern boy. It's you I want. You're my best friend. I can't imagine spending my life with anyone but you. I wouldn't want to. You know my dreams and secrets, my faults…'

'What faults? You're perfect. You always tell me so.'

He grinned and ducked as she brought a hand round to swipe him playfully on the arm. He caught her wrist, held it and brought it to his lips, kissing the soft skin where her pulse beat fast. Small scars stood out white on the mounds at the base of her fingers. He ran a fingertip over each one, then kissed them, too. She shivered and her eyes blazed with a desire that matched Robbie's own, tormenting him with the anticipation of a lifetime of discovering each other's passions. For now he had to content himself with this small moment, but he promised himself that as soon as they were alone he would devote himself to showing Rowenna how thoroughly he desired her.

He faced the adults, trying his best to ignore the varying expressions of delight and triumph that their faces bore. They were his family and the tenuous bond would only grow stronger through the marriage between himself and Rowenna.

'They'll marry and inherit Wharram Manor,' Hal said, pouring wine for everyone. 'Two Danbys together. Imagine what a pair they'll make.'

'The legitimate daughter of a bastard and the adopted son of the legitimate heir? I'm not sure that is what Father hoped for.' Roger grinned. 'But I think he would have found it amusing.'

'We'll be content with nothing besides each other.' Robbie sprang to his feet, pulling Rowenna with him. 'Roger—Father—has many years ahead of him.'

He kissed her, still more briefly than he would have liked, but with a lifetime ahead of them he could afford to wait. 'Will you come see the world with me, Ro?'

He drew her to him, sliding his hands to her waist. She stood on tiptoe and wrapped her arms around his neck. She rose up to meet his lips again.

'I will.'

* * * * *

COMING SOON!

MILLS & BOON

Coming next month

MISS LOTTIE'S CHRISTMAS PROTECTOR
Sophia James

'Are you married, sir?'

'I am not.' Jasper tried to keep the relief from his words.

'But would you want to be? Married, I mean? One day?'

She was observing him as if she were a scientist and he was an undiscovered species. One which might be the answer to an age-old question. One from whom she could obtain useful information about the state of Holy Matrimony.

'It would depend on the woman.' He couldn't remember in his life a more unusual conversation. Was she in the market for a groom or was it for someone else she asked?

'But you are not averse to the idea of it?' She blurted this out. 'If she was the right one?'

Lord, was she proposing to him? Was this some wild joke that would be exposed in the next moment or two? Had the Fairclough family fallen down on their luck and she saw his fortune as some sort of a solution? Thoughts spun quickly, one on top of another and suddenly he'd had enough. 'Where the hell is your brother, Miss Fairclough?'

She looked at him blankly. 'Pardon?'

'Silas. Why is he not here with you and seeing to your needs?'

'You know my brother?'

Her eyes were not quite focused on him, he thought then, and wondered momentarily if she could be using some drug to alter perception. But surely not. The Faircloughs were known near and far for their godly works and charitable ways. It was his own appalling past that was colouring such thoughts.

'I do know him. I employed him once in my engineering firm.'

'Oh, my goodness.' She fumbled then for the bag on the floor in front of her, a decent-sized reticule full of belongings. Finally, she extracted some spectacles. He saw they'd been broken, one arm tied on firmly with a piece of string. When she had them in place her eyes widened in shock.

'It is you.'

'I am afraid so.'

'Hell.'

That sounded neither godly nor saintly and everything he believed of Miss Charlotte Fairclough was again turned upside down.

Continue reading
MISS LOTTIE'S CHRISTMAS PROTECTOR
Sophia James

Available next month
www.millsandboon.co.uk

LET'S TALK
Romance

For exclusive extracts, competitions
and special offers, find us online:

For all the latest titles coming soon, visit
millsandboon.co.uk/nextmonth